PRAISE FOR "SOLID"

This is a great story for MG and YA readers, and fans of James Patterson's Maximum Ride series will enjoy the adventures of this new group of kids who are just a little 'different.' ~ Book Noise

On first seeing the cover and reading the summary, I thought that "Solid" would be something new, different, and intriguing - and it was.
~ Between the Covers

Reading its summary will unquestionably get you interested. And reading its contents will get you hooked and addicted.
~ Reading Lassie

Ms. Workinger is worthy of her own place in the science-fiction/Fantasy genre, because this really is an original and stand-out novel.
~ Magic of Reading

Brimming with entertaining, loyal characters, a gripping, mysterious back story/plot, teens with superhuman abilities, and a satisfying ending that cleverly paves the way for a pine-worthy sequel.
~ Paranormal Indulgence

If I had to describe "Solid" in one line, it would be - YA version of Robin Cook novels but much more fun and exciting!
~ My Love Affair With Books

Readers who would like a sci-fi adventure with a heroine that is real and realistic rather than a knock-off of a cable TV channel vixen, this is the story for you! ~ Litland

A hint of romance, a splash of mystery, and the super hero powers that they are just coming into, and you have yourself an entertaining, and page turning read. No sex and no swearing, so even the younger tweens may enjoy this one. ~ Minding Spot

While the plot might be the foundation of this story, its characters were the heart of it. ~ *Escape Between the Pages*

"Solid" is a wonderful book that brings in a batch of fascinating characters and an intriguing plot that will keep you guessing.
~ *Confessions of a Bookaholic*

It's always a good indication when you like the main character immediately. ~ *One Book At A Time*

The story line is very entertaining with a cast of quirky, loveable and memorable characters…comic relief as well as romance. If you like the X-men *or* Heroes, *I think you will like this book.*
~ *To Read or Not to Read*

A different approach to geeky-high-school-girl-turns-special.
~ *A Musing Reviews*

I fell in love with her characters and had no difficulty completely immersing myself into "Solid." An amazing read that is enticing and captivating. It kept me gripped from the first place to the last. I highly recommend this book! ~ *My Bookish Fairytale*

This was a solid (no pun intended) story, and I'm definitely interested in reading the sequel "Settling" when I can get my hands on it.
~ *Royal Reviews*

I honestly think that for a book that is as good as it is, I don't think it will get the full attention that it truly deserves. ~ *Reading Chic*

The story moves at a fast-pace and the characters come to life in a way that will have readers caring about them. I devoured this book in just a couple of days. ~ *Socrates' Book Reviews*

SETTLING

SETTLING

ISBN: 1-460-98172-3
EAN-13: 978-1-460-98172-6

Printed in the United States of America

First Edition

To my ever-understanding family and friends, who supported my disappearance into the "Solid" world for another year.

ONE

W*hy rush?* I reminded myself, purposely slowing my steps toward the dining hall. Not that I was worried about the food; it was actually a million times better than I'd expected at an Army camp. No, my *relax today, race tomorrow* motto had nothing to do with dinner and everything to do with Monday morning. I may not be embarking on some exotic global adventure, but my new assignment would be my-world changing and today was sort of feeling like the last day of vacation.

And a well-deserved vacation at that. It felt like my whole life had been on fast-forward since I got to campus. I'd started the summer by moving a thousand miles from home along with a hundred other kids; we'd taken the same leap by coming to this strange place, also strangers to each other, showing up for the first day of school where every kid was the new kid.

When I thought back to those first couple of weeks on campus, I felt like so much had happened so fast that I must have missed half of it. The camp of self-discovery we'd signed up for had quickly turned from an inviting lake to a whirlpool of secrets and super-abilities, friends and villains. We'd all kind of clung to the first solid things that floated by just to keep our heads above water.

But once the current had calmed – and the danger of being eliminated by Janet for revealing her secret had subsided – I'd looked around at what I'd grabbed hold of in my panic and felt enormously lucky. Of all the people I could've surfaced with, I'd somehow found the best five fish in the pond. One may be a barracuda, another a clown fish, and the others various species in between, but we made up a swimmy school.

I burst out laughing at my own ridiculous thoughts. Now all I could envision were my friend's faces photoshopped onto scaly, neon bodies with giant cartoon eyes and puckering lips. I guess I had my mom to thank – it was *her* imagination that I'd inherited, after all. It used to bother me that while I'd gotten her creativity, and even her knack for picking up vocabulary, her ability to put ideas into lyrical prose had skipped right over me. And as for what happened by the time my tangled thoughts hit the air, forget about it.

But the unfortunate breakdown that occurred somewhere between my mind and my mouth was a worry for another time. Today was about all the good things I had going on, and I readily returned my focus to them.

Yup, Calliope Grace Kaid, I said to myself, *your life is pretty freaking awesome.*

Even the survivor-like metaphor I'd been relating to – before I'd distracted myself with the fish – hadn't been all that bad. Going back to that brainwave, I reminded myself how once

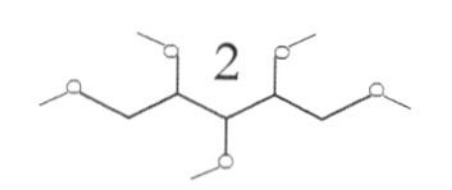

the wild water had cleared and I could let go of all the life preservers I'd grabbed onto, I hadn't wanted to. It was only the rapids themselves that had been rough, not other people and equipment. I still may not know the how and why of a lot of those early days, but I was pretty happy with the right now.

And now that life was moving in real-time instead of warp-speed – now that we'd begun to settle a bit – we could actually just *be* here without constantly stressing over those *hows* and *whys*. To be honest, sometimes I almost forgot the reason we'd been brought here in the first place, because the *here* was no longer the secret and hidden unknown that'd it been when we'd first arrived. The campus had become a familiar place, full of friends. *A home.*

I knew it must seem totally bizarre to people beyond the gate to think of a classified Army camp full of military kids as any kind of homey environment, but that's how it felt to us. And that we all felt the same way spoke volumes.

With every kid on campus a genetically-altered freak of nature – or in our case, crazy scientific experiment – the playing field sort of *evened-out*, as Garrett would say. Finding a place where everyone was so different – in every sense of the word – that nobody stuck out was like a gift to kids who'd spent their lives constantly moving and thus *always* sticking out.

I blended so well into my new surroundings that being able to vanish, to make my solid self *disappear*, wasn't even that exciting anymore. Besides that, like sixty other kids could do it, too; when compared to some of the other latent talent, vanishing wasn't even that impressive of a skill. In the shadow of lighter-than-air jocks, stone-walling heavies, and blindingly brilliant stars, disappearing almost, well, disappeared.

And really, the invisibility hadn't changed my life all that much. I was still seventeen, heading into my senior year of high school; I still needed to get my driver's license and apply for college.

Plus, it's not like I used my ability on a daily basis. In actuality, I'd probably used it more in my old life, before I'd even known what I could do or how to control it. So many times I'd wished my gym teacher would pass me by, repeating in my mind, *You don't see me; I'm invisible*, until she'd picked someone else to play. At the time, I thought I'd gotten lucky; now I knew better. Although here, I no longer had anything to hide from. *So ironic.*

And even though it sounded nuts, figuring out that I could disappear had been kind of eclipsed by everything else that had happened to me at the same time. Finding a place to belong, real friends, a *boy*friend – the new experiences were so entangled that it was hard to single any one thing out as the best.

Now, as I looked through the doorway into the crowded dining room, I felt a rush of excitement at what I'd become a part of – and what'd also become a part of me. The positive buzz shared by every student here was like nothing I'd experienced at any of the schools I'd gone to.

Not that this was a school. Not *yet*, anyway. But if everything worked out, that would change come September. Our campus was about to turn into a very small, very private boarding school with only one real admission requirement – a seriously messed-up ninth chromosome.

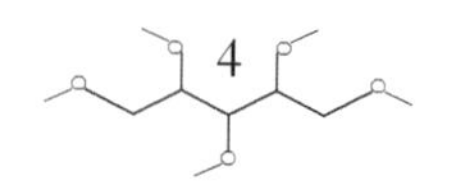

I could hardly wait.

TWO

"Thar she blows!" As I entered the dining room, Garrett hailed me from the table we'd now permanently claimed.

"Did you just call me a whale?" I responded with a calculated snarl once I'd reached him.

"Why are girls so hyper-sensitive?" he groaned. "You take everything so seriously."

"Why are boys so obtuse? They can't even tell when we're joking." I replaced the faux-offense with a wide grin. "Good to see you're branching out, though," I went on. "Did you read the whole book?"

I took his choking as a negative answer, and modified my question. "Movie?"

"First four minutes," he admitted once his airway was clear. "That's all I could take."

"Where've you been?" asked Miranda, the sharpness in her tone every bit intended. I tried to think of it as her own brand of charm.

"I fell asleep." I tried to portray an appropriate amount of sheepish regret, but, in truth, I'd relished every one of those extra z's I'd snagged before dinner.

"Mmm, I love naps," my best friend Bliss mumbled, one delicate hand over her mouth as she finished chewing.

"Where's Jack?" I asked about the person I always most wanted to see.

"Getting food," answered Alexis, the sixth and final member of our group. I followed her indicative gaze until I spotted the back of Jack's tousled brown hair. Despite our having spent the whole morning together, a thrill danced up my spine at the sight of him. Even from across the room, I could tell that his untucked t-shirt and plaid shorts fitted him like everything he wore – so well that he could model them for J.Crew.

Restraining myself from skipping over to meet him at the salad bar, I paused to tuck a long strand of dark red hair behind my ear. My hand froze mid-way when I realized that I'd blown past the mirror without a glance between waking up and coming over here. I quickly forced myself to stomp down the worry since there was nothing I could do about it now.

I felt mostly full from eating through half a box of granola bars while making my notes for tomorrow, but still looked for something to snack on. I snatched an avocado and a peach from the display and deposited them on Jack's tray in a silent hello.

"Looking for an encore performance?" he asked, greeting me with his easy grin. And thankfully taking no notice of my disheveled state.

"Not today," I answered, although his fruit-juggling ability was one of the most endearing things about him. "Just didn't want to get a whole 'nother tray."

"Okay, I'll share, but only because I'm good like that." He nudged me playfully with one elbow so as not to jostle his load.

"And I knew you would, 'cuz *I'm* good like *that*," I tossed back with an elbow-bump of my own.

"Done with your notes?" he asked, sliding down to the next food island to grab a burger.

"Yup," I said, matching his steps. "I think that fourth set is the winner." *It better be, anyway,* I thought, *since I'm out of time. And new ideas.* "How 'bout you?"

"No notes," he admitted. "I'm just riding in on my sparkling personality."

"I wish I had one of those," I responded, half-seriously.

"Here, have some of mine," he teased, and before I knew what was happening, he'd planted a solid kiss on my lips that left me blushing and wondering who'd seen.

And also *alone*, since he'd already headed back to the table. I hurried to catch up and we slid into the last two open seats. Funny how we always took the same seats at the same table, settling into such a family-like routine after all being together less than a month. I guess learning your chromosomes had been secretly altered before you were born had a way of bonding people.

"Everyone ready to report for duty tomorrow?" I asked the rest of the group. Once we'd all decided to stay on campus, even after our near-death experience a week into the summer, we'd shifted priorities from just hanging out here to becoming a part of things. Most of us had planned on working or volunteering at home this summer anyway, so sitting around doing nothing would've left a major gap on our college applications. Jack had been the one to come up with the idea of making our own internships, and Colonel Clark, as head of the program, had readily consented.

"Sooo ready," Miranda answered at the same time Bliss moaned, "Not."

Miranda, who would normally grab any opportunity for self-promotion, was momentarily distracted by Garrett's meal. Fueling his athletic form was practically a sport in itself, and he'd built a small mountain out of what must be some of everything the caterers had put out for dinner. Besides green stuff. "Didn't you get anything that's not processed?" she criticized.

"Look, there's a little guy." He used the edge of his loaded fork to roll a small beige ball toward her without disrupting his plate-to-mouth momentum.

"What is that?" Miranda gave the odd morsel a skeptical look.

"Chickpea?" Garrett offered hopefully.

Miranda stabbed it with her own fork and it crumbled to dust. "That's not a chickpea, you doof; it's a piece of peanut butter crunch cereal."

Garrett kept his eyes on his plate, not interested in engaging in a food battle where nothing was being thrown or dumped over somebody's head.

"Standards seem to be slipping around here," Miranda huffed, partially under her breath. "They don't even clean up after breakfast anymore."

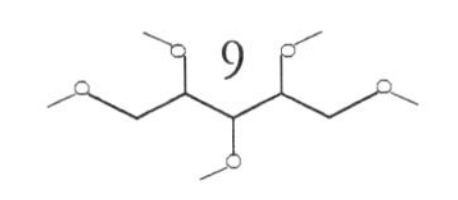

"Really?" I contradicted, reminding her of the newly added international food station. Lucky for me, a few years of Cajun food had given me some decent spicy training. Otherwise, last night's delicious but deadly vindaloo would've produced a not-so-attractive runny nose, which would've taken even me to a new level of self-embarrassment.

Bliss paused mid-bite to blurt out, "You're not working with catering, are you?" She and I both knew that a menu planned by Miranda would be unequivocally catastrophic – worse than prison food. Like fat-farm prison food.

"Of course not." Miranda wrinkled her perfectly pointed nose in distaste.

Relieved, Bliss returned to her dinner – a sundae-like scoop of egg salad sprinkled with poppy seeds and topped with a single grape tomato. Free for the first time from her major-general mom's strict meal regimen, she just couldn't resist playing with her food.

"I have much bigger things to attend to," Miranda continued her dramatic build-up.

"Media relations, perhaps?" Garrett suggested in his most patronizing tone.

"No, that'd be me," Alexis chimed in, half raising her hand. She'd already finished and was leaning back to digest both the food and the conversation. Besides her being the only one not eating, the impossibly black hair framing her pale face gave her the disquieting beauty of a movie vampire.

"First of all," Miranda dismissed the interruption, "that would keep me *behind* the camera, which would be a total waste of my face." She brushed her gold tresses back with both hands to give us a clearer view of the product.

Garrett took advantage of her pedestal-climbing to shovel in as much food as he could before she circled back to him for a second attack.

"Would you like to tell us about your job?" Jack tried to gallantly escort Miranda to her point.

"Meet your new social director," she announced, twirling her hand in a mock-bow.

"Do we need one of those?" I asked, ignoring Bliss's sudden stiffening at my right. I didn't need to look at her to know that her wide, grape-green eyes were asking, *Did you really just say that out loud?*

"Hello? Were you *at* the spring fling-ding disaster?" Miranda asked, her stormy eyes even a darker critical blue than usual.

She knew how to shut me up quickly; the last thing I wanted was to be reminded of the embarrassing welcome dance when I'd almost blown things with Jack.

"Any big plans?" Jack asked her, saving me from the awkward moment in the way I'd come to depend on.

"As a matter of fact, yes," she practically purred. "I'm putting together a Fourth of July blowout for Saturday night."

"Isn't Sunday the fourth?" Garrett asked through a mouthful of hamburger.

Her annoyance with him renewed, Miranda shot back, "Sunday is a terri-bad day for a party."

"You can't just move a holiday," ever-logical Alexis

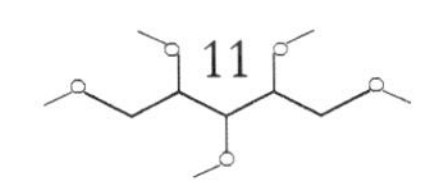

pointed out.

"Watch me," Miranda corrected her. "Look, nobody's going to want to stay up all night Sunday now that we work Mondays. So we'll party all afternoon Saturday, and I'll drag the fireworks out until midnight, which will then officially be the fourth, okay?"

Miranda was easily soothed by our collective murmurs of agreement. As much as we liked ruffling her feathers, we'd learned a long time ago that peacocks do bite if you push them too far.

"There's going to be a barbecue and a band...," she started to fill us in on her plans.

"And you'll be coming by tomorrow to clear all that with security, right?" Jack interrupted, though not rudely.

"You're kidding, right?" Miranda tried to blow him off. "How could rock stars pose a threat? They need their own security."

"M, it doesn't matter to Major Lombardo if your stars have no arms or legs and play kazoos on mouth stands. He's gonna want to check them out, so you better come by or you won't get anybody." Since she could tell he was only trying to help, not hinder her, Miranda gave him a grudging nod.

"You must be pretty excited to work with security, Jack. Isn't that what your dad does?" Bliss jumped in, always unsettled by tension that hardly fazed the rest of us.

"Yeah, he's Special Forces," Jack confirmed. "I'm guessing that's the only reason they're letting me in." The opposite of Miranda, he took no credit for his own deservedness.

"I bet they've got some sick James Bond technology," Garrett mused.

"I'd say I'll let you know, but I won't. Top secret." Jack shrugged to show it was out of his hands.

"No worries, bro," Garrett forgave him. "I'm gonna be bagging plenty of training secrets of my own."

"So you're like reverse-recruiting or something?" I asked Garrett, not entirely sure what his assignment entailed.

"Mm-hmm," he answered. "Looking for coaches."

"What's wrong with the guy you have?" Miranda asked, not understanding something that held such little interest for her.

"Sikes is just an ex-Army football coach; he's no Vince Lombardi," Garrett told her. "He knows a little about most sports, runs some drills, keeps us in shape and all, but he's no pro. We want the best."

"Will famous coaches come here?" Bliss asked with wide-eyed innocence.

"Who wouldn't want to train the dream team?" Garrett responded, touting the super-athleticism of his particular C9x group. The rest of us called them the "jocks," although that gave little credit to the gravity-defying physical feats they could perform.

"If y'all don't start giving some props to my mad skills," he warned, "I'm not gonna return your calls when I make the show."

"You're bringing in scouts?" Jack was thinking ahead of more people who'd need background checks.

"We have to send out tapes first. That's what I'm doing

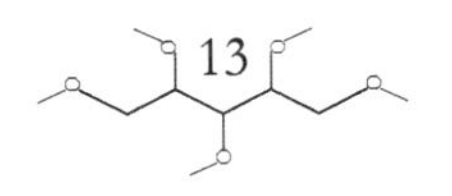

tomorrow – starting to put together highlight reels," Garrett answered. "But yeah, eventually we'll bring 'em in. I'm banking on someone offering me a full ride somewhere."

"Cocky much?" Miranda couldn't resist taking a shot at him.

"Hey, it's not my fault I got superhero chromes and you didn't," he lobbed back.

He was right; the jocks were the only C9x group with showcase-able abilities and would surely all go on to become pro athletes. And while the heavies' blocking ability wouldn't get them far, they all boasted musical and artistic gifts that came from either their genetic alteration or the isolation they'd endured because of it. As for the rest of us, good luck finding careers based on disappearing or sparkling.

"I hate thinking about what we're supposed to do with our abilities," Bliss voiced the collective concern of the stars and vanishers.

"We don't have to figure it out now," I reminded her.

"You're more than just what you do," Alexis chimed in, although as an early-acceptance to Juilliard, she couldn't really relate.

"I think we should save the world!" Garrett boomed loud enough to turn several heads at surrounding tables.

"Let's just focus on saving campus for now, okay?" Jack reined everyone back in.

"I hate to bail," Alexis apologized, "but I've got rehearsal tonight since we'll all be too tied up to meet tomorrow."

"And thanks for the heads up," Jack said with a

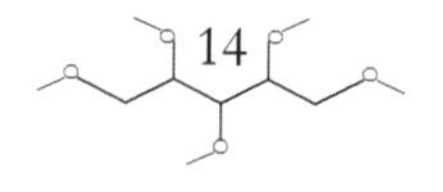

conspiratorial wink. "Your media people've all been cleared."

"You're going to be insufferable," Miranda groaned.

"Aim high – that's our motto," Jack replied.

"Isn't the Army motto: *Be all you can be*?" Bliss's extraneous question got five eye rolls in response.

Alexis's raven-violet eyes, however, betrayed no hint of annoyance as she waited patiently for everyone to refocus. One of the self-proclaimed "heavies" due to a bizarre stone-wallish blocking ability, things rarely rippled her deliberate calm. Basically, she was immune from my personal gift of blurting out stupid things, which made her my idol.

"Anyway," she said when finally given a chance to continue, "I don't have any people coming yet. It's just Captain Dolan and me for now, and sometimes Major Godwin."

"Ah, Miss Crystal, the Rock Goddess," Garrett noted, more than approvingly.

Everyone looked at him, the group movement an unspoken question that he didn't hesitate to answer. "That's what we call you in the gym – we're the jocks, you're the rocks." *We should've known.*

His explanation earned him a groan from everyone but Alexis. "I'll take it. We do rock," she said, surely thinking more of her group's musical talent than their blocking ability. Or maybe she was mimicking Garrett's cockiness – her way of few words always left room for interpretation.

"Wait, before you go," I called out to her, "does your group need anything from Graham – instruments or any other equipment?"

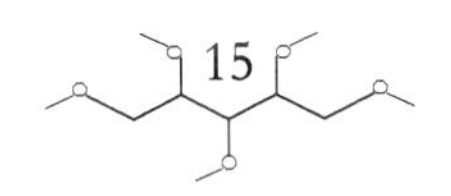

"I don't think so," she answered. "Everyone who plays something brought it with them."

"Okay. If you think of something, let me know." After she nodded, I spread the invitation around the table. "Same for all y'all."

"Did you seriously just say *all* y'all?" California-based Miranda had little tolerance for Southern-isms.

"Yes, she did," Texas-born Bliss jumped to my defense. "She wasn't just talking to y'all," she said with a small wave that included just Jack and I, "but *all* y'all." She illustrated the difference with a sweeping gesture that indicated the entire group.

Miranda's head shake conveyed her unspoken *whatever*, so I reached across the table to pat her hand. "Don't worry," I assured her, "it's contagious. You'll be saying it before long, too, just like me." I could tell she did not take great consolation in the idea.

Alexis took this as her cue to leave, simultaneously pushing back her chair and pushing forward a plate of untouched brownies. "I don't even know why I got these."

"Because you love me," I said, taking the top one and sighing when I found it was still warm. *That Snoopy guy was close when he said 'happiness is a warm puppy,'* I thought, *but happiness is really a warm brownie.*

As the rest of the group started getting their stuff together, Jack turned to Bliss. "Have you found a job yet?" As our least vocal member, she was often in danger of being overlooked, so Jack made sure to never let that happen.

"Not yet," she admitted. "I want to do something that

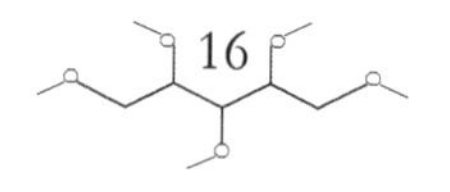

will help people, but I don't know what that could be."

We tossed out some of the same ideas we'd given her before – "Counselor?" "Candy striper?"

"Anyway," she continued when we quieted, "I'm meeting with Colonel Clark at the med center in the morning, and we're going to try and figure something out."

Never one to hang onto the spotlight, she quickly turned her head – and the subject – to me. "You're taking on the whole curriculum, right? That's a big job."

"I'm a big girl," I assured her as I reached for another brownie.

"You will be if you eat that!" Miranda swatted my hand.

I joined the others in stacking the trays and dropping them at the counter by the door on the way out.

"We'll obviously need a health program – nutrition, yoga…," Miranda issued orders for me to pass on to Lieutenant Graham.

"Most def – make Larson teach sex ed," Garrett added, naming the zero-personality head of the medical center and also the faculty person assigned to live on his and Jack's floor in the dorm. The man fell further down my list of preferred physicians than Dr. House. He wouldn't have even *made* the list if he hadn't been taking pretty decent care of Colonel Clark.

"*Ew*," Bliss squeezed her eyes shut to banish the thought.

"Which one of your two brain cells came up with that?" Miranda scolded.

"I'd say they were cells from a little further south," Jack suggested, first giving Garrett a fist bump, then turning to me

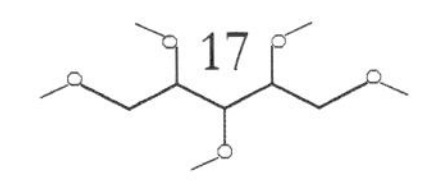

with a guilty shrug that said, *It was too easy; I had to take it.*

"Again, *ew.*" Bliss threw up her small hand in a backwards wave as she started off. When the boys turned toward the path to the gym, I fell into step behind the girls to go back to our rooms.

We'd only gone a few feet across the courtyard when Jack called out, "Clio! Wait up."

I turned immediately at the summons, glad at a second chance to say goodnight.

He came to stop, his face solidly within the kissing zone. "I just wanted to warn you that I'm kidnapping you tomorrow afternoon," he said, brushing a stray hair from my cheek. He wound it gently back around my clip before his eyes returned to mine for a response.

"I feel like I should protest or something to preserve my reputation as a lady," I answered, trying to flutter my eyelashes demurely.

"By all means, go right ahead," he teased. "But let it be known that I will thwart thy futile protestations with my sword of chivalry." He darted in for a too-quick kiss on my grinning mouth, then dropped into a low, swashbuckling bow before jogging off to catch up with Garrett.

THREE

I didn't need to hurry to catch up to Bliss and Miranda; they were waiting for me by the door and made no pretense of pretending they hadn't been watching our little romantic scene.

"He's so sweet," Bliss sighed.

"Ugh, if you're into that." Miranda had apparently not been impressed by the theatrics.

"I thought you were trying to be nicer," I chided.

"Yeah, I keep forgetting that." Her words were dismissive, but her smile was soft. I was starting to think she might actually like being called out when she was being overly harsh because she wasn't really a mean person and didn't particularly want to be thought of that way. She just had strong opinions. *And a tendency to force them on everybody else*, I allowed, but only to myself.

"By the way," she changed tack, "I heard someone calling us 'dis-apps' this morning."

"Really?" My nose wrinkled all on its own.

"Uh-huh," she continued, mirroring my distaste. "We

need to get out in front of that before it sticks."

Bliss and I exchanged looks that said, *Looks like somebody's found herself another crusade.*

"So, I checked the online thesaurus," she said, to which I mentally replied, *Of course you did.* "But every word for disappearing or vanishing was about getting smaller or weaker."

"Oh, no," Bliss's small words held big disappointment. Belittlement of the "dis-apps" was sure to result in serious Mir-acklash against her as a star.

"What about *Urban Dictionary*?" I suggested, and Miranda's thumbs hit cyberspace before all my words had even reached airspace.

"Oooh," she crooned as she scanned the page and I knew I'd scored.

"*Vaporize, phantom, disapoof…,"* she read us the list.

"You could be the *poofs*!" Bliss called out in delight.

"Poof that," Miranda snapped, then offered a synonym more to her liking: "Evanesce."

"Like the band?" I asked.

"Oh, right." She shook her head and kept going. "*Houdini, ninja, stealth….*"

Bliss and I stopped to absorb the last one as Miranda repeated it, testing how it felt on her tongue. "Stealths." Her face broke into a wide smile and her third test-speak came out like a proclamation, "Stealths! Got to put this in motion, girls. See ya!" She turned and headed back down the stairs, descending two at a time.

Bliss and I continued up to the fourth floor and pushed

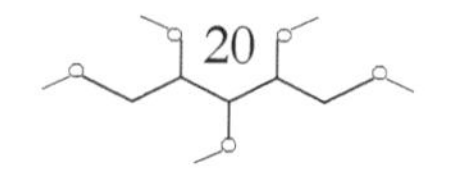

open the door out of the stairwell.

"I like it," I admitted, turning onto our wing and stopping at my door, the first one on the right. "Jocks, rocks, stars, and stealths."

"Me, too," she agreed. "I'm going to work it into my status update and get some points with Miranda," she said, giving me a wave and continuing down the hall to her room.

As I turned my key in the lock, I looked over at the chalkboard posted on the door across the hall. It read, *Back late*, and I felt a twinge of disappointment that Trudy was out. I'd gotten into the habit of checking in with her for a quick chat before bed each night and hated to miss it.

From the day she'd moved in, Gertrude had blown right past "monitor," "guide," and "advisor," dubbing herself hall "mother," although "grandmother" would've been more accurate. She thanked her past nursing career for her strong presence, both physical and emotional, and she'd made it clear from day one that her sole mission on campus was to be available for us girls at all times.

Of course I'd wanted to be leery of her – my blind trust in her predecessor hadn't led me anywhere good – but within five seconds she'd demolished my sad attempt at keeping a wall between us. With her silver-streaked hair, twinkling pewter eyes, and two-handed embracing shake, she'd easily won me over.

Trudy, as she insisted we call her, was definitely a one-eighty from our first guide. Captain Quirk, or Psycho Janet as I now thought of her, had turned out to not only be the daughter of the mad scientist that had secretly drugged our mothers to alter our chromosomes eighteen years ago; she'd also revealed her own twisted, sadistic side by trying to kill my whole group of friends when we discovered her secret. The memory caused my spine to ripple with an involuntary shiver, and I forced myself to shake it off before going into my room to Skype my mom.

I set my iPhone in the stand on the desk facing the bed and scrolled down to my mom's avatar – actually the photo from her last book jacket, which she wrongly claimed was the only flattering picture ever taken of her.

I kicked off my sandals and put my feet up against the edge of the desktop, pushing off my heels so that the chair rocked back and balanced on two legs. I untangled my sunglasses from my hair and tossed them onto the bed that I'd fallen out of habit of making in this parent-less environment. Careful not to lose my balance and tip over, I reached out with one hand to yank the comforter over the rumpled sheets in a half-hearted attempt to straighten up before my mom came into my view and my room into hers.

Within seconds her photo blew up to full-screen size and came to life. She looked even younger than her actual age of forty-one, having bright hazel eyes and shoulder-length hair with my shade of red highlights woven through her dark chestnut.

"Hi, honey!" she greeted me from New York with a wave, thrilled as always to be able to see me while we talked. Our pair of PDAs had been a reactionary purchase after I'd spent the first two weeks on campus completely cut off from the outside world. Even though that situation had since been taken care of, she'd made it clear that she wouldn't take the chance of being

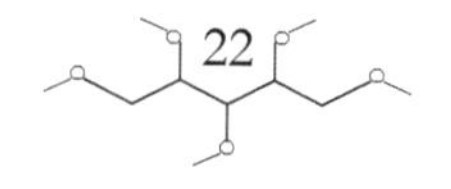

kept apart again.

"Hey, mom!" My response was equally enthusiastic, as I'd never been away from her this long before – almost a full month now. "You packed and ready to go home?"

"I don't have to leave, remember," she made her daily offer. "If you want me to stay, I will." We both knew it was kind of strange that we'd spent the last couple of weeks within fifty miles of each other without ever meeting in person, but both kids and administration had made the united decision to keep campus closed and secure. It may not be the most convenient situation, but we all agreed that the wave of weird letters and threats that'd followed the news of the attack and the purpose of our "camp" had made it necessary.

"Mom, it's crazy for you to sit in the city when we could have these exact same conversations with you home in New Orleans," I reminded her, then admonished, "You also promised me you were not going to stay in your hotel room all afternoon waiting for me to call."

"I didn't," she quickly assured me. "I took a notebook and blanket to Central Park and got some work done." She paused as if choosing her words carefully before continuing. "I started fleshing out an outline for a fictional young adult series based on the C9x experiment and the campus…if that's okay with you, of course," she added quickly.

"I think it's a great idea," I answered. "You're the one who always says how truth is stranger than fiction, right? I don't know if even you, the best-selling Wendy Hart, could've dreamed this up," I teased, using her pen name.

She smiled softly, but remained quiet for a long minute. When she finally spoke, her voice was heavy with guilt. "I am so sorry that this happened to you."

"Regina," I scolded, this time using her real first name. "Stop beating yourself up, will you? I'm fine. Actually, I'm better than fine – I'm *Super Invisible Girl.*" I held my arms out to my sides and gave a model spin, but not a demonstration of my ability. Even though I'd shown her a couple of times before, and assured her repeatedly that most of the other kids could also disappear, I knew it still freaked her out.

"I get it," she promised. "I just want to be sure that you're staying because you want to."

"I swear I'm not being held against my will," I said, meaning every word. "Nobody is."

Yes, the Army had brought us here to figure out what had been done to our bodies. But in all fairness, we wanted to know as much as they did, if not more. And C9x had been the work of one rogue officer, so they hadn't really owed us any of this, but they'd still wanted to make up for what we'd been through. They'd given us everything we could've asked for – kept us "fat and happy," as Miranda once so eloquently put it.

So we'd gone from a state of initial shock upon arrival, through a honeymoon-phase of loving our new digs, followed by a rebellion against what felt too good to be true, before finally settling into our new normal.

I reminded my mom of this now. "It's like we got here and started discovering all these new sides to us and what we could do, then Janet wigged out and almost took it all way." I

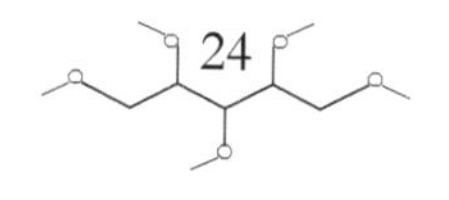

wasn't an idiot; I knew that now they'd seen what we could do, someone else in the organization may be dreaming up another plan to use our special skills. But I also knew that, with the whole world watching, it'd be hard for anyone to take of advantage of us like that again. "I just need to be here with everyone else," I told her. "We need to finish what we started, you know?"

"I know. It's just hard being away from my baby," she said, and I let her have that one without argument.

"And even when I'm a hundred, I'll still be your baby," I added, trying to keep my voice free of mimicry.

Satisfied, she segued into the next topic. "Speaking of starting things, is everyone ready for tomorrow?"

"Yup. We all even came back to the dorm after dinner to make sure we will be well-rested, responsible interns when we report for duty," I assured her, then went on to detail everyone's assignment.

Explaining the jobs to her made me realize how serendipitous it was that there just happened to be a position perfectly suited to each of my friends, even though not every kid on campus had elected to take one on. Working with security was perfect for Jack, the protector; phenomenal athlete Garrett would be a natural at recruiting; Alexis had found her niche in media after siccing them on Janet to literally save our lives; and no one could do a better job of dictating our social calendar than Commander Miranda.

"And Bliss?" Mom asked, quick to notice she hadn't been on the list. I'd told her enough about the others that she practically knew them all, but she'd actually met Bliss via Skype and, of course, already adored her like a second daughter.

"She still doesn't have an assignment," I admitted. "You know how she is – she wants to help people, but doesn't know how to make an internship out of it. She's meeting with Colonel Clark tomorrow to try and figure something out."

"Good for both of them," she answered. "Hopefully, finding the right fit for her will take his mind off his recovery for a little while." She was referring to the colonel's prolonged stay at the campus hospital while his intestines healed from the recent bullet wound. Mom didn't have to ask me how he was doing, both because I'd given her updates and because she spoke with him frequently as well. She'd known Randall Clark since he'd served with my dad in the Gulf War and, like he'd checked in on us over the years after my dad's death, she returned the consideration now.

"And how's Jack?" she asked, not all that casually. I hadn't shared that much about him as far as the "us" of he and I was concerned, but she was perceptive. Very much like Jack in that way, actually.

"He's good," I answered, unable to stop the goofy grin from spreading across my face.

"I'm still waiting to meet him – via satellite, that is," she reminded me.

"I know. Once we get settled into our new routines and all," I agreed, not meaning to sound so noncommittal when I felt fairly confident that they'd get along great.

"How 'bout you – met any cute boys?" I teased, although it had seriously crossed my mind. She'd only been twenty-four

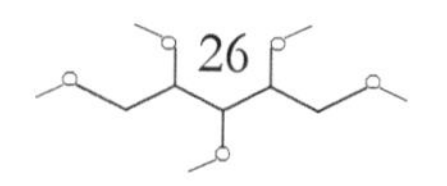

when my dad'd died, and she'd never dated another guy. She always said she was just still in love with John Kaid, which was sweet in a hopeless-romantic sort of way, but, being only a year from graduation, I wanted to see her find someone.

"Oh, stop." She blushed and quickly changed the subject. "Back to you. Are *you* ready for tomorrow?"

"I've got a binder of notes thicker than your last novel." I tossed the assurance over my shoulder as I crossed to the closet and pulled out the outfit I'd selected for my big meeting. The closest things to business-wear I could scrounge up, I held a white button-down under my chin and charcoal pants at my waist for her inspection. It was intentionally basic and boring – all the better for me to be taken seriously.

"Bliss and Miranda helped me put it together," I told her. "What do you think?"

"Very professional," she approved, and I thanked her as I hung everything back up.

"So does that mean Bliss and Miranda have worked things out?" she asked. She knew all about the rift caused by the emergence of extremely-shy Bliss's blinding brilliance and how the extroverted and more obvious "star" Miranda had instead fallen into my group of vanishers. The transposition was the only situation I knew of on campus where the C9x manifestations didn't match up with kids' personalities, and it had almost killed their friendship.

"It doesn't really come up, now that we don't meet as groups anymore," I answered, hearing the relief in my voice. "We don't go around morphing or phasing or whatever, so they can kind of pretend nothing happened."

"Normally, I'd say they shouldn't shelve their emotions and tell you to make them face it," she began, "but I think you all have enough to deal with already."

"Yeah," I agreed. "Right now, trying to justify to the government why they should set up this program for us is a full-time job."

"At least they're keeping their pledge to make things right," she stressed. "Although Randall says it'd be too embarrassing for them to toss you out and close the doors now."

"Works for me," I replied cheerfully.

"As long as you're all safe and sound," she clarified.

"Yes, mom," I answered dutifully, then asked, "Any exciting plans for your last night in the city?"

"I'm having dinner with the other parents who are still in town. I think even the last of us hold-outs are leaving tomorrow." She'd kept me up on the city side of things, so I knew that most of the parents who'd rushed to our area after the story of Janet's deception broke had since returned home, only a couple taking their kids with them. Since our exact location was never disclosed, and they weren't allowed past the gate anyway, some parents had been satisfied with satellite calls and had never come east at all.

"Well, have a safe trip back," I said, secretly glad that my mom hadn't been one of those.

Once we'd both said, "I love you" and disconnected, I turned off the phone to let it charge and dropped onto my bed for a much-needed charge of my own.

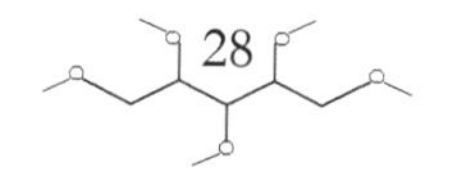

FOUR

*T*oo anxious to get any real sleep, I found myself up Monday morning much earlier than optimal. So early, in fact, that even after the shower had steamed the pillow creases out of my face, I was still faced with a good chunk of time to kill. This meant that fortunately – or maybe not so, depending on how you looked at it – I had time to hit the Starbucks kiosk in the lobby of the main building.

By the time it was reasonable to show up for my meeting, I was more than halfway through the ginormous Frappuccino that had *looked* like a great idea, tasted even better, but left me with a racing heartbeat and accelerated nerves.

"Come in." I ran out of time to smack myself around for the poor choice when Lieutenant Graham responded to my light knock on the office door.

"Good morning," I replied, slightly uncomfortable with the formality that I had not experienced during previous visits to this office when it was Colonel Clark's. Also adding to the awkwardness was the fact that the colonel was dad-aged, while the lieutenant was only a couple of years older than me.

And chiseled like a statue. Like all the officers, he wore regular clothes instead of a dress uniform, but even jeans and a polo shirt couldn't hide his powerful build. Or the laser-blue eyes that burned right through me. I hoped in equal parts that he wasn't making me this unsettled on purpose, and that, despite my unease, my brain would for once be able to control my mouth.

I hadn't seen Lieutenant Graham since the post-shooting press conference, and hadn't actually ever been alone with him except for the very first day when he'd escorted me from New Orleans to campus. And of course I'd been too preoccupied that day with what kind of genetic deformities I might have to pay too close attention to him. Now I wished I'd tried harder to get to know him then.

"Miss Kaid. Have a seat," he said, gesturing to the open chair that faced him across the desk, then returning to his own seat.

"Okay," I answered, placing my binder on my side of his desk.

"Looks like you've done some homework," he noted.

"Yes," I replied, unsure why he seemed so surprised. I didn't have to wait long to find out why.

"I was a little worried," he admitted, "that you were only assigned to me because of your history."

Ugh. "Please don't tell me stories about my dad and your past with him." It seemed like every Army person I met had known my dad and felt obligated to share what was almost always TMI.

"I meant your history with Colonel Clark," he clarified.

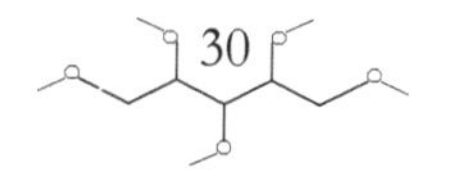

"That he tends to show some favoritism when it comes to you."

"Right. Sorry." I hadn't meant to snap, but sometimes it was too much having so many people wanting to reminisce over a man I couldn't remember.

"How could I have known your dad? He was old enough to be *my* dad, too," he pointed out.

"How old are you?" I asked, thankful he'd opened the door for me to gather a piece of personal data that I very much wanted for my mental file.

"Twenty-one. Almost twenty-two," he answered.

"So how'd you get here?" I didn't mean to be pushy, but I wasn't sure about the math.

"I came straight from West Point with Colonel Clark," he informed me. "Just graduated."

"Colonel Clark was at West Point?" I'd had no idea.

He frowned slightly, as if this were a fact I should've already learned. Maybe he'd forgotten that between discovering super-abilities and trying not to get killed, I'd been a bit too preoccupied to read staff bios.

"He taught there," he filled me in. "He was Head of the Department of Behavioral Sciences and Leadership. Since I majored in leadership, he was my mentor."

"Huh. And he gave that up to come here?"

"Without hesitation. This was his baby." *This* meaning *this campus*. That part I did know from snooping in his office back when I was suspicious of his motives for being here. Before he'd taken a bullet and proved me wrong.

"You must've been at the top of your class, then," I

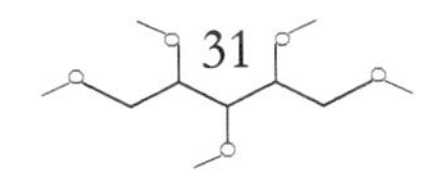

guessed, "for him to bring you here."

"I think it's pretty clear now why he didn't know who he could trust, even within the ranks," he noted, speaking of Janet, who'd been a seemingly upstanding officer before she'd completely lost it.

He continued, "Since I'd been under him for four years and hadn't served in the field yet, he banked on my not having had a chance to be corrupted."

"I guess there's probably a lot I don't know," I conceded.

"Well, now there's less," he wrapped up the line of discussion.

"If we're going to work together every day, can't we be a little more 'at ease,' as you'd say?" I asked, risking a smile.

"Sure. Call me Graham," he said, and I grumbled inwardly, *Right, because dropping the 'Lieutenant' part makes all the difference.* He was harder to talk to than the old Alexis, and it made me determined to break through his wall, even if I had to let my stupid out to do it.

"You know, I'm not a guy, or a jock," I began, "so I'd rather not work on a last-name basis. Do you have a first name?"

"Not that I care to share," he answered in a tone that was not harsh, but definite.

"I'm not asking to be *besties*," I said, cringing at how the caffeine-fueled nerves sabotaged my attempt at a professional demeanor. "Just tell me."

He didn't budge. "Let's consider it need-to-know information."

"Aren't you supposed to be part of the new 'open-book'

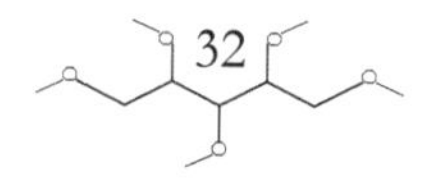

Army?" I framed the words with my fingers in case he didn't speak sarcasm.

"Boy, you're a pain in the ass," he replied.

Okay, so maybe the ball might be moving in the wrong direction, I realized, *but it's better than no movement at all.* Now that I had some momentum going, I just needed to figure out how to push it back the other way.

"This is only a big deal because you're making it one," I pointed out. "Calliope's no golden ticket, either."

"Right," he grumbled and shuffled some papers as an excuse to divert his eyes – an avoidance tactic I was quite familiar with. I waited out the pause until he eventually muttered, "Rutherford."

"Ruth-er-ford?" I drew out, not entirely sure I'd heard him correctly.

He grunted in response, still without meeting my eyes, probably hoping this would pass without commentary. He must've realized it wasn't his lucky day when I involuntarily let out a small giggle.

He jerked his head up – the movement sharp, but a smile threatening at the corners of his mouth. "Where's the sympathy, *Calliope*?" I was glad to see he did speak sarcasm, after all. It would definitely help our communication.

"Nice try, but so not the same thing," I countered.

We fell into another pause, though not awkward or tense like before. Just when he must've figured he was in the clear, I asked, "As in Rutherford Hayes? President number…," I trailed off, having no idea where he fell in the lineup.

"Nineteen. Republican from Ohio. Served 1877 to 1881." He reeled off the facts like a Wikipedia article.

"You know a lot about him," I noted.

"You pretty much have to know about someone you're named after," he pointed out. "People always ask."

"Well, I thought Calliope was a constellation until I got here...." I stopped when I realized how dumb that made me sound.

Even though he was gracious enough to let that pass, I not-so-graciously resumed the name game. "So...Rutherford. That's rough."

"The worst was the year everyone called me the stinky cheese kid," he confided, apparently deciding it'd be easier to stop fighting me. The humor in the memory lit the back of his eyes, softening his face and showing how young he really was.

"I don't get it," I said.

"You would if you were a ten-year-old boy who thought *Rutherford* sounded a lot like *Roquefort*," he explained.

"Oh," I giggled, then stopped quickly so he wouldn't think I was laughing at him. "I bet they wouldn't dare say that now," I said, hoping it came off as complimentary as I intended it to be.

"Thanks," he answered.

"Ford?" I asked, tentatively at first, but more confident in my follow-up. "Can I call you Ford?"

"I think I can live with that," he said, halfway to a smile now.

"Good," I replied, as pleased with myself as if I'd brought

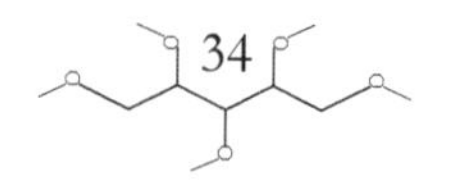

peace to the Middle East.

"Now that we've got that squared away…." He looked back down to his papers.

"What about your middle name?" I couldn't help myself. Though if he'd seemed truly irritated, I'd have tried harder to behave.

His shoulders sagged in defeat before he answered, "No middle name."

"It's so bad you don't want to tell me," I stated, rather than asked.

"I owned up to Rutherford, didn't I?" His exasperated eyes solidly met mine.

"I'm not sure I believe you." This time I didn't worry about the sassiness in my voice, growing more and more confident that he didn't mind my impertinence as much as he pretended to.

"Oh, for crying out loud." He reached into his back pocket, pulled out his wallet, found his military ID, and tossed it face-up between us on the desk.

I kept my hands in my lap and my eyes locked on his as I leaned forward to examine the card, only breaking the gaze when I got close enough to read the tiny print. Sure enough, it read *Rutherford NMN Graham*. Before straightening up, I took the opportunity to check out the picture as well. Turned out he photographed almost as well as he looked in real life. That must be why they put him in front of the camera for all the news stories.

"Satisfied?" he asked, returning the card to his wallet,

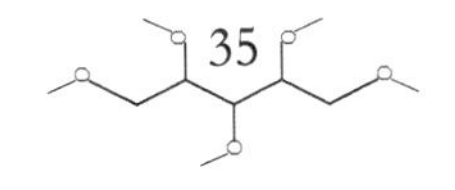

wallet to pocket, hands to desk.

"Yes," I said, nodding. Then, like I was having an out-of-body experience, I reached across the desk and patted the back of his hand. "That wasn't so bad, was it?"

"Don't press your luck," he half-snarled, but there was no force behind it.

Duly admonished, I returned my hand to my own side of the desk, tempted to actually sit on it to keep from poking him again.

He picked up the top sheet of paper on his pile, making another attempt to advance the actual meeting agenda. "Now that we've sufficiently wasted half the day...."

I rolled my eyes at the faux drama. He may have begun this meeting all-business, but he'd shifted to my level with very little gear-grinding. Even a blind man wouldn't buy his irritated grizzly act anymore.

"Please," I said pointedly. "In my regular life, I wouldn't even be up yet."

"That's because you're soft," he teased, his smile stretching to three-quarters.

"If I didn't know better, I'd think maybe *you* were softening toward *me*," I replied.

"Focus, Kaid," he ordered.

"Aye, aye, Captain." I gave a mock-salute. "Er, Lieutenant. Graham. Sir."

"I thought we agreed on Ford," he corrected, this time with a real, full smile.

Mutually satisfied, we got to work comparing notes, going

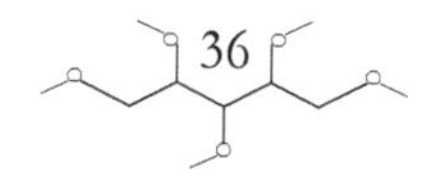

over schedules. We talked about long-term plans for a full school semester, about state requirements and national standards. There were so many rules to go over and lists to review that we hardly made a dent in my notes. Our meetings were only slated for mornings so that he could dedicate his afternoons to his duties as acting commander, but by the time we reached a good stopping point, we'd completely blown through lunch.

"One more thing," he said, plucking a yet-untouched post-it from the corner of his desk. "We have two new kids coming to campus. Not that two people are going to change much as far as scheduling or curriculum, but I wanted to let you know."

"They just suddenly decided to come now?" I'd wondered a lot about the handful of kids that hadn't reported to campus along with the majority of us. Even these two showing up left three more unaccounted for. That we knew of, anyway.

"That's right," Ford confirmed.

"I guess I never really thought we had a choice," I said hesitantly.

"Come on, Kaid," he laughed. "It's not like some MPs showed up and threw you in the back of a Hummer."

"I know," I returned, "but you are the Army."

"Don't forget the kinder, gentler part," he added with a deadpan look, but light tone. "So, if you'd thought there was a choice, you wouldn't have come?" he asked.

"No, I still would've come," I answered without hesitation. "I want to find out what happened to me. And what's going to happen next."

"We're working on it," he said, reassuring me even more than he knew.

"I'm not that worried," I told him.

"Good. So, Xavier Wittman and Rae Mahoney are both arriving tonight. Preliminary interviews placed one with the musicians and the other with the athletes."

"Both boys, huh?" I noted with interest, seeing as how our current girl-to-guy ratio was like eighty-twenty.

"No, the athlete's a girl – Rae, Reagan. She's a snowboarder from Utah." *Interesting.*

"That could be tough," I said, voicing my concerns both about her being the only girl jock, and also that her sport of choice wasn't one she could do much training for on the East Coast in July.

"Yeah," he agreed, "so if you want to keep an eye out for her, her room's on the fourth floor like yours, just a different wing."

"Will do," I assured him, resisting the urge to salute.

"You know, I think we're going to do alright," he noted, nodding as if he hadn't been sure that would be possible until right now.

"I think so, too," I agreed with a whole-hearted grin. Then, feeling an inexplicable urge to prolong the conversation, I found myself extra-slowly gathering my papers and babbling, "So, back to things I should know, but don't – I know we're in Jersey, but where, exactly?"

"North Jersey." He didn't seem too put-off by my random question. "Sussex County, near New York and PA."

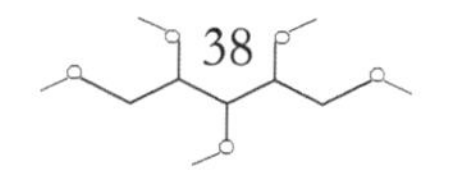

"So how do you keep all this hidden, when we're so close to major cities?" I probed.

"Believe me, this is an extremely secret location," he assured me, "and you're not the first project to be housed here. There're over fifteen thousand acres of wildlife management areas, plus seven state forests and parks. Plenty of cover."

"You make it sound like we're wild animals on a game preserve," I pointed out.

He chuckled. "More like a protected species."

By now we were at the door, and I was starting to feel guilty for taking up so much of his time when I knew he had more important things to attend to. I also felt a slight urge to apologize for my non-best behavior.

"I'm sorry if I was kind of smart-mouthed before; I'm not really like that." I started on the right course, but predictably veered off. "Okay, I am like that, just usually not out loud."

I was through the door and well past him when he called out, "Good afternoon, Clio."

I turned to see him propped in the doorway, one hand high on its frame, the opposite hip leaning into the jamb, completely relaxed and grinning wider than ever.

"Good afternoon, Ford," I called back, returning the smile in full. I gave a little wave before walking away, totally thrilled at how my new job was working out.

FIVE

I headed back to my room to drop off my notes and change into better picnic attire. The khaki shorts and olive ruched halter I ended up in were the result of some serious deliberation, though hopefully didn't look that way.

By the time I skipped back down the stairs, Jack was waiting out front *like a gentleman caller* as Trudy would probably say. Even on such a hot day, seeing him spread extra warmth from my cheeks to my toes.

If someone had told me a month ago that I'd be practically glued to a boy, no matter how cute he was, I'd have laughed out loud. I valued my alone-time, probably the main reason I'd done okay as an only child, and I thought spending every second with another person could only make me sick of him.

But when I met Jack, I had to push aside those definite no's to let in some amazing yeses. Being with him made me feel *more* myself, instead of less. It wasn't as if I lost myself in him, but more like he banished my faults and let me be only my best. As he stood before me now, framed in a halo of afternoon sun, even his shadow stretched toward me. Everything about him called to me. His soft brown eyes had a way of looking not just at me, but *into* me, making me feel not exposed or vulnerable, but treasured. It was as if he could see something in me no one else ever had; I only wished I knew what it was.

He'd come equipped with an actual wicker basket, which he shifted to his left arm in order to offer me his right. I slid my hand into the crook of his elbow and let him guide me away from the path that we usually took. The idea of going off somewhere alone with him made me practically giddy. We spent a lot of our time together with our friends, which was great, but I also liked having him all to myself. Except that I actually cared when I spilled something on myself in front of him, he was as much my best friend as Bliss was, and even one day apart gave us a lot to catch up on.

"I found a great spot on my way back from the treehouse," he said, squeezing my hand in his elbow.

"What's the treehouse?" I asked, squeezing back.

"That's what they call the security office," he explained.

"Is it really a treehouse?" I found the idea intriguing.

"Kinda, sorta," he said. "I'm only half-kidding when I say you're not authorized to know; I can't really give you the details, sorry." His lightly dimpled smile almost made me wish he had more things to apologize for, so I could see it again and again.

"That's okay – I get it," I assured him.

"Besides, I'm sure we can find better things to talk about," he said with the characteristic wink he saved just for me.

"Like the new kids," I said, it suddenly dawning on me

that he must've heard they were coming, too.

"Right," he confirmed. "They're probably meeting with the one-woman welcoming committee as we speak."

"Bliss," he said in response to my confused frown. "You didn't know?"

"No, I haven't talked to her all day." *And she better have gotten the assignment while I was at work*, I thought, *or she's going to be in big trouble later for not telling me.*

"That's right," Jack said, nodding as he remembered, "Colonel Clark was going to ask her to do it this morning. Major Lombardo said that during our briefing; we probably all found out about it at the same time."

"Should we go back and help her?" I suggested, feeling a little guilty.

"You can't do everything," he reminded me. "Anyway, she's just taking them on a quick tour, then bringing them to dinner. They might not even want to eat with her once they meet some of the other heavies and jocks."

We'd reached our destination, so he set down the basket and turned to me. "So, hi," he said, pulling me into the giant hug that'd had to wait until his hands were free. His arms wrapped around me, gentle but powerful – his hold somehow stronger because of its softness. My own arms wound their way around his waist and I relished in the perfect fit of us. It was like he'd been made for me – shoulders just enough wider than mine, tall enough for me to rest my head in the curve of his neck and feel protected but not engulfed.

He kissed my hair just above my ear before pulling out of

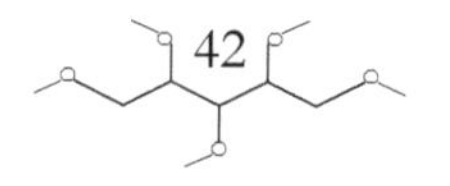

the embrace to unpack. I took advantage of the chance to watch him, noting how his hair had gotten a little long from not having had a chance to cut it. With my own low-maintenance style, I hadn't really thought about the things we were missing on campus, like a barbershop. Besides, it suited him, giving him a carefree boyishness that made him even more adorable than usual.

He pulled out the blanket first – a movie-prop sheet of red- and white-checked cotton. "Don't tell Miranda," he confided conspiratorially. "It's one of her samples for the fourth."

"So how'd you get it? Lock-picking again?" I alluded to one of our earlier escapades.

"Of course not," he said with feigned offense. "Everything she orders has to go through security. And with all the stuff that's been coming in, Clark must've given her the go-ahead for this event weeks ago. I think we'll be putting in some long nights to check it all."

His iPod was next out of the basket, and I tried to guess what new and interesting music he'd brought to share with me. It was sure to be some little-known indie artist with a new take on jazz or some other old style; something both classic and unique – something very Jack.

I waited patiently as he plugged in the speakers and selected the playlist. When the music started, the opening notes were very soft, but easily identifiable.

"James Taylor?" I asked, surprised at how far off my guess had been.

"Yeah," he confirmed. "I thought of him because he kind

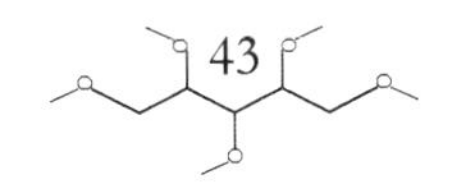

of leaves the music in the background and lets the lyrics really be the soul of the songs."

"Like our duet would be," I said, getting his point without him having to explain.

"Maybe," he shrugged with a sly smile, as if the idea hadn't occurred to him.

"How's the song-writing going, anyway?" he posed casually, not wanting to pry.

"Not really at all," I admitted. "I'm supposed to get together with Alexis Thursday night to talk through some things; that's the soonest we could both fit it into our new schedules."

He nodded while continuing to unpack. "Sunblock?" he offered, pulling out a yellow tube.

Despite how appealing the prospect of having him rub it into my shoulders sounded, I didn't need it and told him so.

"Don't redheads freckle in the sun?" he asked.

"I don't know; I never do," I said with a shrug. "Maybe it's because I'm part Greek, on my dad's side."

"Hence the mythological name, *Calliope*," he drew out the word that he claimed to love, though I most definitely did not. Of course, he was a vault for those sorts of classic romantic works and ideals. He was so much of an old soul, I sometimes wondered, *Could someone be truly wise at seventeen?* I only knew that I felt more interesting just being around him.

He pulled out the food next, like bunnies from a top-hat, and my mouth began to water at the choices presented to me. I couldn't have planned a better menu myself: roast beef po-boys with horseradish mustard, blue tortilla chips – way more fun than

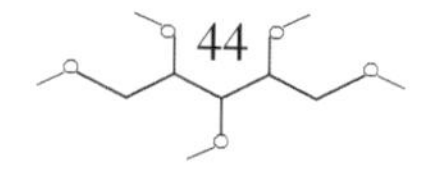

yellow ones – and guacamole that, when opened, released a slight whiff of Tabasco, a secret ingredient I'd never seen anyone else add.

"Good guess?" he asked, reading my smile.

"Perfect," I confirmed. As always, he'd thought of everything. A lot of times – *okay, pretty much all the time* – I didn't think I deserved him.

It hardly seemed fair that he could have it all – be everything any girl could want in a boy rolled into one. But then again, like the rest of us, he had been an unwilling participant in an illicit genetic experiment. Maybe the cosmos had decided to make him so perfect to kind of even things out. And in that case, maybe *my* reward was getting to be with him.

I was so caught up in my thoughts that I hadn't realized he'd closed the basket and was quietly watching my face. "Your eyes are really light green today," he noted.

"That's because I'm happy," I answered.

"I've noticed that they change," he agreed.

"Yeah, they get darker when I'm upset," I confirmed.

"I don't ever want to see that again," he said softly.

"Everyone says it's pretty disturbing," I answered.

"No, I mean I don't ever want to see you upset again," he corrected, holding my gaze.

"As long as you keep feeding me like this, you won't have to worry about that," I joked, breaking the intensity of the mood in typical me-fashion.

Jack just rolled with it, eternally forgiving of my flaws. "So how was your day, dear?" he tossed out lightly, taking a bite of his sandwich while he waited for me to answer.

I took a moment to swallow the chip I was chewing and remind myself that I was supposed to be working on my romantic-crippledness. Since I'd known him, he'd been perpetually sweet, which I returned with perpetual moron-icy. Any other guy would probably have given up, but Jack stayed patient and understanding – making the whole thing cyclical, really. Hopefully I'd get a chance this afternoon to redeem myself a little.

I gave him an overview of my day while we ate, finishing up in time for dessert.

He took his turn to tell me about his day while fishing out a pint of mint chocolate chip ice cream and two spoons. The container gave a little beneath his fingers and he apologized for its partial melted-ness.

"That's how I like it," I assured him, but he looked doubtful. "No, really – at home I nuke it in the microwave until it's like ice cream soup with a couple iceberg-y chunks." I stopped myself before it got worse, self-lecturing, *Why do you always have to sound like such a weirdo?*

Unfazed, he filled me in on more of his first day in security – as much as he could, anyway. I found all the rules and codes and procedures pretty fascinating, but it wasn't long before he used his typical smoothness to turn the subject back to my work.

I got so caught up with sharing the gazillion ideas Ford and I had come up with just this morning that I was shocked to suddenly find the ice cream container empty and the sun

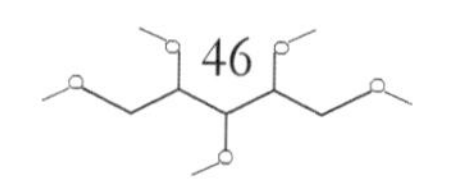

markedly lower on the horizon.

"I can't believe I monopolized our whole conversation," I apologized, embarrassed.

"Not at all," he said, not a patronizing note in his voice.

"Come on, nobody wants to hear me go on and on all afternoon," I pointed out.

"I beg to differ," he countered.

"Right, because I'm so utterly fascinating?" I rolled my eyes to illustrate the point.

"Yes," he said without a hint of sarcasm.

"So is this it?" I asked, somewhat out of the blue.

"What do you mean?" he asked, needing clarification.

"We stay here, we work, we go to school…," I trailed off.

"And?" he asked, still not seeing where I was going.

"Well, do we ever get any answers?" I knew it was almost a rhetorical question.

"Yes," he answered slowly, thoughtfully. "But it might take a while."

"What if it takes forever?" I persisted. "What do we do until then?"

"I have an idea." He crept closer with each word, the last bringing his face within millimeters of mine.

Before I had a chance to destroy the moment, he closed the remainder of the gap, using his soft kiss to ease me down gently until we were laying side-by-side, facing each other.

He shifted an inch to adjust his arm beneath us at the same time a breeze wafted a rogue hair across my nose. I flinched slightly, sure that I was going to sneeze and horrified that even my hair seemed out to sabotage me. But Jack swiftly tucked the stray tendril back behind my ear. I marveled at how the warmth of his sun-kissed skin stood in such contrast to the minty cool of his breath as my lips found their way back to his.

When we parted several long moments later, I grinned and said, "You should've cut me off a lot sooner."

"Oh, I cut you off?" he balked, dropping onto his back. He neatly folded his arms behind his head and crossed his feet at the ankles so that he was completely out of physical contact with me.

"Hey!" I delivered a flat-handed smack to his ribcage.

"No, by all means," he teased, "please pick up where you left off."

I leaned very close over him, putting my hands on either side of his smirking face, and let my hair fall into a curtain enclosing us. "I think," I said slowly, "that this is where I left off."

"Are you sure? Because I swore you were talking about social studies...." He continued to keep his hands and lips to himself, and I couldn't help but think that I might like the goofy, teasing side of him even more than the thoughtful, caring part.

"You want some social studies?" I was happy to come up with a decently coy response.

"Oh, I'm pretty sure I need it." His was better.

Now it was my turn to use words to inch closer. "Okay, I'll give you more social studies than you know what to do with," I said, ending by pressing my lips down on his. I could feel his impish grin even as he returned the kiss.

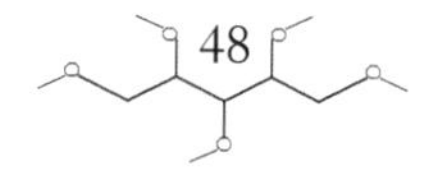

Unfortunately, it was only a few moments before the evil moment-ruining demon inside me roared its ugly head. I pulled back slightly and asked, "Which president was Rutherford Hayes?"

"What number?" he asked, slightly disoriented.

"Yeah," I said.

"Nineteen," he answered.

"Ugh." I made an involuntary groan.

"Is that bad?" he asked, still confused.

"Just one time I would like to know something you don't," I admitted. We'd talked once about how he liked to know a little about everything so that he could talk to anyone. And it was true – he could talk sports and movies with Garrett, music and technology with Alexis, even health with Miranda, for whom talking to at all was a challenge for most people.

"You know lots of things I don't," he said with complete conviction.

"Like what?" I challenged, unable to name one thing.

"Like the words to more songs than *Lyrics.com*," he answered. *That's true,* I conceded inwardly, *though not all that useful of a skill.*

"And how to become invisible," he continued, looking slightly more serious, even a little sad. I hated that he was still the only one on campus to have manifested no special ability. He'd tested positive for the C9x mutation, and his mom's name was on Heigl's list, but nothing had happened and I knew he thought that meant there was something wrong with him.

Before I could offer any words of reassurance, he moved

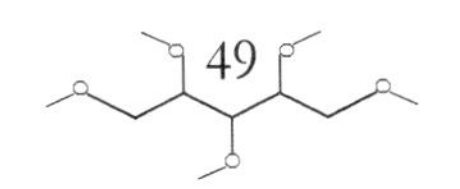

on to his last example. "Best of all," he finished, "you stop time whenever I'm with you."

He had a way of quieting not just my mouth but my mind, and my heart melted instantly into the chocolate brown of his eyes. He might be too good to be true, but I knew better than to tempt fate by saying that out loud and risk having him be the one to vanish. I abandoned all thoughts entirely until the world took its turn to disappear.

SIX

Now that we'd gotten most of the getting-to-know-you stuff out of the way, my Tuesday morning session with Ford was much more productive. Thanks to our initially awkward – but wholly necessary – breakthrough, we'd been able to pick up where we left off and jump into work with an easy rapport. Not only had he not flinched at my less-than-stellar remarks; today he'd actually laughed out loud at the cleverer ones. I'd even filled him in on Miranda's campaign to get everyone to call the disappearing group "stealths."

"Not bad," he'd said, turning it over in his mind.

"It made me think that maybe the campus needs a name, too," I'd suggested.

"It has a name," he'd been quick to inform me. "U-S-C-T-S-A-I-N-J."

"Huh?" was the only word my brain had been able to send out.

"United States Cosmic Top Secret Atomal Installation, New Jersey," he'd responded, filling out the acronym without taking a breath.

"You say that whole thing every time you talk about this place?" I'd already forgotten half the letters by the time he'd gotten to the end.

"Of course not," he'd answered. "We call it the campground."

"I'm not sure I can sell that to Miranda," I'd admitted. I still wasn't all that sure how I felt about the nickname myself, but I was thrilled that he'd shared one of his code words with me. That Progress – *with a big P* – had given me major confidence in our ability to put together a valid school program as well.

Wrapping up early, however, had left me with a wide-open afternoon, but all of my friends still occupied. Even Bliss was working her "job" today – checking in with both the jocks and the heavies to see how her new charges were fitting in. If I were one of the new kids, I'd just release her from duty and self-navigate, but I kept that to myself since she was so excited to finally have an actual assignment.

So I had no reason to turn down the sun, which was embarking on the second half of its journey across the azure sky, when it beckoned me outside for a walk.

Just outside the back door of the dorm, I queued up the newest playlist on my iPhone, giving thanks yet again for the return of internet access and my new online friend, *Napster*. I scrolled down the list until I got to *Just Jack*, which started with the Teddy Geiger tune from the first dance and our almost first kiss, included some Jamie Cullum from the starry first date that resulted in our *actual* first kiss, and ended with songs that just made me think of him, like The Script's *I'm Yours*. I took another minute to add a new track by James Taylor to commemorate yesterday's perfect picnic.

I mused over how I'd compiled such a collection for a boy I'd known for such a short time. I knew that part of the reason I'd fallen so fast was because we'd gone through so much so quickly, navigating more obstacles together than most people would face in a lifetime. But I also knew that the universe had brought us here, now, to find each other.

I had just popped in my ear buds and started the music when Garrett sprang up behind me, heading the same way.

"Hey, Peaches," he called, flicking my ponytail. By the time I turned around to see who was there, he'd already circled back to where I'd started. I ended up doing a bumbly three-sixty before finally ending up facing him.

"Peaches?" I practically hissed my objection.

"Sure. I had to check-swing 'Foxy,' so I'm gaming something new." He feigned a jab at my stomach, but my resulting back-step was more recoil from the ridiculous moniker than self-defense.

"And that's what you came up with?" I made it clear that he'd gone from worse to…worser.

"You're southern, peaches are southern…," he left off the implied *duh*. "Hey, I'm no wordsmith."

My responding laugh came out with an unintended snort. "I don't think I've ever heard anyone under seventy-five say 'wordsmith,' G."

"Scoring my point," he agreed, pulling one knee to his chest after the other to warm up his muscles. "Wanna run?"

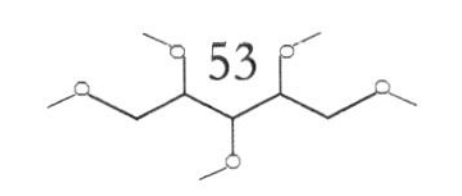

I laughed even louder this time, pointing out, "As if I could keep up with you. Besides being like a foot taller than me, you're super-humanly fast, remember?"

"So I'll run backwards," he negotiated, not one to be easily deterred. "That way you can geek the physique." He dipped his chin briefly to direct my eyes down his torso in case I hadn't caught his meaning.

Admittedly, it was a great view – he stood a full six and a half feet tall with sun-lit sandy hair, North Pacific eyes, and, of course, the flawlessly cut form he'd pointed out. In truth, if he wasn't so goofy, I'd have been way too intimidated by his looks to have ever even talked to him, let alone become friends. And yet, even with all the perks, he was still no Jack.

"Okay, let's go." I acted like I was giving in, but I really hadn't needed much convincing to hang out with my favorite guy friend. His timing was kind of good, actually; I'd planned on using music to work through something that was bothering me, but he could fill in.

"You know," I began, dropping my phone into the front pocket of my not-running shorts, "I've been thinking a lot lately about what Janet planned to do with us."

"You mean with the others?" he corrected. "'Cuz she planned to shoot us."

"Right," I conceded, "but what do you think she was going to do with everyone else?"

"Turn them into her own personal Army," he answered. "She told us that."

"But to do what?" I persisted.

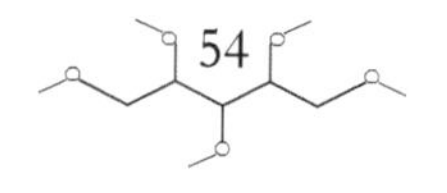

"Conquer the world, I guess. Or at least New Jersey." He shrugged off the idea. "Who cares?"

"I just think about it sometimes, don't you?" I asked.

"Nope," he answered without missing a beat. "Ding-dong, that witch is gone. I only think about good stuff."

"Like…?" I gave him a lead-in.

"Like now that I'm a superhero and all, it may be time to start wearing my underwear on the outside of my pants."

"Don't be ridiculous," I contested.

"Right. I should just give up the pants altogether…," he thought out loud, and I didn't dare encourage him by responding.

"You better tell me if I'm about to crash," he warned before we took off on our jog.

"Don't worry, I'll watch your back – literally," I assured him.

As we started down the path, I found myself in awe at how easily he moved in such an unnatural manner while still maintaining complete control. His ability had to be the best one – the closest to being an actual superpower, anyway, instead of just an oddity.

"So, what're you scheming for the *cur-ric-u-lum*?" He jokingly drew out each syllable as if pronouncing a foreign word.

"What do you want to see?" I returned, honestly looking for his input.

"Some sick math," he answered immediately.

"Seriously?" I asked him.

"Yeah," he repeated, as if I should've seen the obviousness of it. Since I hadn't, he explained, "Sports is all

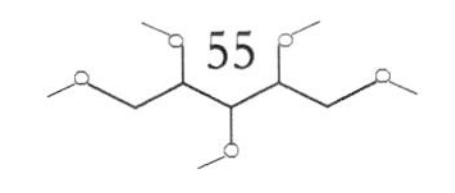

math."

"It qualifies for maybe second grade math," I countered.

"PML," he groaned.

"Pretty much legit?" I ventured.

"Peeing myself laughing," he corrected. "I mean projective geometry, calculating angles…." He checked to see if I was adequately impressed by the big words, since I'd warned him a thousand times that if he kept talking crazy, no one would ever know how smart he actually was.

"Alright, I can see that," I said, rewarding his intelli-speak.

"And then there's strategy," he went on, wiggling his eyebrows maniacally. "Don't even get me started on the G-Lee of abstract math…."

"Okay, Bert, I get it," I tried to rein him in.

"Sure, Ernie. Who's Bert?" His response was sharp and even, though I was starting to get a little winded.

"Bertrand Russell," I explained. "The guy who said that math possesses not only truth but beauty. It's painted on the wall at my school."

"True dat." He fist-thumped his chest and I could see that his daily allotment of profound conversation was officially played out.

"So how's work?" I asked, hoping to elicit a long enough response from him that my breathing could catch up.

"Not bad." *No such luck.*

"How's your new teammate?" I tried again. I'd gotten back too late last night to quiz Bliss on our new floor-mate.

"Rae's cool," he answered, offering no further description.

"Did you find out why she didn't come in June like the rest of us?" I was dying to know.

"Training," he said, again short on detail.

"I never considered not coming," I admitted.

"I did," he contradicted.

"Really?" I was more shocked than I probably should have been.

"Yeah. If we'd made play-offs...."

"What?" I interrupted with exaggerated horror. "You're a *lew*-ser?"

"Not even," he blew off the slight. "Our pitcher threw out his shoulder and we didn't have stellar back-up."

"I'm sorry," I apologized.

"No worries. It landed me here at Camp Fabuloso," he teased, sticking out his tongue.

"Well, I'm glad you're here," I told him sincerely.

"Same here, Hot Sauce," he shot back. *Getting too serious; point taken*, I acknowledged inwardly.

"So how does Rae fit in with the guys?" I returned to safer subjects.

"She's lying low," he answered. "Scouting the talent."

My cattier side wanted to ask if he meant scouting for workout partners or *partner* partners, but I kept it to myself. I'd learned my lesson about judging people with Alexis, and I knew better than to guess about Rae's intentions before I'd even met her. Although, if she was as toned and gorgeous as the guy jocks,

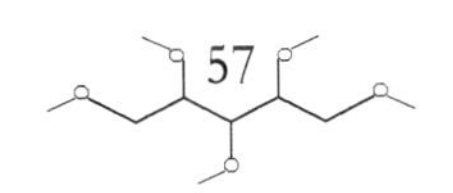

she might pose an obstacle to Bliss in her tortoise-paced pursuit of Garrett.

"So how's work at the big house?" While I'd been busy trying to derail my newest runaway-worry train, Garrett had moved on.

"I already told you," I reminded him. "How's the recruiting going?" I tried again to get him talking, thinking maybe this'd be a more leading topic.

"Same. How's Jack?" *Not just no dice, but no fair.*

"Same. How's Bliss?" I flung back.

"Well played," he conceded. "A good offense can be the best defense." He couldn't possibly think I'd let him get away with that.

"Subtlety's not getting anyone anywhere," I pointed out, talking about both this conversation and his *non*relations with Bliss. I knew that she may never be able to get up the nerve to do anything about it, but I wasn't exactly sure why he hadn't. I decided to offer some advice. "You know, sometimes you've got to stop circling the block and just pull in the driveway and honk the horn."

"Huh?" His puzzled act had zero believability.

"Don't play games with me," I admonished. "Everyone thought you were getting together back at the dance. Then things just kind of stalled."

"*Sesame Street* and *Hot Wheels*? You know, I can probably keep up even without the pre-K metaphors," he assured me.

If I didn't have to focus all my energy on keeping pace, I'd have stuck my tongue out at him for the snarky remark. And

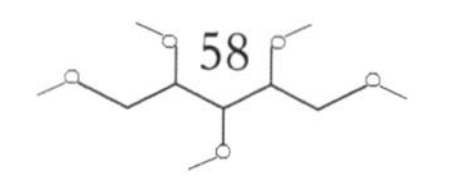

for his ability to backpedal at a speed that winded me forwards.

"What, are you scared?" I managed to get in a shot between breaths.

"You're playing with fire, girl," he warned.

Before he could summon up a good chaser, I gave a little gasp and darted my eyes over his shoulder.

He froze mid-stride and whirled in a one-eighty to face the non-existent danger I'd pretended to see. "Gotcha." I smiled, coming to a stop beside him and bending forward to rest my hands on my knees. "I need a breather."

He laughed and hip-checked me, though not hard enough to knock me over – basically acting like the brother I'd never had.

We'd come up on the gym, so he made a show of checking himself out in its mirrored façade. He lengthened first one long leg behind him in a leisurely calf stretch, then the other.

I didn't venture down this way often enough to get used to the incredible structure. Even though our dorm matched the gym's four stories of height, its sandy brick walls were nowhere near as impressive as this glass monument to athleticism.

I didn't need to go inside to be reminded that the interior was even more mind-blowing than the outside; all four floors were wide open in the great glass room and the football-length shiny blue floor reflected the light upward, creating the illusion of a box of sky. It couldn't have been a more perfect design, since the spectacular feats performed by the jocks were as close to flying as a human being could get.

While I copied his moves to loosen my own unpracticed muscles, Garrett asked, "How 'bout field trips? We goin' down the shore? I'd like to show *The Situation* what's up."

"Hey, do you see something over there?" I broke in, looking over his shoulder toward the treeline on the far side of the building.

"Like I'm falling for that again," he said, shaking his head.

"No, really," I insisted and pointed while walking in the same direction.

He covered the ten-plus yards in only a few strides and then stopped so abruptly – as if he'd slammed into Alexis or another one of the heavies – that I almost crashed into his backside when I caught up. He instinctually put up his arm to shield me, but not before I'd gotten a clear glimpse of what had stopped him so suddenly.

It was a dead body.

SEVEN

"**W**ho is it?" I whispered, apparently concerned about rousing the dead person.

"I don't know – I can't tell from here." Garrett came as close to snapping as I'd ever heard him. *That's not good,* I thought. *If the joker can't keep it together, I'm toast.*

"We need to get closer," I nudged.

He managed to move forward without actually getting any closer to the body. "That's a lot of blood," he pointed out uneasily.

"Mm-hmm," I agreed through closed lips as I moved up behind him. My hand closed over my nose even though there was no discernable smell. Yet.

Garrett finally braved one giant step to make the ID. "It's Dr. Larson."

"Is he really dead?" I asked.

"He sure looks dead," Garrett answered tersely.

"Should we check?" I might have said *we*, but we both knew I only meant him.

"What, like check for a pulse or something?" Garrett

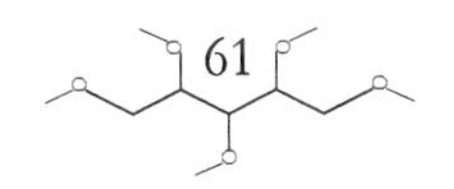

grimaced at the idea.

"I don't know – maybe." I heard my voice teeter toward hysteria.

"I don't think we're supposed to touch him," Garrett disagreed. "That's what they always say on cop shows. We could destroy evidence."

"But what if he's still alive? What if he just needs CPR?" I posed hopefully.

"Do you *know* CPR?" Garrett asked sharply.

"No, but I'd give it a shot if it would help," I snapped back.

Garrett used one toe to nudge Larson's leg just above the ankle, then jumped back when the foot flopped listlessly to the side. "He's definitely dead," he pronounced.

"And I definitely saw some evidence fall off," I responded sourly.

"Seriously?" he criticized my bad timing.

"I learned all my bad behavior from you," I assured him, though I wished I could take back the crass comment.

"We have to go for help," he decided in the joint pause.

"You go," I told him. "You're faster."

"I can't just leave you here," he argued.

"Why? In case he comes back to life?" The tense situation continued to bring out my snarkier side.

"Yeah, because then he'd need that CPR that you don't know how to do!" he fired back and I shot him my dirtiest look.

"I meant that the killer could come back," he said evenly.

"So if I hear someone coming, I'll vanish," I assured him.

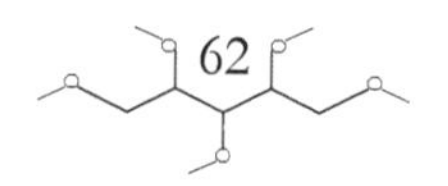

"But what if it's me?" he countered.

"Geez, Garrett, then yell, 'it's me' so I'll know!" I barked.

"What if it's the killer, but he says he's me to trick you?" he stalled.

"Just go!" I shouted in frustration.

"Okay," he finally agreed, "but don't move."

"I'll stay still as a heavy," I promised, and he took off at a dead run.

Alone with the body, I couldn't help comparing my life to a bad TV special. A month ago, I'd been a regular high school student, getting ready for senior year. *And look at me now.*

Despite my taunting of Garrett, I was tempted to roll the lolled foot back to where we'd found it, but the thought of actually touching the body quashed the urge. I wanted to look away, but my head refused to cooperate. I'd never actually seen a real live dead body before... *Okay, that might not be the best way to put it.*

The complete stillness of the air emphasized how unnaturally still Larson lay there. Plus the sweat from my jog, combined with the July humidity, made my skin so sticky it almost felt like the blood was on me. But even the resulting nausea wasn't enough to make me turn my eyes away.

I noted how his stiff, cropped hair remained stubbornly in place, and that his gray eyes seemed locked in a blank yet piercing stare. His hulky, soldier-strong form was now nothing but an empty shell. *Not that he was so filled with life before*, I thought wryly, then immediately admonished myself.

Examining his vacant face made me feel even guiltier for

having never liked him. Yes, he'd been kind of clinic-creepy, but he'd also taken good care of Colonel Clark. Just because he hadn't been the friendliest guy, didn't necessarily make him a *bad* guy. I hadn't given him a fair shot, and now I wouldn't get a chance to.

It wasn't long before my thoughts wandered from guilt into more selfish territory, asking, *What does this mean for us?* Dr. Larson had been in charge of all campus research, had personally collected the data and samples for his studies. *Will his successor be able to pick up where he left off, or will we be back at the start?* I couldn't let myself think that there might not be a successor. Or a campus.

It suddenly occurred to me that he may have already discovered something. *If so, would he have told anyone? And could it have been worth killing him over?*

I hadn't realized I'd taken a step back with each new thought until I found myself right in the path of an oncoming vehicle. I jumped out of the jeep's way, relieved to see Ford at the wheel and Garrett beside him in the passenger seat. He must've gone straight to the main building instead of the medical center, which made sense since Ford's office was much closer to the gym. He probably wouldn't have even been able to get past the over-automation to get into the med center anyway, let alone find an actual human being to help.

Ford simultaneously threw the jeep in park and jumped out. Before he'd even reached the body, Major Lombardo roared up on a four-wheeler, followed by Trudy on another one.

While Lombardo hung back to survey the scene, Trudy headed straight for the body. Ford quickly yielded to her and her expertise as a nurse.

She plucked one limp wrist from the ground and held on long enough to confirm that Larson was indeed gone. Ford then signaled Major Lombardo with a solemn nod, and the two men picked up the body to load it into the back of the jeep.

Garrett climbed out and followed them to the back, hovering near the bumper but not quite able to offer any help. I saw that he was looking a little green – probably because theaters didn't show films in 4-D with smell, and moving the body had stirred up a pretty rank odor.

Ford took off for the medical center, leaving Lombardo behind to secure the area.

"Come on," Trudy called to Garrett and me as she climbed back onto her ATV.

"Uh, no thanks," Garrett muttered, putting up his huge hand as if he could block it all out. "I'll hike it."

I didn't know if his refusal was more about not wanting to ride behind a chick, or the need for privacy so he could hurl in the bushes on the way back, but I decided not to ask and have him think I was making fun of him either way. Plus I wanted to stop wasting time and get to the med center.

I climbed on behind Trudy and we flew up the path toward the center of campus – the most direct route to the med center's location on the opposite side of the property.

I couldn't help but ask questions as we drove, even though common sense told me there was no way Trudy, or anyone else, could have any answers yet.

"Could you tell when it happened?" I shouted over the

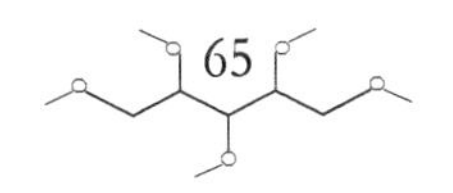

engine.

"He's only been dead a few hours," she yelled back, turning her head to aim the response in my direction.

As I processed that, she added, "You couldn't have saved him, if that's what you're thinking."

I hadn't gone that far in my thinking, but still found relief in the unsolicited pardon.

"Why do you think he was over by the gym?" I asked once we reached flatter ground and I didn't have to scream.

"Maybe he runs," she suggested.

"But he wasn't wearing running clothes," I pointed out.

"Maybe he walks," she amended.

"Or he was meeting someone," I theorized.

"Possibly." She remained noncommittal.

"Why didn't anyone know he was missing?" I launched a new line of questioning.

"Since he usually works alone, there might not've been anyone looking for him," she answered.

I mulled that idea over before asking, "Does he have any friends?"

"I don't know." She gave another unhelpful response and leaned on the gas.

"Why aren't you more shocked?" I challenged, my voice rising again to compete with the motor.

"I'm absolutely mortified," she hollered back, "but melting down isn't going to help anyone. Not him, me, or you." She brought the four-wheeler to a stop, but kept the engine running. "I just want to get to the health center and see what the

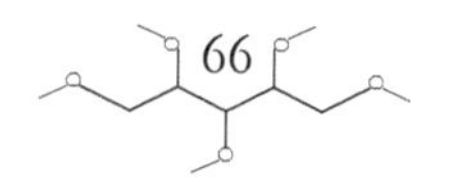

other doctors have to say."

"Colonel Clark, too," I added. I didn't know anything about any other doctors, but I had confidence that he'd know what to do.

"Right," she agreed, but didn't move the vehicle.

"We just need to talk to him," I said again, then finally realized we were idling next to the dorm. Confused, I asked, "We're not driving the whole way?"

"I am, but you're getting out here," she issued a soft but firm order.

"Why do you get to go, but not me?" I knew I sounded like a spoiled brat, but I was too infuriated to care.

"Because I'm on staff," she pulled rank.

"So?" I countered. "I work for Lieutenant Graham; that's like being on staff."

"No, it isn't," she maintained.

"Close enough," I continued to argue, so she cut me off.

"And because I'm Randall's mother," she said with staunch finality.

Randall…Randall Clark…Colonel Clark…, my mind stumbled down the connecting path as if trying to decipher a foreign language. My eyes also had a hard time focusing – I looked from Trudy to the four-wheeler, thinking, *Are there fumes coming out of that thing?* Something was making it very hard for me to process this new revelation.

How could it have slipped everyone's mind to share this vital piece of information with me? That Trudy was actually Trudy *Clark*? Maybe they'd assumed I'd put the names together

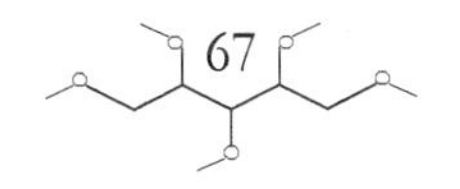

on my own. Which, yes, if I'd had that information, I would have. But I was certain Trudy had never told me her last name, and now surer still that she'd left it off on purpose.

"Why?" I yelled, cramming all my frustration into the one word.

"Calliope, this is not the time," she insisted. "I promise we will talk about this later, but I have to go now." Having no other choice, I let her drive off. I was finding it hard to put up a mature and understanding front when I felt neither.

As soon as she was out of sight, my thoughts scurried like freed lab animals with no idea which way to run. The burning anger rising in my throat stirred up the nausea that adrenalin had been keeping at bay, but trumping them both was the dread of walking into the hornet's nest that waited inside. The last thing I needed right now was to endure an interrogation by the morbidly curious masses over my involvement in yet another violent episode.

As a *flighter*, not a fighter, my first instinct was to run to Jack. Unfortunately, I knew there was little chance of me getting anywhere near him at the treehouse. I should probably find Garrett, but he'd surely been enveloped by the swarm of gossipers with no hope – or real desire – for escape. I vowed to catch up with him after he'd completed the interview circuit, but right now I needed to figure out how to get to my room without being seen.

I'd barely taken a step when the Homer Simpson-like realization hit me so hard I almost palm-smacked my own forehead. *You don't need a plan, dummy*, I reminded myself. *You have a gift.*

Worried my anxiety might keep me from disappearing, I tried to focus on clearing my mind and evening out my breathing. *Nobody can see me; I'm invisible*, I chanted inwardly. *If anyone comes along, they'll just pass right by like I'm not even here.* I repeated the mantra that I'd always used to escape dream monsters as a child, and that would hopefully help me in real life now, too.

Did it work? I asked myself, knowing full well I wouldn't be able to answer. My biggest disappointment since discovering this vanishing ability was finding out that I couldn't see myself change. There was no tingling or other sensation during the transition, and my parts looked to me to be as solid as ever. All I could do was have faith in myself and my gift – not exactly the easiest thing for me to do.

I didn't see anyone as I made my way to the door, but the minute I was safely inside the stairwell, the front door banged open again behind me. One of the stars – Kim, I think her name was – blew in and headed straight for the stairs. *And me.*

While keeping up the internal monologue, I slid all the way to the left of the step I was on, hoping she'd respect the pedestrian-driving rule and stay to the right. I held my breath – along with every muscle in my body – as still as a board. She continued texting without looking up, getting closer and closer until I thought she'd either smack straight into me or I'd pee my pants and give myself away.

And then she passed right by. *It actually worked!* my mind shrieked giddily. Either that, or she'd been blinded by cyber-haze. Not bothering to waste time debating it, I jumped into her wake and headed for my room.

EIGHT

I spent a long night tossing, turning, and trying to ignore both the nightmare images that kept flashing across my mind and the whispers in the hallway outside my door. On one side, I was mad at myself for having taken the cowardly route by disappearing, literally, into my room. Avoiding detection had unfortunately also meant having to stay silent and sit in the dark; I'd even turned off my phone for the first time since I'd gotten it. No music and no reading had left me with nothing to do but relive every detail of the gruesome afternoon.

Half my thoughts were of things I wanted to forget – the shreds through Larson's white shirt, the blackening of the blood as it dried. The other mental pictures were purely constructs of my spasmic imagination – maggots streaming from empty eye sockets, a severed hand picking its way toward me through clotted grass, and other crude horrors. But as bad as all that had been, it was still better than the interrogatory alternative.

My friends had considerately given me my space, mollified in part by the gory details Garrett had been eager to provide, so breakfast would be my first public appearance since the incident.

I walked into the dining hall to find them in a protective circle around our table, but I knew it was only a matter of time before I'd have to pony-up some answers. I took a detour to mound some stomach-settling grits into a bowl before joining them.

"You know what the coolest thing about yogurt is?" Miranda was asking as I took my seat, her spoon paused halfway to her mouth.

"It's alive," Bliss, Garrett, Alexis, and I all chorused in response.

"Are you going to tell us that every time you eat it for the rest of our lives?" I asked, trying to act normally.

"Mm-hmm," she admitted through the mouthful.

"Great," humphed Garrett, not quite back to his usual jocular self.

Bliss piped up, "I'd rather talk about live food than dead people." *Well, that didn't take long; guess my pass was even more temporary than I thought.*

"We can't just pretend nothing happened," Miranda scolded her for what I was sure couldn't be the first time today.

"So what do you think happened? Who killed him?" Now that the door'd been cracked, Alexis wasted no time pushing it the rest of the way open.

"My money's on *Army Conspiracy Part Deux*," Garrett volunteered.

"There was no first Army conspiracy," I reminded him. "Quirk soloed that mission." Janet had taken full credit for being

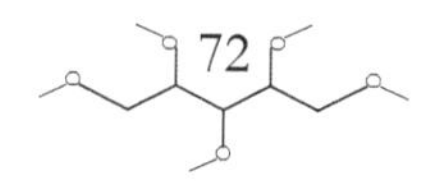

the only officer involved in that plot against us, and I'd believed her. Still did. She was like a cop who had to get a dog because no one else would work with her.

"And she's locked up," Bliss pointed out.

"Unless there's been a prison break we don't know about," Garrett suggested. When Miranda gave him a look, he went on, "Hey, it's not like they don't hide stuff from us all the time. They've probably got the yeti tied up out there," he said, tipping his head toward the window facing the woods.

"Do you really think so?" Bliss's eyes widened. "That she could be back, I mean."

"Would you feel better if it was a random lunatic? Or one of us?" Miranda asked, earning a look of horror from Bliss. "Not one of *us*," she mimicked, "but one of *all* y'us." She flicked her wrist to indicate the entire room of kids.

"That was uncalled for," I reprimanded her.

"I'm just saying," Miranda concluded, "that maybe we need to start watching our backs, too."

"No." Bliss shook her head, refusing to listen. "It was a freak thing, and it's over. We're fine."

Miranda snorted, but refrained from further comment.

"There's going to be a meeting, right?" I turned to Alexis, the most likely of us to have inside information. "A debriefing or something?"

"Uh, we had a floor meeting last night, didn't you?" Garrett threw in.

"You missed ours," Bliss informed me quietly. I was surprised Trudy had let me get away with that, but at least it

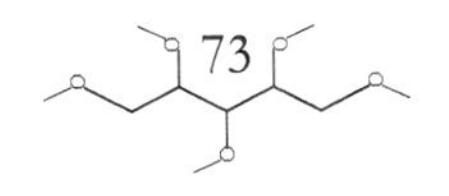

explained all the activity I'd heard outside my door. "You didn't miss anything, anyway," she added, then amended, "Well, except the part about never going anywhere without a buddy."

"You probably *saw* more than they told us," Alexis assured me. "But I've been thinking about what Captain Dolan said about Larson getting a lot of threats," she moved on. "Letters, emails – saying we're all genetic freaks that should be destroyed."

"Ooh – I change my bet. Move my chips to the crazy stalker box," Garrett threw over his shoulder as he headed back to the omelet station for a second round.

"How can he be so calm?" Bliss asked the rest of us once he was out of earshot.

"He's a guy, that's what they do – put up a good front," I assured her.

"Yeah, I'm sure he's shaking on the inside," Miranda agreed sarcastically as we all three watched him shove an entire cinnamon roll into his mouth.

"Doubtful," Alexis said. "With the amount of food he packs in, any internal disturbance would turn him into a vomit volcano."

"Thanks, that's just what I want to visualize while I'm eating," Miranda complained.

Just when I'd decided I'd had enough of the bickering and began looking around for an exit strategy, Jack appeared and collapsed into the chair next to me. The purple bags under his eyes were as dark as bruises, like he'd taken some hard hits over the past few hours. I instinctively reached over to smooth his

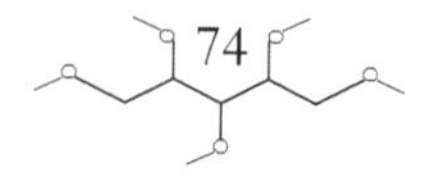

rumpled hair, noting, "You look beat."

"I am beat," he admitted, "but you could pretend I don't *look* it."

Before I could stammer out an apology, he smiled softly and squeezed my knee to let me know he was teasing.

"Have you been up all night?" Bliss asked with concern.

"Yeah," he confirmed. "When Lombardo got back to the treehouse, things went to DEFCON One."

"You've been there this whole time?" I asked. *So much for* my *bad night.*

"I didn't want to leave if there was something I could do," he answered tiredly.

"Good," Miranda huffed, blowing straight past sympathy to self-service. "Someone is supposed to actually be keeping us safe."

"Did you find anything?" Alexis asked him, well-practiced in swerving conversations around Miranda's wrecks.

He sighed when all four sets of expectant eyes looked to him. "Not really," he admitted, looking so wiped it felt almost cruel to keep questioning him.

When no one said anything, he went on, "We know Larson was stabbed, probably by one person. And the cuts slash upward, so the killer had to be shorter than him, which pretty much everybody is. Or the attacker came from somewhere below him, like a hiding place or a crouch."

"Are you supposed to be telling us this?" Bliss asked, her voice rising sharply at the end of her question. Putting together the squeak and the pointed look she exchanged with Miranda, I

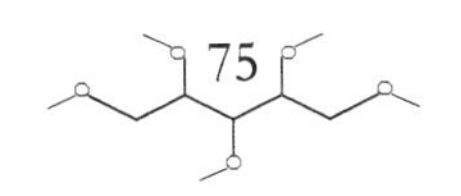

guessed she'd taken a hard kick under the table.

"It's okay," Jack answered. "That's stuff Lombardo's cleared for release. And that the killer was a rightie," he added, almost as an afterthought.

"Boo ya!" Garrett's returning cry made me jump in my seat. "Clears me," he said, holding up his left hand. "Southpaw."

"The killer couldn't really be a kid," Bliss said again, watching Jack's reaction. "Could it?"

"They can't rule it out," Jack hated admitting to her. "From the angle, it's possible. And it's not like anyone here was a big fan of his. But," he went on to ease her nerves a little, "Lombardo says this kind of brutal assault most likely points to an adult."

"They're not actually letting you 'work the case' or whatever you call it, are they?" Miranda asked with sudden realization.

"I'm helping," Jack answered, too exhausted – and too *Jack* – to take offense. "It's probably not anyone's first choice for me to be there, but they need every set of hands and eyes they can get, especially since Clark and Graham said we can't bring anyone in from outside."

"I'm sure you're a huge asset," I assured him. "With everything you know from your dad, you're probably just as trained as the rest of them."

Jack was more humble. "I'm pretty sure if my dad wasn't Special Forces, they wouldn't have let me through the bullet-proof door."

"Did you say bullet-proof door?" Alexis asked him.

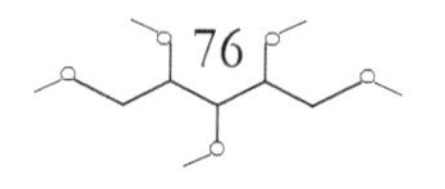

"Right, like a plane cockpit," he confirmed.

"Wow," Bliss and I vocalized our joint amazement.

"Yeah," Jack agreed. "They added some pretty intense gear after the Janet breach. You have no idea. I sit in command central, and *I* have no idea."

Garrett leaned forward to examine Jack's shirt. "Did they sew a spy-cam in your collar?"

"Not that I know of." Jack rolled his eyes and pushed him away. "And since I've been wearing this shirt for two days now, that would've been pretty hard for them to do without me catching on. You jealous they might suit me up for the A-Team?" he teased.

"Nah, those mini-cams aren't all that," Garrett bluffed. "I saw one in the airplane mag on the way here for like fifty bucks."

"So what were you doing all night?" I asked Jack, out of both concern and curiosity.

"Reviewing camera footage, mostly," he answered.

"They got the murder on film?" Bliss's hopes rose along with her voice.

"No," Jack corrected the misinterpretation. "It happened in a blind spot where there's no camera."

"Which means the killer either got really lucky, or he knew exactly where to set up," Alexis surmised.

"They're leaning toward the second one," Jack replied.

"So there's really no way it could've been an accident?" Bliss threw out one last attempt at optimism.

"He said he was stabbed, dummy," Miranda snapped. "He didn't just fall on a knife that was sticking up out of the

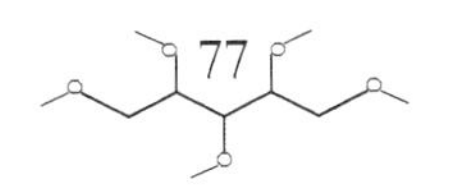

ground."

For once, I couldn't blame Miranda for getting so exasperated. Bliss's naïve hope for the best was usually endearing, almost admirable in other circumstances, but right now it was just annoying.

"What tapes are you looking at, then?" I turned back to Jack.

"All of them," he admitted. "Footage from every camera on campus, from the ones closest to the crime scene to the ones at the front gate. All different times, too," he added. "We're going back days even, looking for anything suspicious." His slumped shoulders and glazed eyes showed the frustration he felt toward the daunting task.

"Could it be an outsider?" Alexis revisited the theory she'd started to propose earlier. "I know you said the Army hasn't brought anyone in, but what if someone got in on their own?"

"It'd be virtually impossible for someone to come onto the grounds without us knowing," Jack told her. "If you tried to get on campus anywhere other than the main gate, you'd hit the invisible fence."

"As in *force* field?" Garrett asked excitedly. "Now there's some hi-tech I can get behind."

"No," Jack laughed, while at the same time Miranda came to her own conclusion.

"Like for dogs?" she spat in disgust.

"The same idea, I guess, but different functionality," Jack answered, going on to explain, "You have to put on a wristband to cross the boundary, or it sends a silent alarm to security."

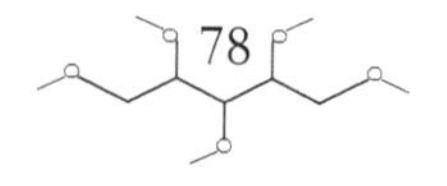

Before we could ask, he added, "And no, there are no camera blind spots on the fenceline."

"What if someone used an EMP?" Alexis posed.

"And carried it in his pocket?" Garrett snorted. "Did you even see *Ocean's Eleven*?"

"Yes, I saw it," Alexis retorted, "and no, an EMP does not have to be as big as a truck. You can get a palm-sized one on the internet for less than half of that mini-cam you scoped out."

"Seriously?" Garrett looked equally surprised and impressed.

"As a WAP collapse," Alexis confirmed, using a metaphor only she understood.

The ensuing pause gave me the chance to ask, "Um, what exactly *is* an EMP?"

"Electromagnetic pulse," the techie and the cine-junky responded in unison.

"What does it do?" Bliss asked the follow-up.

"Interrupt the electric signal." Again, both Alexis and Garrett had thrown out the answer, but this time he ceded her the floor.

"The break in current would give someone a chance to cross the invisible fence," Alexis finished.

"But the disruption would've triggered the alarm and registered on the monitors," Jack pointed out, looking almost guilty for having to shoot down her idea.

"Yeah," she agreed, "and the fence signal would've taken time to come back up – it wouldn't have recovered instantly."

"Okay, so if it's an inside job, what are you doing about

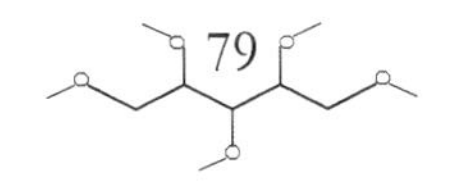

it?" Miranda's question to Jack was clearly more a demand for results.

"Security's questioning all the staff again right now," he informed her. "I, on the other hand, have been ordered to get some rest because they don't want me in on that. They're all going to have to re-take the polygraph, too."

"There's a *polygraph* machine here?" I asked, impressed.

"It's a pretty simple machine," he told me. "I think we have more than one."

"Again, *Skymall*," Garrett said dismissively. "I could've brought one, too."

"Well, I'm gonna follow orders and go get my zzz's," Jack said, getting to his feet.

"You didn't eat anything," I pointed out.

"I'm not really hungry," he answered with a shrug and a half-smile. "I'm sure G ate enough for both of us."

He paused long enough to drop a kiss on top of my head that said both *Goodbye* and *We'll talk later*, so I didn't follow him out the door.

"I've got to go, too," Bliss piped up. "If I'm supposed to be helping Reagan and Xavier adjust, I should fill them in on all this, too. I feel bad," she added. "They just got here and now they're going to want to leave."

"Whatever," Miranda said, her mind having already moved on to other things. "Don't forget, ladies – tonight's mani-pedis in Clio's room."

"Why not your room?" I complained as we both stood up to leave.

"Because I'm remodeling," she reminded me. "Extended stay equals massive overhaul. And," she aimed at Bliss, "that foul tangerine paint in *your* room makes me ill. You should really do something about that."

While Bliss digested the suggestion, Garrett took the opportunity to duck out unimpeded.

"Maybe I *should* paint," she thought aloud. "I could do a yummy color, like Clio's caramel."

"I highly doubt 'mayo' is a paint color," I told her.

"Just don't ask me for help," Miranda interjected, holding up one never-worked hand to make her point. "I only do nails, not walls…."

NINE

When Miranda and Bliss reported for nail night at seven o'clock sharp, I'd only just finished cleaning my room. Not that it'd been a complete disaster, but it wouldn't have been *un*fair to say I'd been a little inattentive lately.

Or should that be nineteen hundred hours? I wondered. For a military installation, nobody seemed to use the Army-isms.

When style-tornado Miranda blew the door right out of my hands, Bliss reached out and stopped it from ricocheting back into me. I marveled at how proficient she'd become at navigating in Miranda's wake.

"Rule number one, girls," Miranda established right away, "no grave gab tonight." For anyone else on campus, that would've been an impossible request, but then they didn't have Miranda to enforce it. And I was happy to get on board; my brain needed a break from all the dead body talk, especially when there was no new information to discuss.

As un-fashion-conscious as I was, I found myself warming up to beauty night. Jack was back at the treehouse, Garrett had gone to the gym, and I wasn't interested in spending another evening with only my anxiety for company. Maybe, for the first time, Miranda had called for an event that was actually warranted. *Who knew?*

I closed the door and joined the girls on the gold chenille rug where Miranda was busily arranging her wares like some kind of desert-nomad Avon lady.

"Alexis just texted me – she's not coming," I let them know.

"Who cares," Miranda blew off the update.

"She's our friend," Bliss admonished.

"That's not how she means it," I said, translating the Mirand-itude for her. "She's just mad that Alexis wiggled out of her makeover trap."

"I don't want to trap her," Miranda contested. "I want her to *want* to change. It's hard to fix someone when they keep trying to get away."

Bliss decided to let it go and move on. "Why isn't she coming?" she asked me.

"Major Godwin called a meeting. I think they're filling her in on whatever they plan to tell us tomorrow about the mur…*campus climate*." I caught myself before I broke Miranda's commandment and earned some lashes.

"Yippee," Miranda cheered sarcastically. "Let's hear it for *Thrilling Thursday*."

I didn't know whether to chime in or keep quiet, but Bliss changed the subject by pulling out a white bakery box that she must've had delivered. "I brought snacks!" she announced.

Before she'd fully opened the lid, Miranda threatened,

"Don't you dare. You can't eat this late."

"I'll stay up lat*er*," Bliss growled back – a mother bear protecting her dessert instead of cubs.

"Trust me; eating after eight will totally obliterate your metabolism," Miranda re-issued the warning.

Bliss defiantly pushed the box toward me with one hand, the other already unwrapping a chocolate-dipped Twinkie. I grabbed a second one from the box and tossed it at Miranda, who watched stone-faced as it bounced off her chest and fell into her lap. I tensed in preparation for the back-fling.

She recovered from the shock of the assault to retrieve the pastry missile, pinching it between her first finger and thumb as if handling toxic waste. She tilted her head to investigate the label without letting her face get too close to the offending item.

"Food *product*," she announced with disgust. "You're aware that they can't even call this actual food, right?"

"Mm-mm-mm," Bliss hummed through her frosted lips to drown out the lecture.

"It's only three past seven," I pointed out to Miranda before taking a Twinkie for myself. "You've got fifty-seven minutes to shove some down."

She refrained from further comment as she unceremoniously dropped the odious item back in the box and went back to arranging her tools.

I decided to reward her self-control by turning the conversation to her favorite subject – herself. "I have to say," I began, "I'm shocked you didn't call in your own nail person."

"She couldn't clear security," she answered matter-of-

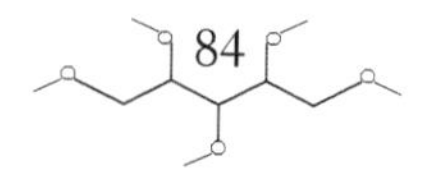

factly, ignoring the teasing in my voice. "To get in here, they have to interview your family and friends. She couldn't take the chance they'd tell her husband about her boyfriend."

"That's terrible!" Bliss cried out. "You're going to find a new manicurist, right? One that's not a *cheater.*" She said the seven-letter word as if it had only four.

"Like that has anything to do with doing great nails," Miranda dismissed the idea without looking up from her task. "Toes first, girls," she instructed. "Pick your polish."

She'd put out a ridiculous number of bottles for three people, but the color spectrum itself was quite restrained. There were no flaming reds or obnoxious oranges – only rows of neutral shades. Swallowing the last bite of her second Twinkie, Bliss reached forward and selected a pink blush that perfectly complemented both her coloring and her personality.

Miranda chose a glittering gold that instantly brought to mind the brilliant star she wished she was. Like I'd told my mom, since we didn't meet in groups anymore and never really "showcased" our abilities, I thought the tension between Bliss and Miranda had mostly gone away. Now I wondered if there might still be some resentment gurgling below Miranda's smooth surface. For the sake of girls' night, I decided to leave that pot unstirred.

The shade I chose for myself couldn't even be described as such; I took the hardener that brushed on clear, thinking that with everything that was going on, some strengthening was definitely in order.

Miranda began passing out nail files and picnic plans at

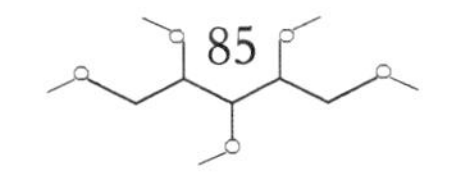

the same time. She started by going over her list of necessary props – everything from organic cloth napkins to hemp picnic baskets – then paused to ask if we thought she'd missed anything.

"You're asking what *we* think?" I pretended to swoon in disbelief.

She narrowed her eyes to show that she didn't find the funny in my facetious. I knew that she probably only deserved half of the grief we gave her, but she also only half-listened to it, so it all zeroed out, really. Her problem was that, even if her intentions came from a good place, her delivery flat-out sucked.

All facts, no tact – the perfect description of her plight suddenly popped into my mind. Unfortunately, the grand revelation caused me to shout aloud, "Aha!"

I tried to recover quickly. "You use the rough side," I said, holding up the file. I should've been relieved when Bliss and Miranda both took the poor lie at face value, but I wasn't. I knew I was a little glamour-challenged, but their acknowledgment of it kind of hurt.

Miranda went right back to her event plans, but I had a hard time focusing. Even the menu, which would normally catch and hold my interest, wasn't enough to keep my mind from wandering. And the first place it drifted to was yesterday morning in Ford's office.

I hadn't seen him since – he'd cancelled today because of the attack – but for reasons known only to my subconscious, he'd been on my mind all day. Again, I found myself replaying our last conversation, particularly the point when he'd asked me what I most wanted to see in the curriculum.

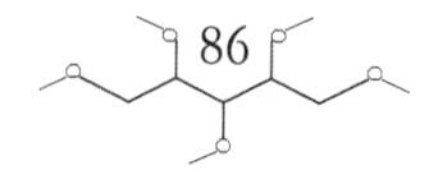

Not having put that much thought into it, I'd said, "Maybe writing, I guess, but that's probably just because of my mom. I have no idea what I want to do with my life."

"You're not supposed to know," he'd responded. "You're only seventeen years old."

"When you were seventeen, you knew you were going to West Point," I'd argued. "And here you are, on your path."

"You're on your path, too," he'd countered. "You just haven't seen where it goes yet."

I'd been surprised by his philosophical outlook – it was a sharp contrast to the matter-of-fact lieutenant I'd thought I had all figured out. Now I'd seen a much deeper part of him that I felt compelled to delve into.

"Hello? Earth to Clio?" Miranda called me out of my reverie.

I could tell I'd missed a big enough chunk of conversation to forget about faking my way back in, so I offered an apologetic smile. But instead of letting me slide, Bliss probed, "What were you thinking about so intently?"

"Jack and Clio up in a tree, k-i-s-s-i-n-g…," Miranda sang mockingly.

"First comes love, then comes marriage…," Bliss chirped the second line of the couplet.

"Let's not go that far," Miranda warned.

"You started it," Bliss defended herself.

"I was in for the making out, not the matrimony," Miranda clarified.

"That's how it goes," Bliss argued.

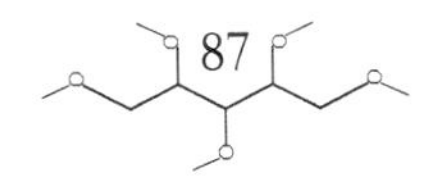

"Eventually, but not with a guy you meet in high school," Miranda disagreed. I stayed clear of the exchange, hoping if I kept my mouth shut, they'd end up somewhere very far from me.

Luck was not with me.

"Do we need to have the sex talk?" Miranda whirled on me like the Tasmanian devil.

"No, I'm good. Really," I assured her.

Bliss continued poking holes in Miranda's argument. "Aren't you the one who said our bodies are temples?" she reminded her.

"It's not like I'm telling you to drop trou or anything," Miranda explained, "but if anyone's planning to do anything, like someone who's name rhymes with Glio…."

"That's not even a word," I mumbled, growing more and more unhappy with where the discussion was going, but not sure how to stop it.

"Of course I have rules," Miranda went on, "but I'm a realist, too. I'm not going to tell you to go buy a motorcycle, but if you're straddling one in my driveway and revving the engine, I'm sure as Hell going to make sure you have a helmet."

Bliss gasped out loud, though I wasn't sure if she'd been more ruffled by the innuendo, or the cursing. When she recovered, she turned to me and asked, "Are you and Jack…?"

"No!" I answered immediately, and even though I hadn't really shouted, they both recoiled as if I'd taken a swing at them.

I wasn't surprised to see Bliss wince at the rebuke, but it shocked me to see Miranda falter as if she's been shoved. She covered the back-step by turning on an unsuspecting Bliss.

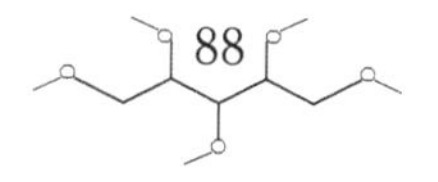

"So where're things going with you and the Okie shortstop?" she asked her about Garrett.

Bliss, caught completely off-guard, flushed the same pink as the half-unscrewed bottle in her hand.

"First base," I spoke up to fill the awkward pause.

"You finally took a pitch?" Miranda asked, surprised.

"I meant that Garrett plays first base," I corrected. "Not shortstop."

"So…?" Miranda asked her again.

"I don't know," Bliss squeaked, trying to dodge her. "I don't see him that much with these new jobs and all…."

Even though I was still a little peeved at her for joining Miranda in the preschool chant, I couldn't ignore the pleading look she threw me.

"Yeah, how are things going with your…," I searched for the right word, settling on, "project?"

"Great," she answered with a grateful smile.

I asked another question before Miranda could regroup. "Do you still meet with Clark, or just stay with Xavier and Reagan?"

"Oh, I see Colonel Clark every day," she answered. "He's terrific. And really easy to talk to. He says he likes having me around."

"That's nice," I said, surprised at the unexpected edge in my voice. *I should be happy for her, shouldn't I?*

"He's like a whole new person," she went on, "now that he's gotten rid of all that baggage."

My rational brain knew she was talking about his history

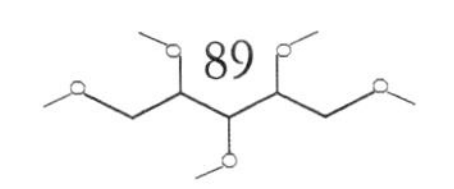

with Dr. Heigl and the secrets he'd been holding onto for so many years, but the hot-blooded part of me shoved cold logic out of the way.

"So by baggage, do you mean *me*?" I heard myself ask acidly.

"N-no," she stuttered, confused. "I just meant that he's okay as long as we're okay."

Her use of the word "we" hit another of my nerves. *I* used to be the colonel's main concern; he was always looking out for me. Maybe I'd been too busy working to check in with him as much as I used to, but that didn't give Bliss permission to take my place. I felt the anger not just rising inside me, but trying to surge out from my body as if trying to escape a pressure chamber.

Even though I didn't say anything further, I could tell by Bliss's confused look that my face said enough. The hurt pushed her into dangerous territory, making her babble, "I was even at the med center when they brought in Larson."

"No *body* talk," Miranda warned her sternly.

"They brought him in on a stretcher and got on an elevator I've never seen anyone use," she went on, as if unable to stop unraveling a ghost story. "There must be like a morgue or something in the basement. It gives me the heebie jeebies when I go there now," she finished with a shudder.

My mouth opened to say, *Then maybe you should stop going there*, but Miranda got her words out faster.

"Are you *trying* to ruin mani-pedi night?" she growled.

I practically jumped at the opportunity to call it a night.

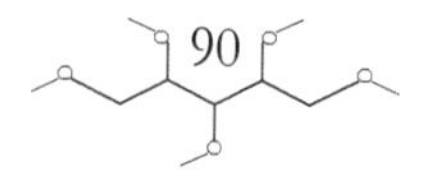

Unfortunately, it was only after I got up to leave that I remembered we were in *my* room, so I had nowhere to go.

"I think we're pretty much done anyway, don't you?" I said, trying to wrap things up and get them moving. "I'm just so exhausted," I added by way of excuse, even conjuring up a yawn to play the part as I started shoving Miranda's beauty bazaar back into her bag. I kept my eyes averted to ignore their bewilderment as I herded them toward the door.

Before they could ask me what was going on, I practically pushed them out into the hall and closed the door. As I sagged against it, I could hear them muttering outside, but I didn't much care. The last thing I needed was to try to explain to them whatever this was that I couldn't understand myself.

Somehow, in the course of an hour, I'd managed to go from fairly relaxed to nearly enraged. And for no apparent reason. Once the girls finally moved down the hall, I began to feel more like myself.

What was that? I thought. *What's wrong with me?* Sure, the Jack talk might've made me a little uncomfortable, but it wasn't anything new from Miranda. And the rush of jealousy I'd felt over Bliss spending time with Colonel Clark was totally uncalled for. I didn't have an answer. I quickly crawled into bed and pulled the covers over my head before a third personality could jump out.

TEN

I was enormously relieved when Bliss and Miranda stopped by in the morning to pick me up for the debriefing. I'd been more than happy to accept their unspoken agreement to forgive last night's scene, not that I felt any better about it. And spending the night thinking about losing my mind might've saved me from another set of Larson-mares, but it sure hadn't helped me get any sleep. I had to force my eyes to stay open and my smile to stay on as we made our way across the courtyard to the main building.

"What's all the buzz about?" Bliss asked as we followed Miranda down the only open row of seats.

"Not this meeting, which will of course be useless and a waste of my time," Miranda commented without looking up from her cell.

"I hope not," I said. I was counting on getting both some answers and some reassurance that everything was under control. Something to give me hope for a return to normalcy. And sanity.

"Done," Miranda announced, pocketing the phone. "I just placed the final food order for Saturday. Not that you two were any help."

"If they haven't found the killer, I bet they're going to cancel the party," I speculated.

"Yeah," Bliss seconded.

"Don't even say that," Miranda snarled. "I've been killing myself Mirandizing the perfect barbecue menu."

"Isn't Mirandizing like when they say you have the right to an attorney and all?" Bliss asked, fully unaware of her comic timing.

"Yes," Miranda glowered, "and *you* have the right to remain silent, got it?" When she was sure Bliss was indeed going to keep quiet, she went back to talking about the food. "We're having nitrate-free hot dogs…."

"Will they be flavor-free, too?" I interrupted.

"They're one-hundred-percent beef, and they'll be delish," she informed me sharply. "We're also grilling free-range chicken and veggie burgers that you can't even tell are soy."

"If you can't tell the difference, why can't we just have meat burgers?" Garrett asked, dropping into the chair next to me.

"And I'm all over the salads," Miranda went on as if he hadn't spoken. "Green ones, bean ones…."

Bliss looked like she was having chest pains until Miranda threw in a potato salad with vegan mayo, which I was pretty sure she'd only added in reaction to Bliss's distress.

"I've decided to forgive you the invite oversight, by the way," Garrett interrupted again, "since you're the ones who lost out on the chance to manscape me. And I'm gonna go one more step and do you a solid and grill on Saturday. Man. Fire. Good," he grunted.

"We have staff for that," Miranda assured him.

"You know, sometimes this being-taken-care-of stuff gets old," he complained.

"Why don't you start washing your own dishes, then?" I suggested.

"Whoa, Nellie, let's not get crazy!" He held up both hands to doubly protest and slid a seat further away from me.

"Did you hear?" Jack asked, appearing just in time to claim the newly vacant spot.

"Hear what?" I asked him. "It hasn't started yet."

"There's been another attack," he dropped the bomb, looking both sorry to be the messenger and to find out we were the last to know. At least it explained all the chatter in the room.

"Who?" Bliss asked at the same time Miranda demanded, "When?"

"Somebody stabbed Nate Gagne last night," Jack filled us in.

Though Bliss, Miranda, and I all made murmurs of surprise, Garrett stayed quiet.

"Aren't you going to say anything?" I leaned around Jack to look him in the face. "He was your teammate."

"No big loss," Garrett said with a shrug.

"It's a loss to me," Miranda griped. "Now who's going to launch the fireworks?"

"You were going to let a criminal set off *fire* rockets?" Bliss shrieked.

"Hey, how come you let him do something cool and not

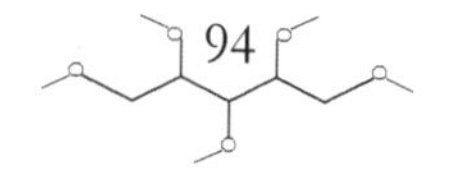

me?" Garrett was insulted.

"Well, since it sounds like he won't be able to fulfill his duties, the job's yours now," Miranda snapped.

"Have you all lost your minds?" I shouted over them. "Somebody was attacked! Here. *Last night.*"

"Clio's right," Bliss agreed. "We shouldn't be thinking about other stuff when someone is dead."

"Not dead," Jack corrected her. "Just critical."

"Circling the drain, eh?" Garrett remained nonchalant.

Before Jack could give us the details, Major Eve Godwin breezed past, her shiny-smooth chignon, toffee skin, and perfectly-tailored suit practically turning the aisle into a runway. Not to mention the crowd-silencing look she gave as she assumed her position at the head of the room.

Like everyone else, I inched to the front of my seat to hear what she had to say.

"I'd planned to discuss the situation concerning Dr. Larson," she began in her rehearsed, even tone, that did nothing to reassure me. "However, as I'm sure most of you have heard by now, there's been a second incident." She paused to wait out the responding murmurs.

"A student – Nathan Gagne – was attacked last night," she went on once the hum died down. "He is receiving top-level care, but he has not yet fully stabilized."

She kept talking over the resurgence of whispers. "I would like to assure you that everything is being done to preserve your safety," she said, raising her voice without shouting to regain control. "And you need to trust in the system we've put in place to protect you. We have an A-plus security detail, supported by incorruptible technology." I wished Alexis had been sitting with us and not Captain Dolan so I could ask her opinion on that.

"Now I know you're all asking yourselves what you can do," Major Godwin continued. "You're wondering how you can help your fallen comrade."

Sure not, I thought to myself. *Never even crossed my mind, actually*.

"We've already consumed much of our blood supply," she went on, "so we'll need type matches, both for Nathan and to replenish the reserve. At the conclusion of this meeting, all A- and O-type donors will report directly to the health center." This was clearly an order, not a request. I wondered if she knew not everyone would've gone otherwise, most of us having no love lost for the kid.

She began reading names from a list, presumably in case someone wasn't sure of his blood type. I tuned her voice down to low, knowing that, as an AB, my name wouldn't be called.

My group wasn't the only one to start whispering amongst ourselves, and I found it strange that Major Godwin didn't call for silence. Maybe she preferred our half-attention; otherwise, we might start questions that she didn't want to answer.

"We have to do something," Bliss hissed, and I realized she must be completely terrified to volunteer for anything even potentially dangerous.

"We could go out on patrol," Miranda suggested, always front-line ready.

"The stealths?" I asked, seeing the merit in her idea. "If we got all sixty kids to do it, we could cover the whole campus."

"It's a bigger area than you think," Jack shot down the plan. "Especially if you add in the woods."

"The main campus is all we really need to cover," Miranda argued. "That's where all the people are."

"They're not going to let you stay up all night to patrol for a killer," Jack tried to reason with her.

"So we take shifts." Garrett came off the bench for Miranda's team.

"It's not the hours," Jack protested. "It's putting everyone in danger."

"We're already in danger!" Bliss reminded him.

"Why are you so against it?" Miranda asked, suspicious. "You're not telling us something."

Jack's responding "No" held little conviction.

"I think he doesn't want to say that they don't trust us," I said, suddenly feeling like *he* didn't trust *me*.

"Or they *suspect* us," Miranda took it a step further.

I hated trapping Jack between us and his duty, so when he said, "You have to trust Lombardo and the team, like she said," I kept quiet.

I hadn't even noticed Major Godwin had finished calling names and was poised to leave until she startled me by announcing, "You're all dismissed."

But unlike the end of most meetings, this time no one seemed in a rush to leave. Maybe it was finally starting to sink in for everyone that we were in real danger. Whether it was because

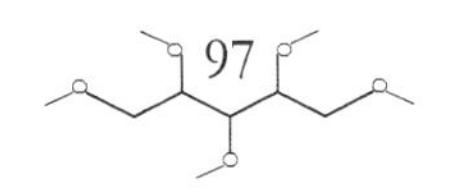

none of us had liked Larson, or that he'd always been so distant from us, we'd almost dismissed his attack as not "real." Not a threat to us, at least.

Now the killer had gone after a kid, though. Someone most of us liked even less than Larson, but still one of us. That was a lot harder to brush off.

After several more minutes of hushed conjecture, everyone started collecting their stuff and shuffling toward the exit. Jack and Garrett were the first out of our row, and we three girls fell in behind them as a second line. I was half-listening to Jack tell Garrett about the crime scene, so it took a minute for me to register the words of the girls whispering behind me.

"That's him," the first girl said quietly.

"I heard he works in security," added the other.

"So he knows everything that goes on here," pointed out the first, "and how to get away with stuff." Now my ears were all on them.

"You know, he doesn't even have an ability," the second girl said with obvious disapproval. "I bet that's why he went after the doctor. Larson probably found something genetically wrong with him, like proof he doesn't belong here."

"Yeah," her partner agreed, and I didn't need to turn around to know she wore a smug smile when she added, "Plus Larson was killed by the gym, and Nate was a jock. I bet he has it in for all the big guys because he's jealous."

Fuming, I whirled around to confront them. Their faces looked vaguely familiar – maybe from past stealth group sessions – but I couldn't quite place them. I knew they didn't live on my floor; they didn't know me and they clearly didn't know Jack.

"Where do you get off, you pathetic losers?" The words were out of my mouth before I could think of classier ones, but I wasn't about to take them back.

They didn't even attempt to respond. One had the decency to blush, embarrassed at being caught gossiping, while the other pursed her lips and looked pointedly away. She was probably just waiting for me to turn around so she could return to her backstabbing.

"Let's go," Bliss said, putting her hand lightly on my shoulder as she tried to diffuse the situation.

"Don't waste your time on these harpies," Miranda added, putting them in their place.

Queen of serendipitous timing, Alexis made her way over to us. I knew by her frown that even from across the room she'd seen something was up, and her determined approach was enough to knock the nasty girls backward while she was still a good distance away. Their shock at the force of her ability was deliciously evident on their faces.

By now Jack and Garrett had also turned around, but I didn't want them to get involved. Miranda read my thoughts and deftly stepped between the boys, taking both by the elbows and propelling them toward the door.

I walked out between Alexis and Bliss, trying to unclench all the muscles in my body.

Once we were all outside, Jack freed his arm from Miranda's grip and turned to me. "What happened back there?" he asked, searching my eyes.

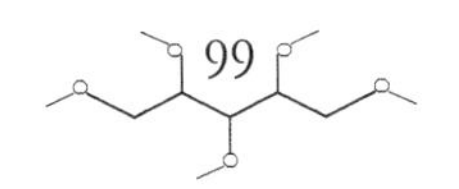

"Nothing worth recapping," I said, forcing myself to hold his gaze even though I wanted to look away.

"You can catch it when it comes out on DVD," Miranda backed me up. We both knew that, as much as the confrontation had upset me, hearing what they'd said would crush Jack. We wouldn't give them the satisfaction.

"You sure?" Jack asked again, concerned about me.

"Totally fine. Really," I assured him, and planted a firm kiss on his frowning lips as proof.

"So who's coming to the med center?" Bliss tagged in, steering both us and the conversation in a new direction.

"Me. A-neg," Alexis answered first.

"A-plus for me," Garrett cheered, as if he'd done something medal-worthy.

"You do know that the plus means you're positively descended from monkeys, right?" Miranda informed him.

"Oo-oo-ah-ah," he taunted her, hunching over to scratch his armpits. Even without knowing what had just transpired, he knew exactly how to make everyone forget it.

"I'm O-positive, so I have to go, too," Bliss said, looking less than thrilled.

"Me, too," Miranda fourthed. "O-negative – the universal donor."

"That can't be right," I teased, forcing myself back into our normal rhythm. "All you ever give anyone is a hard time."

"Very funny," Miranda retorted. "I have, as a matter of fact, been doing my civic duty and donating blood since I turned seventeen, thank you very much."

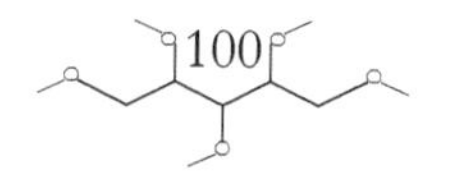

"Wait," Alexis interjected, the wheels of logic turning almost visibly behind her shining eyes. "So Garrett and I are both type A, but we have opposite rh factors. And we have polar abilities – light versus heavy. Then you two," she went on, indicating Bliss and Miranda, "are both O, but again positive versus negative – sparkling versus vanishing. What if our blood types had something to do with how we reacted to Heigl's drug?"

As we paused to consider the idea, she asked me, "Clio? Are you O-negative like Miranda?"

"Nope," I answered, hating to be the flaw in her theory. "AB-negative."

"Really?" Miranda was shocked. "That's the rarest type, you know."

"What about you?" Alexis turned last to Jack.

"I'm B-negative," he said, almost sadly. "More proof that I'm not like everybody else, right? A for *grade A*, O for *outstanding*, and B for…," he trailed off without finishing.

"Below average?" Bliss threw out reflexively, then clamped her hand over mouth when she realized what she'd said.

"You and me both," I pointed out, taking his hand.

"I think," Garrett chimed in, "we need to go for a run."

"Right now?" I asked, puzzled.

"You have to go to the med center," Miranda reminded Garrett sternly.

"They can catch me later," Garrett called back, pulling Jack in the opposite direction. Then he laughed and said, "Or maybe they can't!"

"Are you going back to the dorm?" Bliss asked, turning to

me. "No," I decided spontaneously. "I'll follow you to the med center. I think it's time I caught up with Colonel Clark."

ELEVEN

Alexis, Miranda, Bliss, and I were barely out of sight of the main building when our foursome became a fivesome.

"Bliss!" Rae called from half a football field back, but easily caught up to us at the same time as her greeting.

So this is the girl Garrett, I thought, trying to discreetly check her out while Bliss made introductions. She had short, dark curls – similar to Garrett's, actually, but softer-looking. And even though you could tell by her movements that she was an athlete, she wasn't overly muscular.

Or tall. I guess I'd imagined she'd be a giant like the guy jocks, but her eyes were level with mine when she said, "Hi, Clio. Good to meet you."

"You, too," I answered, feeling hugely guilty that the meeting was a couple days overdue. To be fair, I'd been lucky to grab a few minutes of quality time with even my close friends lately; having everyone in the same place today was like a perfect storm. It was lucky Rae blew in when she did, or it might've been days before our paths crossed again.

As usual, all the over-thinking was only my-sided; Rae's

warm and welcoming autumn eyes belied no hard feelings. And I couldn't help but laugh when she jokingly confided, "I'm a med-center virgin. I might need someone to hold my hand when I board the mother ship."

The medical center that was just coming into view did admittedly look a bit extraterrestrial. The building boasted the same mirrored-glass façade as the gym; curiously, it also stood equally high. I'd been trying to figure out since my first visit why less than a hundred and fifty people would need four floors of health services. Except for our initial check-ups, we'd never been called to the center, let alone all at once. In fact, I was pretty sure that the handful of us who'd visited Colonel Clark, the sole patient-resident, were the only ones who'd returned to the building at all. And unless New Jersey suddenly got sprayed with a plague, I didn't see any way that would change.

"We can't walk through the door with you," Bliss told Rae in all seriousness. "The censor only lets one person through at a time."

I watched Rae's eyes widen as we explained the finger-scan entry and automated doors.

"Okay, I *was* kidding," she said, "but now you're starting to freak me out a little."

"Don't worry, Dr. Creepy's gone now." I didn't know what had possessed me to make such a snide remark, and I instantly regretted it. Thankfully, everyone was gracious enough to let the indiscretion pass without comment.

The dead man, however, didn't get a pass.

"Bliss told you about Dr. Larson and Nate, right? Before

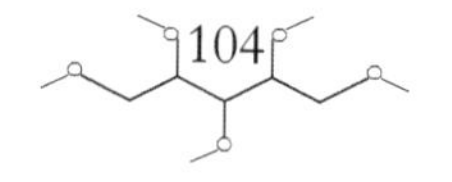

the assembly?" Alexis asked Rae, at the same time looking to Bliss for confirmation.

"Some," Rae answered, "but I have a feeling I got the sugared version."

"Most definitely," Miranda sighed.

"That," I said, tipping my head toward Miranda, "is who you need to see for the soured version."

Everyone laughed but Miranda, who tried valiantly to scowl, and Bliss, who hung onto her injured pout.

"She told me that Nate's still on campus," Rae continued. "Is that true?"

"Unfortunately," "Unbelievably," and "Unjustly," rang out our unenthusiastic replies.

"He hasn't been hanging around the gym?" I asked her. I'd assumed if he'd been out in the open enough to be attacked, he must've been mainstreaming back into campus life.

"Not when I've been there, anyway," she replied.

"Be thankful," Miranda told her. "And take my advice, if he asks you to wrestle, don't."

"I don't think he'll be up for much for a good while," I pointed out. "Seeing as how he's not even conscious right now." It continued to amaze me how Miranda – and, to a lesser extent, Bliss – kept seeming to forget about the attacks that never left the front of my mind.

"I can hold my own," Rae said, dismissing Miranda's warning with a casual shrug.

"You think you could take on one of the guys?" I asked, not sure I believed it.

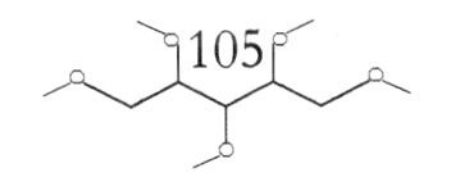

"You mean because I'm a girl?" She rose to the unintended challenge by backing one step away from us and flashing a wicked grin. Without warning – or momentum – she launched into a double back-flip, rolling the effortless landing into a smooth curtsy.

As our minds tried to find their way around the incredible demonstration, Rae was distracted by a call from the end of the student line. The rest of us also turned to locate the source of the low, approving whistle that'd seemed to play an entire song in one note.

My eyes easily picked out Rae's fan – a boy with mahogany-laced black hair and a one-dimple smile.

Even though I'd never seen him before, he seemed to have a following; the crowd of girls he'd turned away from was still hanging on his last abandoned word. And that the group was made up of *stars* was the most shocking part of all.

Back at the beginning of the summer, when we were all one giant group known as the "general population" of leftovers after the jocks and heavies had been singled out, I hadn't remembered anyone sticking out as a snob, or a princess, or a "star." But discovering their special ability had changed everything for the few girls who suddenly felt the Janet-assigned "title" *en*titled them to stellar status.

All except Bliss. Besides sharing their dazzling ability, she had nothing in common with the five-girl clique and they knew it. Even Miranda, who I knew still harbored a secret desire for the brilliant talent, couldn't have stood hanging out with that group. She may be a bit of a know-it-all, but Miranda really did believe

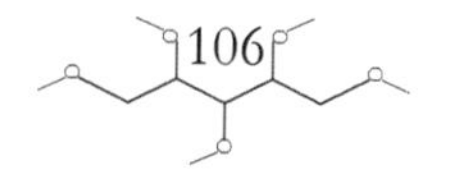

she was helping people with her advice, not cutting them down as seemed to be the stars' m.o. Every time I saw the pack of snickering hyenas, I wanted to remind them that, like everyone else, they'd started this summer with no special ability. And, for all we knew, these talents could all disappear as swiftly as they'd come. But I'd never bothered to say anything to them, knowing full well that they blatantly ignored everyone on campus. Except, apparently, *this* boy.

Not sure if my friends were following, I found myself walking toward him, pulled as if gravitationally by his well-black eyes.

As I drew nearer, I could see how shockingly good-looking he was – beautiful, in fact, like the reverse of the Monet-effect. But instinct told me there was a deeper force behind my attraction. The inexplicable desire to approach him grew into an overwhelming need to touch him, to make solid contact.

As if compelled, I reached forward.

"Xavier Wittman," he introduced himself, accepting my hand. His smile never faltered, though his eyes widened curiously at the oddly formal gesture.

"I know," I replied in a voice so soft I hardly recognized it as my own. I finally found the decency to let go of his hand, but his gaze still wouldn't release my eyes.

"You do?" he asked, his deep voice ringing as musically as his earlier whistle. He gave me a chance to catch my breath when he turned to look at Alexis.

"Hi, Xave," she said to him. "This is my friend, Clio. She's a dis–"

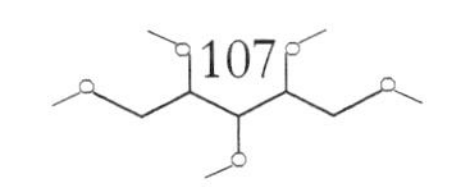

"Stealth," Miranda swiftly cut her off. "We're stealths." She offered Xavier her own hand, along with the sweetest smile she'd ever produced. "I'm Miranda."

"Hey, Miranda," he politely returned the greeting before peeking around her to say, "Hi, Bliss."

"Hi," Bliss sighed, presumably at the way his voice tinkled through her name like wind through chimes. Seeing her practically dissolve in his presence helped me snap out of my own trance-like state. I felt almost embarrassed for her and hoped the others hadn't thought the same thing about *me.*

Then came the real shocker; all five stars chorused, "Bliss!" It took me less than a second to put together that they wanted her access to Xavier. *Badly.*

While Rae and Xavier exchanged "Hellos," Alexis leaned over to me. "He does that," she said in a stage-whisper.

"What, hypnotizes you?" Once my head started to clear, irritation pushed its way to the front and my complaint came out a little louder than I'd intended.

"Not quite," Bliss started to explain at the same time Xavier offered a sheepish, "Sorry."

I looked into his eyes and found myself sinking again into the dark pools. *Is bottomless a color?* I wondered, then shook my head to break free again.

"I thought you were a heavy," I said, trying to reconcile my preconceived idea of him with his real-life self.

Alexis's "He is" overlapped Xavier's "I am," and she closed her mouth to let him speak.

"I fit in with the *rocks,*" he paused to give Alexis a wink,

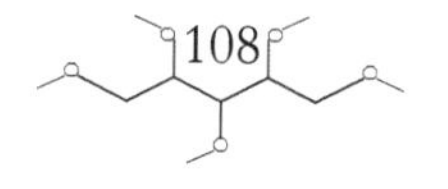

"more than any other group. But I don't exactly share their blocking ability."

"We get that, Captain Obvious," Miranda snorted. I couldn't tell if she was more unnerved by how easily she'd fallen under his spell, or miffed that there was yet another "special" person on campus for her to contend with.

Rae wasn't about to let Miranda plow over her closest friend on campus. "I think you're pretty cool for a freak," she told him, delivering a light elbow to his ribs. I suddenly put together that she, as the only girl jock, and he, as the only guy rock, were quite equally odd. And in *this* place, that said a lot.

"Thanks, Rae," he replied with such genuine appreciation that I felt bad for my earlier annoyance with him. He hadn't chosen his ability any more than the rest of us had, and it wasn't his fault we all lost brain function in his presence. The more I thought about it, the more I could see that while the instant adoration of strangers may have some appeal, the ensuing backlash of people once they'd recovered probably wasn't much fun. I knew my reaction hadn't been the friendliest.

"I'm sorry I didn't come find you and introduce myself," I apologized, trying to make up for it. Then I froze when I realized I'd been unconsciously stroking his forearm as I spoke. *Seriously, how was he doing that?*

"I'm working on it," he said, seeming to read my thoughts. "Lex tells me she has almost total control of her blocking now." I nodded in agreement, thinking how she rarely pushed us away like she used to.

I also noticed that he hadn't pushed my hand away.

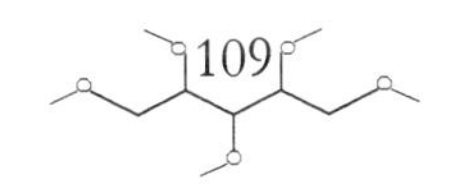

Trying not to be too obvious, I rolled the self-removal into a casual check of my watch.

"Lex?" Bliss questioned the unexpected familiarity of the nickname. "Sounds like you already knew each other." Her hurt at being left out was clear.

"We don't. We didn't," Alexis assured her.

"We both signed up for the same drum symposium this summer," he explained. "I recognized her name. Guess there'll be spots open now."

Huh. Another Juilliard-ite, I surmised. That meant when she went home, Alexis would have someone there for her for the first time since she'd lost her parents. They may have different abilities, but Xavier and Alexis were proving to have one major thing in common – the more I learned about them, the more I found to like.

If we all live long enough to make it out of here, my inner cynic weighed in, rudely reminding me where we were and why we were here. I saw that, while we were talking, the line had moved up. As everyone shuffled forward to fill the gap, I flashed back to something nasty Janet had once said about us – that we were a bunch of stupid sheep. I felt like that's exactly what I was witnessing now – obedient lambs, lining up for slaughter. And not just today, but every day that we kept going on with our lives as if they were normal. Why didn't someone – anyone – just stand up and freak out?

Not that I'd done anything different. Maybe not consciously, but I'd shoved my terror down as far as I could to keep functioning, too. I hadn't been that one person who was willing to step up and say something; I hadn't volunteered to be "that girl who totally lost it."

Apparently, we'd all come to the same conclusion – that melting down wasn't going to accomplish anything. Panic wouldn't stop a killer; crying wouldn't magically produce evidence or bring justice. Our joint reaction was somehow both insane and rational at the same time.

"It was nice meeting you," I called to both Xavier and Rae as I broke away from the group, "but they don't want my blood, and I need to see someone upstairs." *And maybe get us moving in a new direction,* I added to myself.

When Rae shot her pointer finger at me and shouted, "Probe ya later!" I burst out laughing. She actually made me want to stay and hang out in front of the creepiest building I'd ever been to. And I'd *been* on the haunted tour of the French Quarter.

Welcome to Camp, Rae Mahoney, I thought happily. *It's good to have you here.*

TWELVE

I ignored the muttering and dirty looks as I bypassed the line of kids and climbed the steps to the medical center's front door. I wanted to explain to everyone that I wasn't cutting, just going up to see Colonel Clark, but I figured announcing my "in" with the head honcho wasn't going to earn me any forgiveness. I couldn't see why they were so anxious to get inside anyway; this was one event I was more than happy to be left out of.

I wasn't surprised to hear the automated voice project, "Kaid, Calliope," as the door opened to allow my entry. What did give me pause, though, was that it'd happened *before* I'd put my finger in the print scanner to be identified. I looked around for some new body-reading lens, but didn't see anything out of the ordinary. Not that I had a clue what to look for.

I looked ahead to see Job, as I now knew to be the name of the desk-bot, parked in his usual spot at reception. I knew he wasn't about to tell me about any upgrades. After his curtness at our first meeting, he'd quickly devolved into silence, eventually dropping eye contact as well. Why the Army couldn't find a friendly ex-hostess or cruise director to man the desk instead of a guy with no more humanity than his Bluetooth was a mystery to me.

I passed him without acknowledgement, and the elevator doors opened as soon as I pressed the call button. I could've guessed that, especially today, nobody else would have any use for the upper floors. I stepped inside the steel car and waited for the doors to close behind me. I let my hands fall to my sides, as there were no buttons to push; this car travelled only back and forth from the lobby to the fourth floor, which housed the rehabilitation area.

I knew from my earlier "check-up" that the first floor was comprised of exam rooms, but still wasn't sure what took up all the space in-between. Two and three had to be for supplies and storage, at least in part, and Dr. Larson obviously had an office or lab or both in there somewhere as well. At least, thanks to PETA-member Bliss, I knew that there were no lab animals here or anywhere else on campus. She'd fully investigated that before the possibility had even occurred to me.

As the elevator rose, and all the things I wanted to ask Colonel Clark began rushing in, my anxiety climbed along with it. I wasn't even sure where to begin: Larson's murder, Nate's stabbing, the new and different – in every sense of the word – kids. The more worries I let into my mind, the more overwhelming it all became. *Was the world going crazy?* My part of it seemed to be, anyway.

I turned to my go-to calming technique to try and pull myself together. Instead of counting to ten or thinking of my "happy place," I relied on reciting lyrics to steady my nerves. The vertical trip took less time than the opening verse of *Let Me Go*. The 3 Doors Down tune was one of my standards because of the repetitive lines and soothing melody, so I continued singing it in my head as I walked down the long corridor to Colonel Clark's room.

I didn't pass a single person or hear any noise from the rooms and off-shoot hallways I passed, which wasn't unusual on a normal day, let alone this one. Surely everyone must be needed downstairs to process the dozens of kids and blood bags.

And it wasn't like I needed to see another face to know that eyes, albeit mechanical ones, were watching my every step. I resisted the impulse to wave to one of the cameras and send a silent *Hi* to Jack, in case he wasn't the one checking this footage.

The colonel's door was open as usual – a continuation of the constant availability he'd pledged from day one. I reached the opening at the same time I got to the chorus, and I suddenly realized I'd been wrong – the song wasn't irrelevant to my life. *You love me, but you don't know who I am* – the line was ironically fitting for the man I was about to see. Colonel Clark had spent his whole life watching over me like a godfather, without my ever knowing; he'd known all *about* me, without ever actually *knowing* me. I reminded myself to keep that in mind as I questioned him.

"Clio!" He came as close to jumping out of his seat as he was physically able, at the same time welcoming me with a bright smile. He dropped the book he'd been reading onto his chair and shuffled toward the door, one hand on his side to relieve the pressure on his still-healing wound.

It only took one look at the broad grin he wore in spite of his obvious pain for the outraged *You need to tell me what's going on around here* to die on my lips. This was the first time I'd seen him since everything from finding Larson's body to learning that Trudy was his mother had unraveled, and I'd come determined to give him a piece of my mind and demand answers.

Instead, I burst into tears.

He quickly took my elbow and led me to a second chair by the window, somehow managing to find me a tissue along the way. As I wiped the embarrassing wet trails from my cheeks, I averted his concerned eyes by pretending to take in the room.

Not that there was much to see. I assumed it looked like every other hospital room, but my experience was seriously limited. The only time I could even remember being inside one was when my wild friend Chelsea had had an unfortunate – though not unforeseeable – streetcar accident. She'd treated the *Keep your arms and legs inside the trolley* sign as an ignorable suggestion, and her arm had been fully extended out the open window when her elbow'd collided with a metal pole at twenty miles an hour. *Big ouch.*

Over the weeks Colonel Clark had been living at the medical center, he'd added fewer personal touches than Chelsea had in the hours she'd claimed a chair and surrounding feet of clinic floor space with strewn clothes and miscellaneous emptied-purse items. His room remained as stark as the day he'd moved in, but then again, his office had also been devoid of personal tokens.

Because he doesn't have anyone outside of this project, I reminded

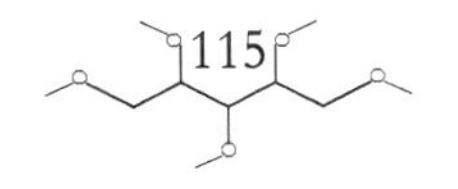

myself. He had no one to care for except me, the girl he'd watched over out of respect for a man with whom he'd served in the Gulf. And despite his loneliness, he'd never intruded in my life, yet here I was, busting into his hospital room to rip him a new one. *Nice work, Kaid*, I chastised myself.

He moved *Going Rogue* from his chair to a side table, but instead of settling back into his seat, he remained perched on the edge in case I should need something else.

I should be the one seeing if there's anything I can get him, I thought, releasing an audible sigh.

"Are you alright?" he asked, his gray eyes as soft as a flannel blanket.

"No," I answered, managing to keep my tone merely miserable and not accusing.

"Oh…," he trailed off. I caught the whispered "s" of "sweetheart" that he'd tried to swallow, but I let it pass; we both knew that he felt more fatherly toward me than I was ready to accept.

"What can I do?" he asked, practiced at staying the line, even in the face of my obvious distress.

"I just want to know what's going on," I told him, keeping my voice as calm and even as I could.

"What did Major Godwin tell you at the assembly?" he asked, looking for a frame of reference.

"Why does that matter?" I retorted. "So you can be sure to only repeat the party line and not accidentally tell me too much?"

I hadn't meant to snap, but before I could take it back, he

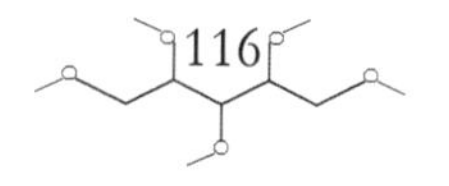

said, “You’re right.” *For real?*

“It doesn’t matter what she said,” he agreed. “I’ll tell you everything I know.”

And he meant it. I could both see in his eyes and hear in his voice that he would say or do whatever I asked – not that I deserved any of it when I’d offered only suspicions and demands in return. He immediately began filling me in, leaving none of the gaps I was sure he would have if I’d been anyone else. This, of course, made me feel horribly guilty for taking advantage of our relationship. Or, more accurately, the relationship with me that he wanted to have. In that humbling moment, I made a silent vow to treat him with more care and consideration from now on.

Unfortunately, he didn’t have anything to share that I didn’t already know. He told me again how they assumed the attacker must be male, due to the force needed to overtake two large guys; he reiterated that forensics estimated the weapon to be between five and six inches in length, unable to be precise since the killer had taken it with him. And the scariest part of all still held true – the isolation of the victims proved the attacks had been carefully premeditated.

As far as evidence, no images had been caught on film, no breach of the fence had been detected, and there were no witnesses to either attack. They had no clues of any kind to work with.

“Our only hope of catching a break is for Nathan to pull through,” the colonel said, not optimistically. I’d never thought I’d find myself wishing Nate would be okay, but the colonel was right. We needed him to recover.

Instead of lifting my spirits, the certainty that Colonel Clark hadn't kept anything from me somehow made me feel even worse. It would almost be better if he'd held back an important lead, rather than be as clueless as me.

I realized the discussion was agitating him, too, and wondered if that was bad for his condition. I knew it couldn't be good, at any rate.

"How are you feeling?" I asked, trying to put him more at ease and lower his blood pressure or whatever relaxing was supposed to help with.

"I'm fine," he said, giving a standard soldier response.

I didn't know if I should ask again, or let it drop. I decided to go with a third option.

"I'm sorry I haven't been around much lately," I apologized.

"That's okay," he assured me. "Lieutenant Graham told me how busy you've been with work."

"He talks about me?" I asked, startled by how my heart fluttered at the prospect.

"Sure," he replied, thankfully not seeming to notice my reaction. "We meet every day to go over campus affairs."

Disappointment washed over me, although my brain told me it had no reason to. Of course they met every day; Colonel Clark was still in charge, and Ford had to implement his orders while he was out of commission. It wasn't like they were gossiping over coffee. And really the last thing I should want was to be the focus of their conversations anyway.

"And Bliss is great," he continued. "She's like a ray of

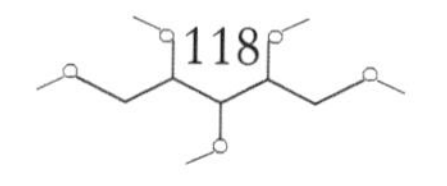

sunshine."

I stifled a groan and said, "I thought she might not come by as much, now that she's got the tour-guide gig." I grimaced at how snarky I sounded.

"Oh, no," he assured me. "She still comes every day. I don't think Ms. Mahoney and Mr. Wittman require a lot of guiding," he added. "Have you met them?"

"Just this morning, actually," I said. I gave him my impression of both Rae and Xavier, making sure to point out how strange it was that she was the first girl jock and he the first guy heavy.

"I'd kind of thought it was a given that our abilities were gender-linked," I admitted. "All but the stealths, anyway; we're the only group to have girls and guys. Guess that's another thing I got wrong."

"We all did," he commiserated. "As far as conclusive C9x findings, we have nothing."

"I was hoping Dr. Larson had found something," I moved forward, glad to leave behind the irrationally touchy subject of Bliss for something that had a chance of being productive.

"If he did, it was so recent that he hadn't had a chance to tell anyone," he said, frowning. "As far as I know, he was still at square one." *So much for my theory that Larson got killed because of some new revelation he'd had.*

The lull in our conversation allowed the hypothesis Alexis had proposed earlier to resurface in my mind. "You know, Alexis had this idea about blood types and abilities…," I said, going on to explain her thoughts on a possible correlation between the two.

Colonel Clark listened intently, processing the idea. When he pulled a pad of paper from the side table drawer to make a note, I rushed to point out the flaw in the theory. "We realized it doesn't hold up," I told him. "For it to work, I'd have to be Type O, but I'm not."

"That doesn't mean it's not valid," he argued, "just that there are exceptions."

"Right," I snorted, "because that's me – exceptional."

"Yes," he answered in all seriousness. I quickly sensed that I should redirect him before this took an emotional turn.

"So are you going to replace him?" I asked. "Dr. Larson, I mean."

"That hasn't been decided," he answered, adding, "but if you're worried about the campus shutting down, don't be. The gates will stay open as long as you need them to."

"What about all the hate-mail?" I asked, remembering what Alexis had told us.

"You know about that?" he replied, seeming somewhat surprised but not alarmed. "It's nothing." He tried to dismiss the subject, so I gave him a skeptical look.

"There will always be people who get angry about what they don't understand," he went on, "but that's not for you to worry about. You just need to remember that the conspiracy theorists or lunatics or whatever you want to call them may be out there, but they'll never get in here, I promise you. And," he added, tapping one finger to the side of his head, "it's up to you

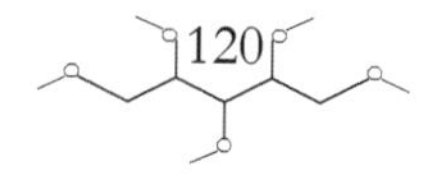

to make sure they never get in *here.*"

I couldn't explain why I'd never even considered the option of leaving, even with a killer on the loose. But what I found most interesting was that the colonel hadn't asked me to.

There was a light rap on the doorframe, and we both turned to see the physical therapist. She looked pointedly at her watch to signal that visiting hours were over, so I got up to leave.

"Are you going to be okay?" Colonel Clark asked me, also getting to his feet.

I felt the sudden need to say one last thing before leaving.

"I haven't been fair to you," I began, "and I'm sorry. You give me a lot more than I give you." I hoped the slight break in my voice clued him in to the depth of my appreciation for not just the physical security he provided, but also everything he did to protect my spirit.

"You don't have to say anything," he said quietly, trying to wave it off.

"Yes, I do," I contradicted, knowing I was in danger of violating my anti-touchy-feely rule, but continuing anyway. "I need you to know that *I* know, no matter what's going on outside, there's one person in this room I can always count on."

"Thank you," he said softly, his eyes threatening to well up.

"You don't have to be so forgiving all the time," I added.

"You got it. Now initiating *Mission Mean,*" he said in a comically robotic voice.

"Don't do that either," I laughed, glad that he'd been the one to lighten the mood. "Don't be too nice or too mean.

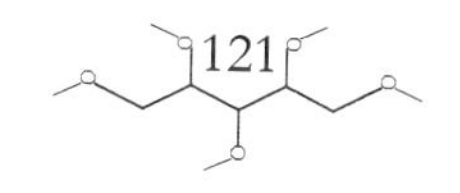

Just…be."

"Yes, ma'am!" He gave a little salute and I felt an unexpected urge to hug him, but settled for just squeezing his arm and saying, "Goodnight." *Baby steps.*

I left the building, turning out of habit toward the center of campus. With everybody either still plugged into donor stations or done and gone, there was no one to see me stop mid-stride, suddenly unsure where to go.

Any other day, I wouldn't think twice about finding a soft patch of grass to stretch out in and breathe in the afternoon as it melted into twilight. But alone-time was no longer allowed. Neither was not telling anyone where you were going, and definitely not closing your eyes and completely letting down your guard. I knew it sounded ridiculous to say the killer was "ruining everything," but those were the exact words that popped into my mind as I thought of how he was murdering my favorite places. At least he hadn't gotten to any of my favorite people. Yet.

I felt paralyzed by my lack of options. I had no interest in listening to everyone else complain about being poked and prodded all afternoon, or to rehash the gory details of the latest attack either. Jack was most likely still unavailable, and I was sick of holing up in my room like the fox Garrett had once compared me to.

Without even thinking about it, I found myself sinking down right there on the grass, wishing that, for a little while, I could be alone with just the sunshine to warm my face and the breeze to carry away my worries. Lost in the desire to do so, I simply disappeared.

THIRTEEN

By the time I reemerged, the sunset was almost complete, but the night lights hadn't come on yet, shrouding the campus with eerie shadows. I felt like the kid who'd hidden so well playing hide and seek that everyone else had given up and gone home.

I hurried back to the dorm, stopping by my room for just a second to grab my notes before heading to Alexis's. I hoped I wasn't late for our play-date.

Pulling my door closed behind me put me directly facing Trudy's. I was torn between wanting to talk to her about everything that was going on and being so mad at her that I could scream. I didn't know why I was so much angrier with her than Colonel Clark for keeping the same secret; I actually hadn't even realized until this minute that I hadn't asked him about it in his room. I'd like to pretend that was because I'd been considerate of his condition, but that wasn't it. For some reason, I felt that she'd violated my trust more, and since I was also pretty sure that if I tried to talk to her, I might not be able to keep my calm, I turned and walked away.

Alexis's door swung in at my touch; as I stepped inside, I saw she'd just turned the knob with one elbow, her hands busy running floss through her front teeth.

"Sorry," she said, pulling out the string and ducking across the hall to throw it in the bathroom trash.

While I waited for her, I let my eyes drift around her room. It was the first time she'd had me over, though we'd been trying to set it up for weeks. I hadn't expected to find the space cozy and inviting, but I'd never thought it would be so plain – nothing at all Alexis – and to have such starkly white walls and even floor.

"Miranda talked me into alfalfa sprouts at dinner," she explained as she came back into the room. "Now I feel like someone sowed my mouth with grass seed *and* I'm still hungry."

"So," she went on, "getting a glimpse at college life?" *Of course.* I should've put it together right away; the room was a replica of her dorm room in New York. Now the tile floor and metal bunk beds made complete sense.

As she crossed to the built-in desk to turn off the music she'd been listening to, I had to ask, "What is that?"

"*Starless*, by Crossfade. You like it?" she asked, surprised.

"Um, no," I answered honestly. But even though I had no love for the metal sound, the band and song names caught my attention. "*Fade* and *Starless*? Could be our campus theme song."

"Huh," she said, "I hadn't thought of that."

That's because I do enough over-thinking for all of us, I thought, making a mental note to look both up later.

"Take a load off," she suggested, so I went over to the

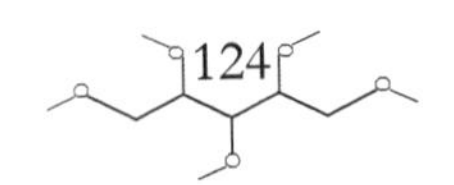

lower bunk, the only seating option I saw in the room besides the desk chair. As I got closer, I saw that what I'd thought was a sheer curtain hanging from the top was actually some kind of wire, woven into a pattern. When I pushed it to the side so I could sit down, it folded into sharp panels along the track.

"Old guitar strings," Alexis explained before the question had even formed on my lips.

"This must have taken you forever," I murmured, fingering the intricate and strangely beautiful design.

"It kept my hands busy after my parents died," she said simply. "And my head." We'd never really talked about her parents and how they'd been killed in what she now knew was a staged accident after her Army-doctor dad had started digging into Heigl's past for Colonel Clark. I could sense that she didn't plan to change that by opening up tonight. As much as she'd gotten control of her blocking ability, some of her walls were still firmly in place.

Sitting down gave me a view of the other side of the room, the part that'd been behind me and the door when I'd walked in. Four shiny copper drums stood in a line, arranged by slightly graduating size.

"You have drums in your room?" I asked, amazed.

"Well, I just have the one room for all my stuff," she answered with a small shrug. "I'm not allowed to play them, though, because of the noise."

"You could put them in storage," I suggested.

"Yeah, but I like having them around," she said, stroking the soft top of the largest one. Then she lifted off the whole

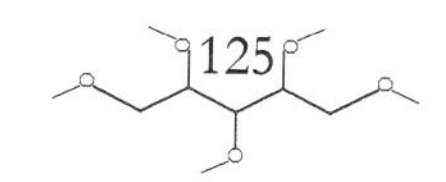

hoop and rested it on top of the next one in line.

"Plus, I need the space for my snacks," she added, pulling out a plastic bag and holding it up for me to see. "Voila. Tim-*pani* becomes tim-*pantry*."

"Nice," I said, clapping my hands in approval. And also to avoid accepting her offering of shriveled green balls.

"They're wasabi peas," she informed me. "Don't judge."

I didn't unwrinkle my nose, but I did uncurl my fingers slightly to make the smallest hand cup I could. She poured in a few of the questionable morsels and I gave one a tentative lick. Once I'd confirmed they were indeed edible, I downed the half-handful. *Not horrible*, I admitted to myself as Alexis plopped down beside me on the bed, *but I won't be asking for seconds.*

"I feel kind of bad, trying to write a song with everything that's going on," I admitted as I wiped my hand on my leg.

"But we planned it a long time ago," she argued, using the practical calm she held onto in every storm. "And we hardly see each other anymore."

"The worst part is," I confided, "that I spend most of my time thinking about silly stuff like this, because if I keep obsessing over the attacks…."

"You'll go crazy," she finished for me.

"Exactly," I breathed with relief.

"Don't you think that's what everybody's doing?" she asked gently.

"You, too?" I felt some of the tension slip from my shoulders.

"Yup," she confirmed with an empathetic nod.

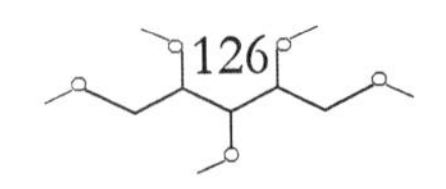

"Well, let's go on and make some music then," I said with a small laugh and a larger sense of calm.

"Bring it," she laughed in return.

"Do you have any time to play anymore?" I asked, unfolding my sheets of scribbles.

"No, I haven't been down to the rehearsal room in over a week," she answered.

"I thought y'all practiced in the great room," I said, wondering if yet another thing had changed without my knowing.

"We met there at the beginning, before we knew anything about each other or what we could do," she explained, "but it didn't take long for us to figure out we were better off playing than talking. After that, we moved into an unused conference room with better acoustics; they even soundproofed the walls for us."

"If you haven't been down there," I supposed, "you probably don't know how Xavier's fitting in."

"Why, are you interested in him?" Alexis teased.

I decided to say nothing and treat it as a rhetorical question, since we both knew it was impossible to *not* be drawn to the human magnet.

When I saw that she was waiting for an answer, I mumbled, "I have enough going on already."

Her eyes darkened with concern beneath narrowing lids and one quizzically arched brow. "Anything you want to talk about?" she asked.

"No." I hadn't yelled, but my response had come out so fast and sharp that Alexis blinked in surprise.

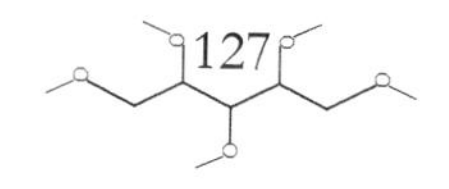

"Well, where do you want to start?" she asked, tipping her head toward my pages and choosing to move forward as if nothing had happened.

"I'm not really sure," I answered hesitantly, both because I didn't know where to begin and because I felt like I might owe her an apology. "I'm new to this."

"Okay," she said, then asked more specifically, "Would you rather work out the melody first, then lay the chorus on top and move out from there? Or do you already have lyrics written down that you need music to go with?"

She must have seen that I found her follow-up even more confusing than her opening question, because she said, "You have to help *me*, help *you*."

"Have you been watching movies with Garrett?" I asked, thankful for her willingness to let me off the hook.

"He says I need the culture," she answered with a completely straight face.

"I guess it feels more natural to me to work out the lyrics first," I decided.

"That's what I figured," she agreed. "What've you come up with so far?"

"Well, every time I try to put down some words, I get caught up with how I'm going to rhyme them in the next line," I admitted.

"You can't let that block you," she advised.

"Easy for you to say," I grumbled.

"Think about Sinatra's *My Way*," she said, checking to make sure I was following. "He rhymed *mention* with *exemption*,

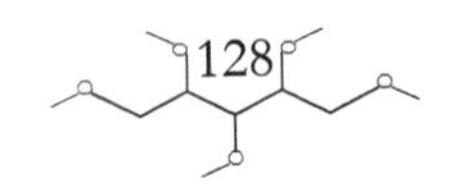

okay? That should've been terrible, but he worked it out."

I nodded, conceding the point.

"So tell me what you're trying to say," she encouraged.

"I want to write about a sense of found…," I stumbled, searching for the right word, "…*ness*? Found*age*? Are those words?"

"You've got me," Alexis said with a shrug. "I'm not a word-maker. Let's just take the idea and roll it out."

"Okay," I agreed. "So a feeling of found*ity*…," I trailed off again, but Alexis twirled her hand to tell me to blow past the word-block and move on.

"Right," I tried again. "So, not in the expected way of *I was lost, but now I'm found*; more like, *I may not know who I am, but I know where I belong.*"

"Mm-hmm," she said, taking some notes of her own while nodding me on. "Go on."

"*I've found where I am*," I continued, "*Here in this, this is here….*"

Alexis kept writing, but I stopped to rethink the line. "I just feel like I keep coming out with stuff that sounds goofy," I complained. "I don't want to go all Hillary Duff, *If the light is off, then it isn't on*, you know?"

"Deep or dumb – it's a fine line," Alexis agreed.

"Can I use that?" I asked.

"No, because I might!" she threw back with a smirk. "You know, you're giving me kind of a Fray vibe. Maybe it's because you're so focused on being 'found' like that one song they have."

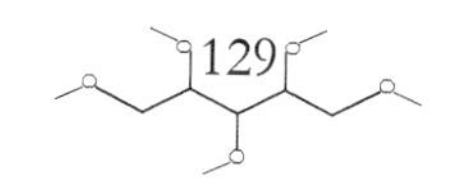

"But their music is so…dark," I objected.

"So?" she asked, not seeing the problem.

"So I don't want to write depressing music," I reminded her.

"Who said dark has to be depressing?" she argued. "You know, when I was little, my mom went through all my books and anytime one said that the dark was *scary*, she blacked it out and changed it to *mysterious*. She told me that the dark is a place where anything is possible, so let your imagination run free."

"That's true," I admitted.

"Plus, when you go in a direction nobody expects, it's much more interesting," she went on, but I'd already caught on to what she meant.

"No arbitrary boundaries," I agreed, putting it into my own words.

"Hey," she thought aloud, "you should check out Candlebox. They're a little older, but they have a really good balance between heavy music and solid lyrics."

"I will," I said, writing the name of the band across the top my first sheet.

Alexis reached around the side of the bed to retrieve the guitar that'd been leaning there. "Let's play a few chords to stir up your brain fluid," she suggested.

As she strummed a basic tune, I let out the first words that came into my mind. "I'm here and I'm good, even if it's not all understood…."

"Um," she interrupted. "I'm *here* and *good* kinda makes you sound like a hooker."

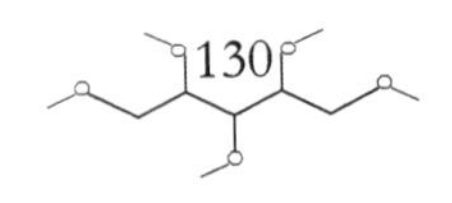

"Scratch that," I laughed. "I haven't really slept the past couple nights, so I think I'm starting to lose it a little."

"I hear you," she said, putting the guitar back down.

"Do you play everything?" I asked her. "Cello for Juilliard, plus drums *and* guitar? You're like a one-man band."

"Like a *calliope*?" she teased.

"Ha, ha," I returned and threw in an accompanying eye roll.

"Yeah," she answered the earlier question. "My mom taught music, so I got to listen to and try everything."

Only because I felt she'd opened the door, I asked, "Do you think about them a lot? Your parents?" I braced myself for the possible push-back.

But there wasn't one.

"All the time," she answered softly, looking away.

"I'm sorry," I offered the only comforting words I had.

"It's okay," she said before gently closing the subject. "I mostly prefer thinking about them to talking about them."

"I didn't mean to snap at you before," I apologized, feeling like I'd been doing a lot of that lately – both snapping *and* apologizing. "I don't know what came over me."

"I don't know if you want to hear this," she said tentatively, "but you sound like I did before I got here. Before I found out what I was, and that what was wrong wasn't really wrong with *me*."

"Are you trying to say you think I'm a heavy?" I asked, though I was pretty sure that's what she meant.

"Maybe," she answered, waiting for my reaction.

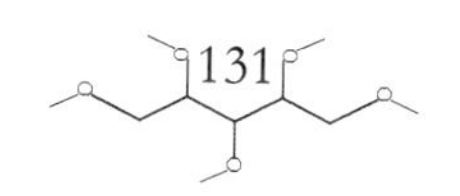

"But I vanish, remember?" I reminded her.

"What if you have more than one ability?" she proposed.

It took Alexis saying it out loud for me to realize that the same idea had already crossed my mind. My recent inexplicable blocking and deflecting had *heavy* written all over them.

"But how can that be?" I asked, as if she held all the answers. I also didn't want to admit I'd been hiding behind a shield emblazoned with *denial* as well.

"Come on, how can any of this be?" she countered. "Remember my theory about the blood types?"

"Yeah, I actually told Colonel Clark about it when I went upstairs," I answered.

"Well, what if it's right on?" she posed. "What if it proves you're different – not just from Miranda and the other stealths, but from everybody?"

"Because that's what I need right now," I groaned.

"Like I said before," she reiterated, "unexpected is always more interesting."

"Right, and I was just complaining about how boring it is around here," I said, surprised at how easy it was to joke about the prospect I'd been so adamantly avoiding.

"I also think," she added, "pushing those girls this morning might have been you, not me."

No way. The possibility hadn't occurred to me until now, but once she said it, I thought about how far away she'd been when they'd reacted. At the time, I'd attributed it to the strength of her practiced ability, but now I wasn't so sure. *Could I have done that?*

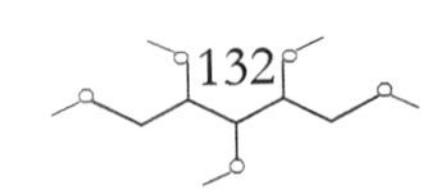

"I'm not going to tell anyone," Alexis assured me, "but if that's what's happening, you can't stop it."

"I know," I conceded, adding a heart-felt "Thanks" before leaving.

Despite the "heavy" talk, I felt somehow lighter as I walked back down the hall to my room. I'd let go of some of my denial, unlocked the cage that I'd banished the possibility of turning heavy to. I still wasn't sure how I felt about it, but I knew there was no way to lock it back up now.

FOURTEEN

The night woods were darker than I'd ever seen them – the branches weaving a thick canopy that blocked even the rays of the moon. But I couldn't let the lack of visibility slow me down; I had to go fast, go far, go *now.* I fought to maintain a dead run despite the treacherous terrain of meaty roots covering the forest floor.

My instinct was to stop and repeat to myself, *I'm invisible; he can't see me. Vanish, and he'll run right by*. Though it'd saved me in every nightmare chase my memory could recall, I somehow knew that, even if my ability *had* grown strong enough to burst into my waking world, it couldn't save me tonight. Not from this predator.

I could hear him swiftly closing the gap between us, could sense that he could somehow see me even in the pitch-blackness and that even disappearing wouldn't protect me from him.

I had no choice but to keep running, though I'd taken such a random zig-zagging course that I'd lost track of where I was and had no way to find my way back. All I knew was that more and more branches seemed to snatch at my hair and tear scratches across my cheeks, telling me I was going deeper into the woods. And farther from help.

I swore I could hear his rough breathing behind me, but didn't dare waste a second by turning to check. Not that a backward glance would do me much good, when I couldn't even see the nose on my own face.

My only hope now was to call out at the top of my voice and pray that, by some miracle, a breeze would materialize out of the stillness to carry my cry to open ears. I forced all the air in my lungs up my throat and out into the night.

No sound emerged. With my mouth still framing the silent scream, my heart took its own upward leap – trying to either shove the yell the rest of the way out, or to make its own escape from my doomed body.

My mind broke away next, absconding to survival-mode, and I felt myself breaking apart….

I bolted upright in bed, struggling to free myself from the sheet that shrouded my head, netted my hair, gagged my mouth. Once liberated from the cotton prison, I scanned my room, only to find it undisturbed and inhabited only by me.

The air conditioning froze the sweat that beaded on my neck and trickled down my back, but I knew the cold wasn't the cause of my chill. Tremors ran up and down my spine like a child dragging a stick back and forth across a xylophone, but my legs had gone past tingling into numbness.

As I tried to shake some blood down to my lower body, I thought about how I hadn't had a nightmare like that in months, maybe years. Not even the Janet debacle had wracked my

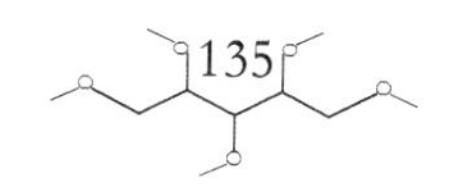

subconscious this fiercely. And even in the worst dreams I'd ever experienced, I'd always been able to disappear and escape the bad guy. *Always.*

I needed to get up and out of my room to try to calm down a little before I could change into dry pajamas. I stumbled out of bed and across the floor on wobbly legs to reach the night-lit corridor. Wrenching the knob as far hard left as it would go, I yanked open the door to find myself face-to-face with a hideous monster. My dream silence finally overcome, I let out a deafening scream that rattled the door in my hand.

"Come on, honey, pull yourself together. This is the true face of beauty." Trudy's voice came from somewhere behind the mud mask, and I searched out her familiar gray eyes, buried deep amidst the mottled green and brown lumps covering her face.

"I'm sorry," I apologized, not sure if I felt worse about shrieking so loud, or because I'd done it in reaction to the way she looked. "I didn't mean to wake everybody up."

"Oh, you girls sleep like the dead," she dismissed the notion with a wave of her hand. "Sorry, bad choice of words."

"But I woke you up," I pointed out. "Was I screaming in my sleep?" I must have been, for her to have already been at my door when I'd come out.

She nodded her head, but forgave me. "It's okay. Once you've had children, you never sleep soundly again." As she talked, she ushered me into her room and settled me into her rocking chair.

"Just something to keep me busy," she felt the need to tell me as she moved the knitting that'd been piled there to her

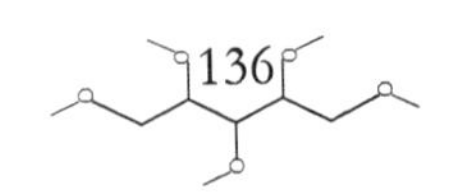

bed. "Don't you go thinking I'm some old maw-maw."

She crossed to the teakettle on the table by the door, and although I wasn't sure I wanted any, I let her pull out a second mug for me. While I waited, I breathed in the familiar comfort of her room.

Trudy hadn't changed much since she'd taken over from Janet – the space remained very simple, though not in the stark, institutional way of Alexis's. Trudy had softened the standard white walls with pearl-blue curtains and stretched deep beige carpeting from corner to corner.

A few personal touches, along with the lingering aroma of herbs, made the room comfy, but not cluttery. She'd hung a driftwood-framed watercolor of an ocean scene over her bed; anchored one corner with a hefty stack of hand-worn, leather-bound books; and hung a shelf next to the chair I was sitting in to hold several knickknacks whose meaning I loved to guess at. I picked up a large, hollowed-out sphere that was half-hidden in the back row. *Ostrich egg?* I guessed.

"It's the eye socket of a whale," she answered my unasked question, and I almost dropped the artifact in my hurry to get it back into its place and out of my hands.

I took the mug she offered me with both hands, not realizing I was still shaking until the surface of the liquid threatened to slosh over the rim.

"Would you like something to eat?" she asked politely.

"No, thank you," I answered, knowing my own grandmother would've been ecstatic to hear me remember my manners in this time of crisis. "I've been so stressed out lately

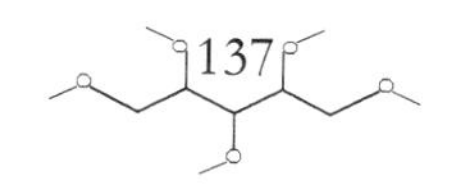

that I can't even eat," I told Trudy. "Do you know how bad that is?"

"Tragic, I'd say," she sympathized.

I nodded in confirmation before taking a tentative sip of the steaming brew. "What's in here?" I asked, finding the tea bold, flavorful, and nothing like the lemony water I'd expected.

"All sorts of things," she said, tasting her own. "Ginger, chamomile, cinnamon, a little catnip…."

"Seriously?" Just when I'd been sure nothing in the world could take my mind away from our current predicament, Trudy'd managed to come up with a zinger.

"It's called *Tension Tamer*," she explained, then asked, "So what was attacking you that we need to tame?"

"The killer," I told her, leaving off the sarcastic *obviously*. "It's driving me crazy how they keep saying how safe we are, when we're so not."

"Would it make you feel better to know there were fighter jets in a holding pattern over campus?" she posited. "Or snipers on top of the buildings?"

When I opened my mouth to respond, she hurried to add, "Not that there really are; I'm just trying to figure out what the Army could do to make you feel better."

"Just tell us *some*thing," I burst out in exasperation. "I don't know why everyone thinks keeping things from us will keep us calm."

"They're trying to not treat you like children, but at the same time not terrify you," she said, trying to explain the administration's position, but I just couldn't see their side.

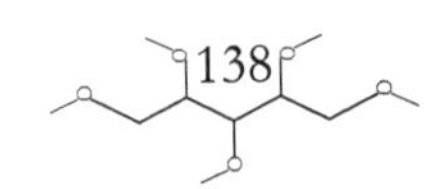

"If they'd just tell us anything at all, I might feel better," I replied, looking for a specific example. "Like, if Dr. Larson had finally learned something about C9x that made him a target. Then at least I'd know I wasn't next."

"Well, if Mark Larson had made any sort of discovery, Randall didn't know about it," she said, and I believed her. "And to be fair," she went on, "it'd be irresponsible to spread guesses."

"His murder just seems to bother me more than Nate's attack for some reason," I told her. "And the more I think about him, the more questions I have – about his research, about *us*. About everything, really. I feel like I'm drowning in them."

"Would it help to share some of them with me?" she offered kindly.

"Sure." I didn't need her to ask me twice. "When are we going to find out what C9x even is? And what other side effects might be coming? Will I wake up one day with six eyes and a tail? Will we ever know the whole story?" I paused for breath and another sip of tea.

"I don't know; I don't know; I hope not; I don't know," she answered in all seriousness.

"Some help you are," I said with a frown.

"You said you wanted honesty," she pointed out.

"I know," I conceded. "And I know we won't get all the answers in one night, but I have a hard time believing nobody's figured out anything at all. Or that the Army's really going to tell us the whole truth when they have it."

"They will," she said firmly.

"Right," I answered, a bit of sarcasm grabbing on to the

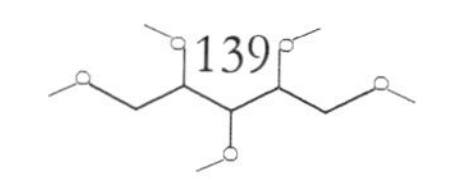

tail end of the word and escaping before I could catch it. And once I'd let out a little, a lot more was right behind it. "Because they've been so straight-forward up 'til now."

"I truly believe that you – *we* – know everything the government does," she said with total conviction. "You're right – it's possible that Dr. Larson found something he hadn't shared with anyone. But if he did, it's gone, and there's no use wishing any different."

"Unfortunately, all C9x research is now on hold," she went on, "and I'm sure you can understand why. But you also have to remember that you're still here, despite very contradictory public opinion. That speaks volumes. The Army has pledged to do all they can, and they will continue to uphold that promise," she finished.

"But how can you be so sure?" I wasn't so easily persuaded.

"Because Randall wouldn't allow anything less," she reminded me. "You have to know that."

"I do," I admitted softly, only to have my voice rise again a split second later to shout, "It's just so frustrating!"

"Calliope," she said, using the conclusive tone of a lawyer delivering her final argument, "I'm not going to promise you that you'll get all the answers you want, because it's possible that you won't. I can only assure you that you remain a top priority of the U.S. government and that you will be privy to their findings."

"I want to believe you," I said, "but sometimes I get so fed up, I just want to leave."

"You don't mean that," she dismissed the idle threat.

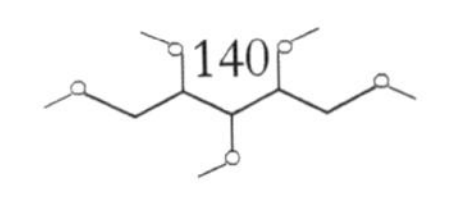

"No, not really," I agreed. "I just wish things would stop constantly shifting and just *settle* a little. Every time I feel like I know something, or that things are on the right track, it seems like the ground just gets yanked out from under me again."

"So is life," she said philosophically.

"They'd probably have to pry my cold dead hands off the front gate to get me out of here anyway," I confided. "You must think I'm crazy for saying that."

"Not at all," she disagreed.

"Really?" I gave her a chance to change her position. "I *want* to stay in a compound where I can't trust anyone and there's a killer on the loose, and you think that's sane?"

"Either you feel in your heart that that's not entirely the case," she posed gently, "or what you've found here is greater than your fear."

"The good parts are amazing," I admitted, "but the bad parts block them out. It's like they're constantly at war with each other." I wasn't sure I was expressing myself all that well, so I tried a different way of explaining my feelings.

"Like, I was having a great day with Garrett…until we found Larson's body. And then I was having a really hard time dealing with *that*, but I spent some time with Bliss and Miranda and they made me feel better. Well, until Bliss made me feel *worse*, but that was really my fault. Then I met Rae, who lifted me up again…until I made an ass of myself with Xavier. So I went and talked some things through with Clark, which made me feel better and worse at the same time. After that, I ended up with Alexis, and I left her room feeling almost *good*, but then I had the

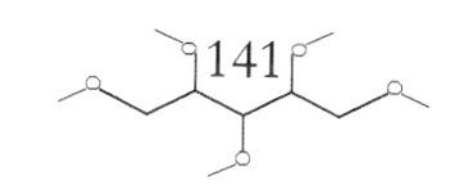

worst nightmare I've ever had."

"Sounds like there's one person you haven't spent any time with," she noted.

"I'm so sorry," I apologized quickly for having gone to everyone but her.

"Thank you, dear," she accepted graciously, "but I meant Jack."

"Oh," I replied, startled by the realization. She was right; I hadn't gone to Jack. But he also hadn't been around. I felt like I hardly saw him anymore – definitely not alone or for any significant amount of time. *Is that the reason I'd turned into such a mess? Because Jack was my source of calm?*

The idea struck me as both true and pathetic at the same time. I'd always thought of myself as so strong and independent, but now I saw that I hadn't been much of either lately. And that wasn't Jack's fault – it was mine.

"Did you two have a fight?" Trudy asked, misinterpreting the extended pause.

"No," I assured her, adding, "I don't know if it's even possible to fight with him. He's so…Jack. Everybody loves him."

"He sounds perfect," she surmised.

"He doesn't think so," I said, unsure how much of his backstory she knew. I decided to fill her in. "You know he's the only one here without an ability."

As I explained to Trudy how hard it'd been for Jack to watch the rest of us discover our gifts while finding none of his own, I was struck by a new thought entirely. *What if there was some significance in Jack being the first one of us to see the abilities emerge?* Not

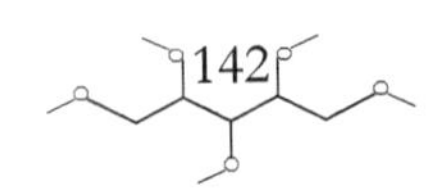

only had he seen us vanish before anyone else had, but he'd had to point it out to us since we couldn't see it by ourselves. The wheels were spinning furiously in my mind and I tried to put the swarm of ideas into words for Trudy.

"He's like an all-seer," I declared at the end. "Omniscient, isn't that what it's called?"

"Close. Omniscient means all-*knowing*," she clarified.

"Oh my God – I have to tell him!" I was half out of my chair when Trudy reined me back in.

"Not now," she chuckled. "It's the middle of the night."

"Oh, right," I said, sitting back down. And maybe I should think things through a little more before I told him my theory, anyway.

"So everybody loves Jack," Trudy returned to the last abandoned subject.

"Well, not everybody…," I amended my earlier claim to tell her about the girls who'd accused him of being the attacker. "I got so mad, I just wanted to start pounding on them and never stop," I said, feeling the rage start to burn inside me once again.

"That's awful," Trudy cried.

"I know. Poor Jack," I agreed. "They don't even know him."

"I meant awful for *you*," she corrected. "You sound like you completely lost control – like you couldn't even recognize yourself."

"I did," I admitted, surprised she could read so much into my few words.

"I hear more than just what you tell me," she said,

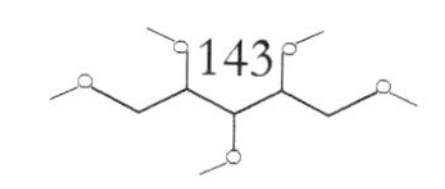

seeming to read my thoughts. "Even when you were telling me how you'd felt, it was like you were talking about someone else."

"That's how it felt to me, too," I said, relieved by her easy understanding. "And it wasn't the first time." I suddenly found myself telling her all about my recent pattern of strange behavior. The possibility was so much easier to talk about the second time that I took the big leap.

"Do you think I could have two abilities?" I asked. "That I might be a stealth *and* a heavy?"

"Absolutely," she assured me. "Hasn't this whole experience shown you that anything is possible? That your potential is exponential?"

"That's kind of what Alexis said," I told her.

"She's right," Trudy confirmed. "And if anyone were to push the boundaries of C9x, it would be you."

"Me?" I asked with a mixture of disbelief and denial.

"Yes, *you*," she repeated. "You've always been the most extraordinary one."

"You've got to be joking," I snorted. "I blend into the crowd like all the other stealths. I'm not athletic, musical, brilliant – no star of any kind. Trust me."

"Well," she began slowly, "you may have been able to blend in in your old life, but I'm afraid those days are behind you. Things have changed, and you're going to have to accept your new role as a leader."

"Okay, now I *know* you're joking," I responded.

"Taking control of the campus school – spearheading the entire movement to stay and establish a program – is the top

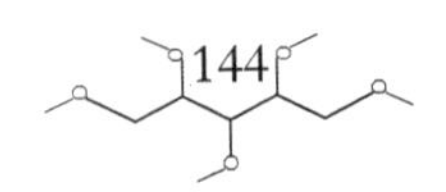

leadership position here," Trudy countered. "You're the only reason there's even going to *be* a school."

"No," I disagreed, "everybody wants that."

"But you're the one who's making it happen," she insisted.

"You're wrong," I said, because I wanted her to be. "I'm not a leader."

"We'll just have to agree to disagree," she replied, not budging from her position.

"Done." I stayed equally set in mine. I was done with this conversation, done with the notion that I needed to lead the other kids, done with having more unsolicited burdens piled on top of my load.

"So does this mean you're going back to avoiding me?" she asked pointedly.

"What?" I tried to act like I didn't know what she was talking about.

"I know that's what you've been doing," she persisted.

Since my faux-dumb act had failed me, I switched to the answer-a-question-with-a-question technique. "Then why didn't you say anything?"

"I knew you must've had your reasons," she said simply.

"But what if I'd never talked to you again?" I pursued. "Wouldn't you have cared?"

"I'd have been devastated," she answered, "but I wasn't going to push you."

"Why didn't you just tell me?" I knew she could tell I was talking about Colonel Clark now, about the secret they'd kept

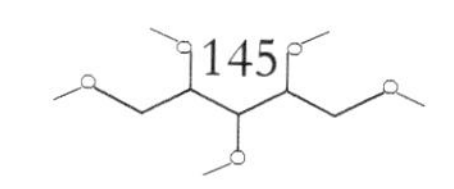

from me that had driven me away from her in the first place.

"We didn't want you girls to think I was some sort of spy," she said. "I wanted you to be able to talk to me without worrying that I'd take what you said in confidence to Randall."

"I just wish you would've told me," I said again, my defensiveness retreating.

"In hindsight, so do I," she admitted. "But Randall had to pull some strings to get me here, and I didn't know which feathers it was safe to ruffle."

"What kind of strings?" This was news to me.

"Placing me on campus, even though I'm a civilian," she explained.

"I thought you were a retired Army nurse," I returned to an accusatory stance.

"A retired nurse, yes, but I never enlisted," she clarified. "Randall's father was in the service, so I got hired on at hospitals in every city we moved to."

I conceded that one; it'd been less of a concealed truth and more of a misinterpretation by me. "I guess that's why you're not as reserved as the other officers," I commented.

"Probably," she agreed, "but give them a chance. They may surprise you."

"Okay," I allowed, though not as reluctantly as Trudy probably thought. My thoughts jumped straight to the one officer I'd already given a chance to, and how glad I was that I had.

"I'm glad you came to me," she said, offering a hug that I walked right into.

"You know, you could've pushed me a little," I added

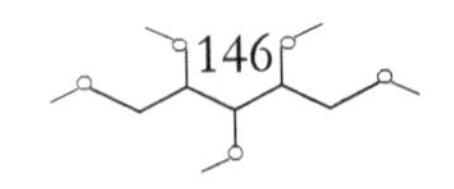

when I finally pulled away.

"Duly noted," she replied. "Now back to bed, young lady."

I surprised myself by thinking how good bed sounded now. Not sure if I should give all the credit to getting so much off my chest or let the catnip take a little, I headed for my pillow without looking back.

FIFTEEN

For the first time in a long time, I woke up with a sense of purpose. Last night's talk with Trudy had really helped me put things in perspective, and I was determined to stop life from jerking me up and down like a Super Shot ride. I knew it'd take more than desire to get back in control of my life, but determination was a good jumping-off point. I threw on some clothes and headed out.

Ten minutes later, I stood face-to-face with a person who looked less than thrilled to find me in his office.

"Clio, what are you doing here?" Ford asked, striding past me to drop a fist-high stack of files on his desk. I chose to attribute his unenthusiastic greeting to the timing of my visit, rather than me.

"Where am I supposed to be?" I came back, fighting to soften the edge in my voice.

"Getting ready for the party," he said simply, taking his seat and opening the top folder.

"I can't believe we're even still having it," I protested, using a pointed look to add, *Am I the only one with any sense?*

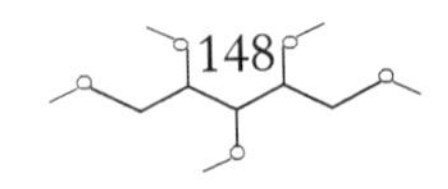

"Me neither," he admitted, closing the file to address me fully, "but Colonel Clark is the C.O., and if he says we go ahead with it, that's what we do."

"Even if it's ridiculous," I asked and answered at the same time.

"He's the boss," he said, closing the subject.

Good, I thought, drawing back my shoulders in a most Mirand-assertive way. I had more important things to discuss with him anyway.

And hopefully a better way of going about it. I'd thought a lot about how my previous info-demand strategy hadn't been all that successful, and I'd come ready to try out a new technique.

"What're you doing today?" I asked casually, initiating my new plan of gathering instead of hunting.

"Polygraphs." Either I'd caught him off guard, or he'd found my question harmless enough. Not that it mattered, so long as he kept answering.

"For who?" I tried to sound innocently surprised, though I'd known about the tests since Wednesday's debriefing.

"You," he said simply.

"Me?" This time I didn't have to fake shock.

"The collective you," he clarified. "The kids."

"All of us?" I reacted to blow number two.

"Everyone except Nathan Gagne," he amended.

"Because he's unconscious," I said somewhat smartly, but unable to help myself.

"Because he took his on Wednesday with the staff," he corrected.

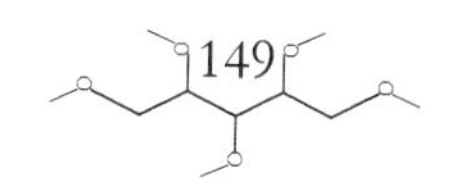

"Did it show anything?" I asked, suddenly excited by the possibility of getting some real information. First day working this new strategy and gathering-me looking poised to bag bigger game than hunting-me ever had.

"Only that the kid is a snake with no moral compass," Ford answered, coming in low on the helpful scale, but earning points for good character assessment.

"But…," I urged leadingly.

"But he didn't attack Larson," he said regretfully.

"So Nate got attacked the same night he took his polygraph," I laid out the pieces thoughtfully. "There's gotta be a connection right? Like he revealed something in the test that he shouldn't have?"

"Or someone thought he did," Ford agreed. "Yeah, the thought definitely crossed my mind."

"And all the staff people came through clean?" I asked, hoping he wouldn't suddenly decide to shut me down.

He answered with one word: "Crystal."

"Crystal Dolan?" I gasped. "You think she's the killer? Did you arrest her?"

"I meant crystal *clean*," he corrected. "Captain Dolan passed the polygraph along with everybody else. Including me."

"But you all know how to beat the test," I argued, pointing out what I was sure had to be true.

"In theory, maybe," he conceded, "but Clio, I assure you that that wasn't the case here. The campus killer is not one of us."

"How can you be so sure?" I countered. "You're all

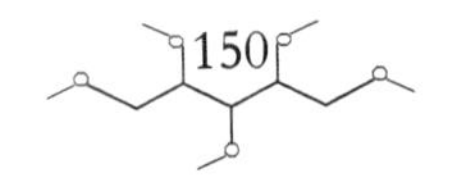

trained killers, after all."

"We're highly-trained *soldiers*, Clio," he corrected. "Killing is only the last resort we'd use to stop an enemy."

"Nate *is* the enemy," I assured him.

"No, he's a kid," he disagreed.

I was torn between wanting to press my argument and risking that he'd say he thought of me as "just a kid," too.

"So now you're going to test the rest of us – every single person," I said, returning to a safer previous subject.

"Yeah," he confirmed, then allowed the tiniest hint of a smile to peek through. "Thorough is my middle name."

"I thought you didn't have one," I quickly joined him in our now-familiar banter.

"It's new. And self-assigned," he threw back with a grin so wide it almost knocked me off-topic.

Almost.

"Even the new kids?" I pursued. "They just got here."

He raised one eyebrow as if to say, *Think about what you just said.*

"Oh." It only took me a second to make the connection. "They just got here…right before the first attack."

He nodded without offering anything further, so I forged ahead on my own.

"How's it going to work?" I asked.

"Alphabetically, starting with Miss Bliss Campbell," he answered, misunderstanding my question.

"No, I mean the machine," I explained. "Will it hurt?"

"Not at all," he assured me. "Here, let me show you." He

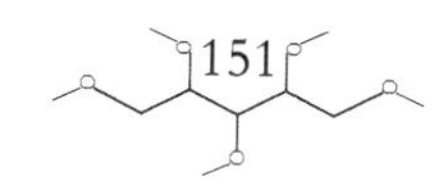

leaned down to open his bottom drawer, which made no sense to me.

"Isn't it some giant machine, like on TV? With a creepy old mustached-guy taking notes?" I knew my questions would've done Garrett proud.

"No," Ford laughed, pulling from the drawer a four-inch white plastic tube with a long cord dangling from one end.

"Here," he said, reaching his other hand palm-up across the desk. I cautiously laid mine likewise on top.

I kept my hand very still as he slid the tube onto my index finger. I waited anxiously for a needle-prick or a pressure-grip, but nothing happened. "How does it work?" I asked, starting to relax a little.

"There are infrared lights on both sides of your finger," he explained. "The blood pumping through your finger matches the pumping of your heart. A change in your heart rate will cause a change in your blood speed and affect the transparency of your finger through the infrareds."

Reading my doubtful expression, he continued, "I know it sounds clumsy, but it's extremely accurate."

"Says who?" I asked, checking his sources.

"*Mythbusters*," he said without missing a beat. He grinned, knowing his choice of authority had surprised me. "They tried thinking happy thoughts when they were lying, or inflicting pain when they were telling the truth, to see if they could skew their responses," he went on. "It didn't work. They concluded that, if administered correctly, the finger-reader is accurate up to ninety-nine percent of the time."

"And you're a good administrator?" I asked, startled at the flirtatious tone behind my question.

"The best." His bright blue eyes met mine dead-on and I felt my heart rate accelerate. I was suddenly acutely aware of his strong hand cradling mine, aware of every bodily change he'd described – my heart pumping harder, the blood in my finger pulsing. I knew he hadn't plugged in the cord, but I waited expectantly for a beeping to start, an alarm to sound – something to alert him to the crazy physical change erupting inside me.

Then, by none of my own volition, I abandoned my chair to meet him in his – uninvited maybe, but not unwelcome. One minute I'd been seated, steady; the next I was traversing the gap between us without touching down. All I knew was that there'd been nothing but air supporting me until I'd climbed onto his lap and connected with the solidness of him.

His response to my assault was not immediate; he clutched the armrests as long as conceivably possible while waging an inner battle between desire and decorum. His conflict – his call to me held in check by his uncertainty – froze his body as if he were petrified. More likely not so much by me as by this new *us*.

Breaking his resistance, I ran my hands up his shoulders to touch his fine hair, prickly soft under my fingertips. On his lap, facing him, I nudged up his chin, making him look into my eyes and see that this was what I wanted, what I needed. Our faces a breath apart, I felt heady inhaling his delicious scent. My heart raced even faster, calling his to match pace. My hunger for him burst forth in an intensity I'd never experienced as I claimed the

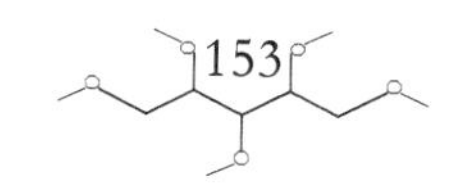

first kiss.

So this is why Eve was the slandered one, the seductress, I thought. That first taste of him, like the first bite of the apple, was the drop that knocked down the floodgates. And in the same instant that I knew there was no going back, that nothing could stop the wave I was riding, he stopped fighting and met me at its crest, joined me in the *us.*

His hands moved smoothly from the armrests to my waist, his broad fingers spreading across my lower back as he settled me more securely onto the seat. My knees slid up to his hips, my legs still folded underneath me but now pressing against the outside of his. And then it was he who deepened the kiss, hurtling from concession to conviction, clutching my backside as I bowed deeper into his chest.

Without fully separating, we both took a necessary gasp at the same instant, seeming to breathe in the same pocket of air, resealing our lips with yet more urgency. *Where does the air come from when desire binds you too tightly to each other to part for even a second? More than just I want you, but I need you – need you more than air?*

As if from a distance, I heard my own throaty moans, vaguely aware I should be embarrassed by the near-growling, but his grip only tightened at the sound. The heat between us climbing higher, his hands followed suit, up my back and sides all at once, over my bursting ribcage, rounding the tops of my shoulders, trailing down to rest lightly on the front of my biceps in an unexpected but tender hold. I wanted the moment to last forever. He was so strong yet soft, vulnerable and safe all at the same time. So intense, so overwhelming, so everything I needed at this moment.

His hands trailed past the curve of my elbow, slowing across my forearms, then wrists. They came to rest on top of mine, still holding tight to the back of his head. He paused for a split second, as if hearing a key turn in a lock, then pulled away, at the same time gently but firmly peeling my fingers from his scalp and depositing them in my lap.

"We can't…do…this," he panted, his raspy breath sounding almost tortured, his sharp blue eyes clouded by passion.

"I know what I'm doing," I insisted, trying to bring him back to me.

"No, you don't," he disagreed. "You're upset, you're confused."

"Don't treat me like a child," I snapped, fighting to keep my lower lip from betraying me with a pout. "You're only twenty-one and I'll be eighteen in February."

"I'm talking to you like a person who's not thinking clearly," he corrected, his breathing beginning to even out.

"I'm clearly thinking that I wanted to kiss you, and you kissed me back," I challenged. "If we were twenty-four and twenty-eight, we wouldn't even be having this conversation."

"Maybe not," he conceded, "but we need to stick to reality."

"The reality is," I pursued, "that I like you, and you like me…."

"And that means we work well together," he incorrectly finished my thought.

"Are you trying to say it's bad to fool around with people

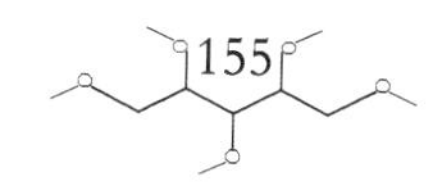

you work with?" I asked. "Because I'm not fooling around."

"Good, because this isn't a game," he snapped before taking his argument in a new direction. "You of all people should understand the position you're putting me in."

"What's that supposed to mean?" I shot back, hearing more anger in my voice than I'd intended.

"Don't you see how we're almost in the same boat?" he asked, practically pleading with me to understand. "Clark has put me in a position that the others think I don't deserve, that he only gave to me out of some sort of nepotism. They think I'm too young and unqualified, and they're just waiting for me to screw up and make a mistake."

"That sure didn't feel like a mistake to me." I'd only heard part of what he was saying, knowing that it wouldn't change how I felt.

"This shouldn't have happened," he chastised, more angry with himself than me now that he was back in control of his senses. "There could be serious ramifications."

"What, like you could get fired? I'll tell them it was my fault," I fought to convince him. "How would anyone even know?"

As soon as my question was out, realization slammed into me like a truck. "There are cameras in here, aren't there?"

He didn't need to answer, just like I hadn't really needed to ask. I felt violated, not just because of the kiss, but because of all the private conversations we'd had, the private time we'd spent here. None of it may have been inappropriate by military standards, but all of it had been intimate to me. The talking,

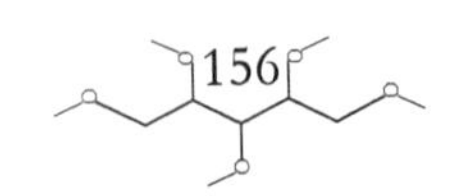

sharing, developing of a friendship, maybe more, had all happened under the scrutiny of the entire security force.

I felt sick to my stomach. I had to go. *Now.*

He didn't try to stop me as I bolted from the room, down the short hallway, and burst through the door into the infuriatingly bright and sunny courtyard. I looked around wildly for the best escape route, but my vision was too blurred by the tears welling up.

What was that? I shrieked on the inside as I started to shake on the outside. *What was I thinking, kissing Ford?*

You know better, I self-lectured, though suddenly I wasn't all that sure that I did. I wasn't sure I knew anything at all these days, particularly myself. I felt like I was losing myself – not just my mind, but also my sense, maybe even my heart.

I hadn't consciously thought, *I'm going to kiss Ford today*, or even been aware enough to think, *I'm going to kiss Ford right now.* I'd just *done* it; my body operating on its own.

And reacting the way I had – being so furious with him for stopping it – was even more out of control. *I*t was obviously a mistake – he knew it, and so did I. *Didn't I?*

And of course my phone chose the worst possible moment to buzz to life. I looked down to see *Mom* listed as the incoming caller. She never called, always careful to give me my space. Apparently my plan to hold her off these past couple of days with texts hadn't worked as well as I'd hoped. Knowing that she must be seriously worried made me feel guilty, but not guilty enough to answer the call. I silenced the ringer, knowing I'd pay for it later.

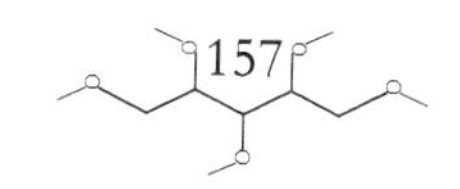

I shoved the phone back in my pocket in preparation to take off, only to turn smack into Rae, who must've appeared from thin air.

"You're not supposed to go anywhere by yourself," she issued a warning and a finger-wag.

"Doesn't look like you have a buddy," I retorted.

"I don't need one. I have cat-like reflexes, remember?" She backed up the claim with a tiger-worthy pounce that landed her cleanly on the other side of me. "I'm a soopa-hero. You, on the other hand, need a buddy, because your only skill is that sad little vanishing trick."

"So sucks to be me," I grumbled back, without turning to face her.

"Hey, I was just kidding," she said as she came back around. "I didn't know you were so upset."

"I know, you're just like Garrett," I snapped. "Everything's a joke to you."

"I'm not 'just like' anybody but myself," she shot back, equally peeved, and I realized it'd been kind of a jerky thing to say.

"Do you want to talk about it?" she asked, offering more sympathy than I probably deserved.

"No," I answered in the nicest way I could. It wasn't her fault I'd commandeered the stupid train again, and I was not in the mood to give tours of the wreckage.

"Okay, we'll just go in silence," she said, linking her arm in mine and turning me around.

"Go where?" I asked, still wanting to just get away from

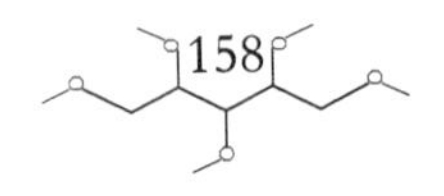

here.

When she said, "Back inside," I tried to yank my arm free.

"We've been summoned to the great room," she explained. "Miranda's got a project for us."

SIXTEEN

The last thing I wanted to do was see anybody, especially the anybodies that I least wanted to find out about what I'd just done. And I knew I couldn't trust my mouth to stay shut; at this point, I was in full-on crazy-person mode, likely to do or say the worst possible thing at any second.

On the other hand, I had to ask myself, *do I really want to be alone right now?* Then I'd have to actually admit to myself what'd just happened and try to figure out what it meant.

For a day that'd started on a mission to take back control, I'd somehow found the surest way to lose it. *Maybe everyone would be better off if I handed back the reins*, I thought, finally letting Rae lead me into the building.

I paused in the doorway of the great room, taking in my group of friends. They hadn't heard me come in, so they remained with their backs to me, lined up assembly-style down two long tables pushed end-to-end.

Miranda stood at the head, followed by Garrett, then Jack, Alexis, Xavier, and finally Bliss at the end. It didn't seem strange to see Xavier planted firmly in the middle, nor for Rae to join the team.

Our six-some had been so random from day one that it was almost a given we'd pick up the newbies. We were like a home for wandering orphans. Aside from Garrett and Alexis, who blended into their ability groups, the rest of us were kind of odd-people-out, like mutant strains who'd diverged even further than the rest. Maybe that was what had subconsciously drawn us together in the first place, and also why we'd become so close so fast.

Crazier still was how we'd just as quickly gone from inseparable to ships passing in the night. *Okay, not that crazy*, I had to admit, since I'd been the one to either irritate, isolate, or avoid each one of them over the past few days.

I quietly – and attemptedly inconspicuously – inserted myself into the small space between Xavier and Bliss. I wasn't sure why I'd picked that exact spot, except to avoid being on the end and open to everyone's attention.

Total backfire, I realized immediately, having drawn seven silent stares by going to Xavier instead of Jack. Even though it'd been an unintentional slip, the tension made it too awkward for me to move.

I felt, rather than saw, Jack's curious look; there was no way I could make eye contact with him under the current circumstances. Luckily, Alexis stepped in on my behalf. Though her voice was too low for me to pick out the words, I could tell by her head tilts and hand gestures that she was explaining Xavier's magnetic draw.

Wait, why didn't Jack already know about him? Hadn't he felt

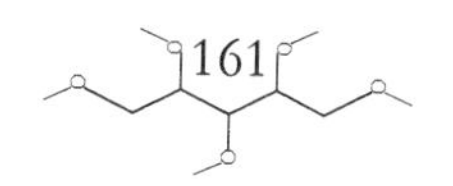

Xavier's pull like the rest of us? Unless my new theory was right – that Jack was the one person to see through our abilities and was therefore immune to them. But he didn't know about this new hypothesis because I'd been too busy making out with another guy to tell him. Coming in here with Rae was looking like a worse idea by the minute.

Out of the corner of my eye, I watched him nod at Alexis in understanding. *Of course. When had Jack ever been anything but?* When I looked his way, he threw me both a wink and a smile, and though I tried to send one back, the fakeness of it hurt.

With all eyes back on me, I felt compelled to say something. I wasn't about to get into everything that'd been going on over the past couple of days, but I could talk about this morning. The public-knowledge part of it, anyway.

"I just came from Lieutenant Graham's," I offered, careful to use his formal title. "He told me our polygraphs are today."

Nobody reacted to what I thought would've been discussion-opening news.

"I know we knew it was coming," I tried again, "but I didn't know today was the big day."

"Didn't you get the text?" Miranda asked, shaking her head in disbelief as if I'd missed a cannon-blast announcement.

"I guess I missed it," I admitted, thinking how I'd been reflexively hitting *Ignore* every time my phone buzzed.

"You've been missing a lot of things," Bliss said softly, making me feel like a total jerk.

"Including you," I acknowledged, sincerely sorry.

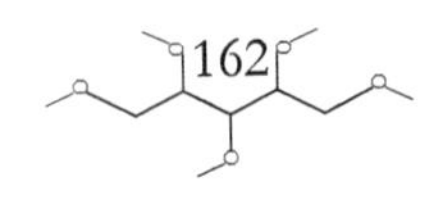

"Yeah, yeah," task-master Miranda interrupted. "We have a lot of work to do, people."

"What're we making?" Rae asked, sidling up on the other side of Bliss.

"Baskets for tomorrow," Miranda answered. "Jack and Garrett are unpacking the supplies," she continued, motioning toward the huge pile of boxes Garrett must've helped Jack haul over from the treehouse.

"Next, Alexis and Xavier load the baskets," she went on, showing me the checklist she'd given him so that he could tell Alexis how many of each item she needed from Jack.

"Then Xavier slides the packed baskets down to Bliss for tagging," she finished, and Bliss demonstrated her job of lacing a tag onto a red, white, and blue ribbon, laying it on top of the basket, and sending it on its way.

Miranda took me by the upper arms to move me around Bliss and Rae to the end, directing, "You go here. Rae will tie the ribbons onto the handles, then you can write the names since her handwriting's ugly and your mom's a writer."

"Uh, my mom writes *books*, not invitations," I pointed out.

"Whatever," she waved me off with her words and hands. "Even basic calligraphy will do."

Right, I thought to myself. *How about legible cursive? 'Cuz that's all you're gonna get.*

I looked over the list of names on the table in front of me. "What's the difference between the two columns?" I asked, noting the left side was patterned name-name-space, while the

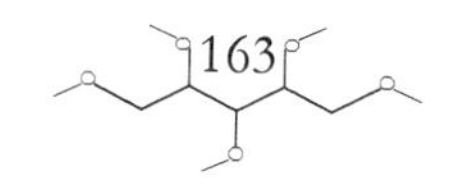

right had a space between every name.

"Couples," Rae chimed in, sparing me from further Miranda wrath.

Of course, I realized. *That couldn't have been more obvious.* Apparently my brain had been putting so much effort into acting normal, it'd dropped basic thinking functions.

Scanning the sheet, I saw at least a dozen couples – way more than I'd known had gotten together. Not that I really knew anybody outside this room and, like Jack and I, most of them probably refrained from in-your-face PDA announcing their couple-hood.

"I don't know if I can fit two swirly names on one tag," I joked, trying to get back on Miranda's good side.

"Two separate tags," she corrected, then turned to Rae to reiterate, "tied with bows, not knots."

"Seems like a lot of rules," I commented.

"You never know who'll break up between now and then," she pointed out, and I took it as a direct hit, though nothing in her face hinted at any hidden meaning behind her words. I took a deep breath, reminding myself that nobody knew about Ford and me. And maybe they'd never have to. As soon as I got a chance to make some sense of that kiss – where it'd come from and what it'd meant – I was sure I could put it behind me. But that would have to wait.

Returning to my task, I found my name paired with Jack's near the top of the page. I hadn't signed up for the double basket, so he must've taken care of it. The usual butterfly-excitement I felt at seeing our names together was replaced by the gurgling of

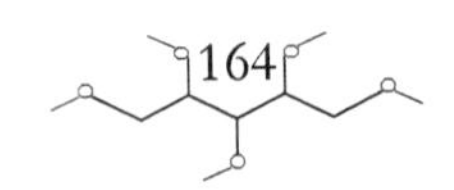

a cauldron where my stomach should be. I had to get my mind onto something else. *Quick.*

As I searched for a new subject, I was startled to find Garrett's name at the bottom of the couples column. But there was no second name, even on the back side of the paper I flipped over to check.

"Garrett, who're you going with?" I called down to him, waiting to hear the announcement everyone else must've already heard – that he'd asked Bliss to be his date.

"My second stomach," he yelled back. "I'm a growing boy, you know."

Ouch. I felt Bliss stiffen at the slight, even though Rae was between us. I also saw Rae subtly reach over and squeeze Bliss's hand in reassurance.

Have I been replaced? I thought, stung. Not that I'd have anyone to blame but myself if I had. I'd dropped out of sight; it's not like I should've expected them to sit around pining over me. I could hear the echo of my mother's voice lecturing, *Be careful what you wish for….*

I'd wanted to be alone, and my wish'd been granted. It's not like I had a right to be mad at Rae for stepping into my place; I'd left it open. Well, I might not be in any position to take it back, but I needed to show I wasn't leaving again.

"So what goes in the baskets?" I asked, looking over to Rae as she tied on another tag.

"Accessories," she answered, pushing the basket to me to sign.

"Picnic blankets, cups, plates, napkins," Bliss explained.

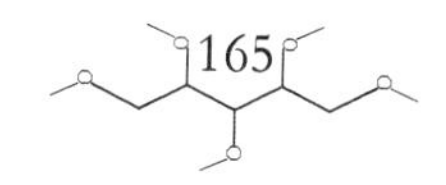

"Wow," I said, peeking inside the one in front of me and finding real glasses, metal silverware, cloth napkins.

"No waste," Miranda informed me proudly. "When you're done, you just ball it all up inside your blanket and shove it back in the basket. The maintenance people will sort it all out."

"Aren't the name tags waste?" I wondered out loud. As soon as the instigating words were out of my mouth, I wanted nothing more than to shove them back in. Just because I wanted to get things back to normal didn't mean I was looking to battle Miranda.

"They're made from one-hundred-percent recycled paper. And this," she said, forcing a shiny fountain pen into my hand, "is filled with soy ink."

"Or we could write the names right on the baskets," I suggested, trying to be helpful.

"This is only our first social event," she sighed, her patience with me all but gone. "We'll have to re-use these for future events, too."

"Plus," she went on, "they're going to keep the baskets in the dining hall for anyone who wants to take a meal al fresco."

"With soda?" Garrett asked, though I could tell he was just messing with her, unable to resist his favorite sport.

She rose to the bait. "Fres*co*, not Fres*ca*, dummy. It means fresh air."

"I thought you were against all those Jersey smoxins out there," I said, caught up in Garrett's game.

"I am *evolv*ing," she said slowly, and I wondered if that was her version of *I was wrong*. "Like we all should be," she

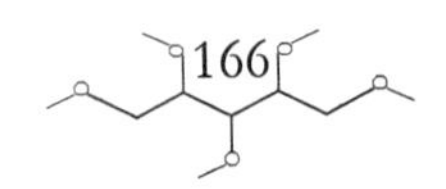

finished, managing to tag on a lesson for the rest of us.

"We also have parting gifts!" She moved on, dancing over to another table and bringing back a box she'd clearly been saving for last. She put it on the end next to me, her eyes begging me to peek. I obediently looked inside and found a pile of shiny metal chains.

"Dog tags?" I asked.

"Aren't they brilliant?" She pulled one out and held it up so we could all see. "Your name's on one side," she pointed out, pausing to twirl it around, "and your group's on the other." The one in her hand said *Andrea* and *Star*.

"Isn't that kind of morbid?" I said without thinking.

"I thought they were unique," she stammered, her face falling with her voice, "and sort of perfect."

"Absolutely," I rushed to undo the damage I'd caused.

Bliss filled the awkward pause by prompting, "So what is everyone's favorite part of the fourth?" She sounded like she'd gotten a conversation-starter-of-the-day app, but I kept my mouth shut since it was my app she was saving.

"Wow, even the conversations around here are organized?" Rae teased.

"There's nothing wrong with directed discussion," Bliss defended herself, and I wondered if she'd really planned it as a way to get up the nerve to talk to Garrett. I could see her doing that, particularly without my having been around to advise against it.

"Carolina barbecue," Jack called out, quick to reward her effort.

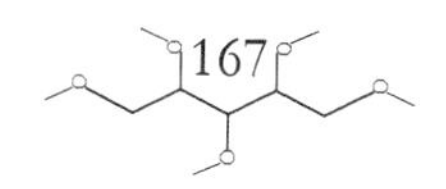

Bliss immediately turned to challenge him over sauces, launching first into a Texas-North Carolina debate of pork versus beef, then vinegar or ketchup, culminating with Bliss's outrage over mayo-less slaw.

I knew Jack didn't really care about any of it – he'd only been in Raleigh for a couple of years. Because of his dad's Special Forces designation, his family had spent most of his childhood overseas.

Having no personal preference either, I let them go back and forth awhile. When their dispute started winding down, I spoke up.

"I love the fourth on the river," I shared. "Me and my mom go out on the Creole Queen to watch the fireworks in the middle of the Mississippi." Thinking of the old paddle-wheeler made me wonder for the first time if my mom would go without me this year.

"I like me some donkey softball," Garrett jumped in, telling us about the Freedom Festival he went to in Bethany.

"The fourth in Utah may not be quite *that* unique," Rae went next, "but the rodeo and pony express race in Tooele are pretty awesome."

"Ugh," Bliss uttered in disgust. "The rodeo is horrible. All those poor baby cows getting knocked down for no reason…."

This time Alexis was the one to interrupt. "I have to give a shout-out to patriotic tunes," she said. "There's nothing like good drumming – rock or march."

"The fourth makes me want to jump off a bridge," Xavier said, almost absently.

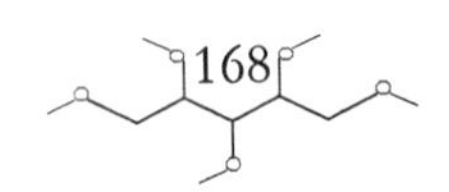

What? I startled. *So much for not being dark – could this be his heavy side finally shining through?*

The others had made their surprised remarks out loud, so he rushed to clear things up. "There's a train trestle over the lake that me and my friends jump off in the summer to cool off," he explained. "We go out there at night on the fourth to watch the fireworks."

"Aren't you scared you'll get hit by the train?" Bliss asked worriedly.

"Nah, they don't use those tracks anymore," he assured her. "And if they did, we'd just jump."

"It still sounds dangerous," she argued. "You could break your neck in the fall."

"It's not that high, plus the water's deep," he said. "I'm not an idiot."

Miranda took this as her cue to lasso everyone back in. "Well, my favorite part of the fourth is – what do you know? – organizing fantabulous events! So back to work, people."

Her order signaled an end to the chatter, so we focused on working in the quite peaceful silence. I concentrated so fully on my loops and swirls that, after a dozen or so baskets, my mind had quieted to almost normal.

I looked down my line of friends – really *looked* at them – and saw what a complete fool I'd been for having pushed them away when I should've been burrowing deeper into their supportive circle. I wouldn't make the same mistake again.

After we'd tagged the last basket and added it to the stack against the wall, I felt not only a sense of accomplishment, but

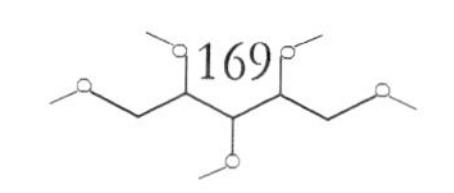

also serenity. In this room was the peace I'd been looking for; I'd just been looking in the wrong place.

When Bliss asked tentatively, "Are you coming to dinner? With us?" I didn't hesitate.

"Absolutely."

SEVENTEEN

I returned to my room that night sure of two things: one, that alone-time could take its bags and get gone; and two, that soda was not my friend. The bubbles that'd burned my throat and the chest-stomping hiccups that'd followed had not been conducive to a relaxed lie-detector-taking experience. Besides being completely embarrassed, I had a sinking feeling that the bodily malfunctions may have skewed the results and I might have to re-take the test.

But I tried to focus on the good part of the day and put the bad part behind me. Having at least faced, if not slain, one demon motivated me to face a second – calling my mom.

As I reached for the phone, I felt a slight chill. "Somebody must've jacked up the a/c again," I grumbled to myself, then started digging through the pile of clothes on my chair to find my favorite hoodie. I could've sworn I'd worn it just the other day, but it wasn't there. Annoyed, I rifled through my drawers next, only to come up empty again. *It must still be in the laundry*, I realized disappointedly.

I shrugged on a different top, settled myself on the bed

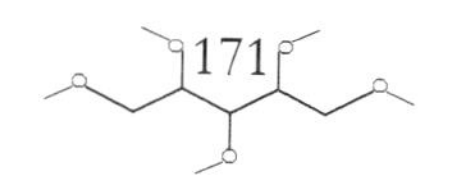

with a deep preparatory breath, and manually punched my mom's number into my cell, both to stall and to collect my thoughts. I knew it was cowardly to avoid Skype, but I already felt bad enough about blowing her off for days without having to actually see the disappointment in her face.

Sure enough, I heard plenty of it in her voice. She answered on the first ring with a flat, bordering on cold, "Hello" that made my stomach clench.

"Hi, mom," I said, unable to keep from closing my eyes and ducking my head against the inevitable onslaught.

But it never came.

"Calliope," she acknowledged, her reversion to my full name as good an indicator as her tone of how upset with me she was.

"I'm sorry I haven't called you back," I launched straight into my apology. "Things have been so crazy here…," I trailed off, waiting for her to interject.

"Mm-hmm," she answered, forcing me to squeeze my eyes shut even tighter. I'd rather endure a screaming tirade than this torturous silence, which of course she knew. I'd have to do some quick explaining to make it stop.

"But I know that's no excuse," I said, using the words she would've if she'd gone the yelling route. Her responding sigh assured me I was on the right path, so I conjured up another of her favorite lines from lectures past. "It was very inconsiderate of me to make you worry," I said, then paused, not wanting to let my mouth get ahead of my head and undo the strides I'd made so far.

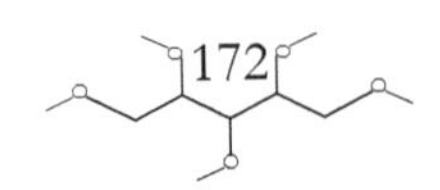

"And very irresponsible," she added. *Not a full sentence,* I noted, *but better than grunts and humphs.*

"And very irresponsible," I echoed, doing my best to sound sincere and not mimicky.

"Your only saving grace," she said with deliberate slowness, "is that you did check in with Randall and Gertrude, so I knew you were alright."

"You called them?" I felt slightly annoyed that she'd gone around me, although I knew I'd sort of asked for it by dodging her calls.

"Oh, yes," she confirmed. "And Lieutenant Graham as well."

Now that was going too far. "You called Ford?" I practically shrieked.

"I called Lieutenant Graham," she corrected, and I froze at the edge in her voice. Was she mad at what she saw as a lack of respect for authority? Or had my worst nightmare come true and he'd told her about the kiss?

"He caught me up on the investigation," she continued, and I nervously waited out the seconds until she concluded, "but I'd rather have heard about it from you."

"I know, I know," I apologized in a rush, grateful to have dodged the bullet.

"I thought we had a better relationship than that," she said softly.

"We do," I assured her, thankful the anger portion of the conversation had passed, and now anxious to move beyond the guilt part as well.

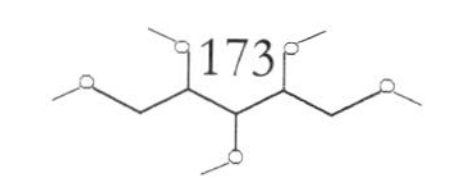

"So...," she said leadingly, and I ran into the opening, filling her in on everything from discovering Larson's body through today's polygraph. Everything except the kiss, of course, and the enormous relief I'd felt at having fallen into Lombardo's test group this afternoon and not Ford's, which probably would've killed me. I exhaled a huge breath at the end of my speech, relieved to have caught her up and to have gotten everything out. *Mostly.*

After taking her own breath in response to the enormity of it all, she opened her mouth to say something, but I spoke first. "Can I call you right back?"

"You'll really call?" she questioned suspiciously.

It took a solemn promise from me to get her to hang up her phone.

I docked mine and summoned her by Skype.

"Well, there's my beautiful daughter," she cheered, delighted by the communication upgrade.

"I just wanted to say goodnight in person," I said, feeling a little silly.

"Good," she replied, "because I needed to see your face to be sure you were really okay."

"I'm a lot better now that we've talked," I admitted.

"That's always the case," she agreed, nodding wisely.

Her words stuck with me long after our call had ended – after I'd changed into my pajamas, crawled into bed, and turned off the lights. Lying there in the dark, I couldn't keep my thoughts from going back again and again to the kiss I'd shared with Ford.

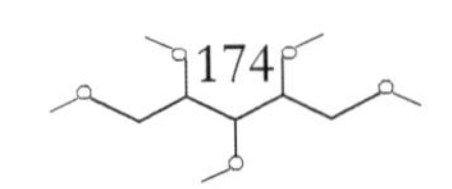

What'd possessed me to attack him like that? And how did he really feel about it? Then there were the cameras to worry about – I had no way of knowing if anyone'd really been watching, or if he'd just said that to get rid of me. *But he'd kissed me back; he'd wanted me, hadn't he?*

And what did I want? To be with him? Instead of Jack? The thought of even trying to compare them felt horribly wrong. They were both kind, smart, funny, gorgeous. *But who's the better fit for* me*?* I hated that I couldn't answer, even to myself.

Jack was perfect. So perfect that really only the law of opposites could say we belonged together, with me a full one-eighty in the other direction. It almost made me question if I'd fallen for him, or the *idea* of him. Or, more accurately, the *ideal* of him.

My feelings for him had been immediate – striking like lightning in the way we all dream of from the time we watch our first princess movie. *But what if that was all wrong?* I'd thought my heart had leapt for him, to him, because it'd been meant to be, that we'd been brought here to find each other.

But couldn't I say some of those same things about Ford? I sighed, frustrated to have circled right back to where I'd started. I had to stop *thinking* about it when there was nothing I could *do* about it right now. Maybe it would help to work on something I *could* change.

I got up long enough to turn the lights back on, grab a pen and some paper, and bring them back to my bed. I flipped to the back of the binder, searching for a clean sheet.

My mom was right – talking through my worries always

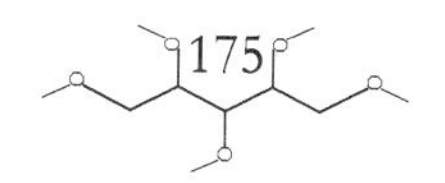

did make me feel better. But what helped even more was putting them down on paper. I knew that writing out my thoughts about the attacks would not only sort out my mind, but might also reveal something that I'd been missing in the mental jumble.

Not sure where to start, I decided to treat it like a writing assignment. *Just get the pen moving, and the ideas will follow*, my mom's instructions came to me. *Write what you know.*

I decided this first meant naming, then eliminating the possible suspects. I started with my friends, since they'd be the easiest to write off.

I started on the left side of the first line with *Bliss.* Obviously there was no way she could be the attacker; besides not being strong enough to take down a grown man, she didn't have the nerve for such a bold act, nor the inner ugliness required. I drilled my reasoning down to two words, writing *too weak* next to her name.

On the second line, I penned *Miranda.* Again, I just couldn't see it. Not because she lacked the guts, or even the physicality – I had a feeling she could summon the strength of a grizzly if pushed far enough – but I couldn't help feeling that she wouldn't put herself at risk. Her own safety – and manicure – weren't worth it. I put *self-absorbed* by her name.

My third entry, *Garrett*, rounded out the trifecta of impossible suspects. The idea of him stabbing someone was absurd; he was so happy and full of life that the only way he could kill somebody was with bad jokes. *Ridiculous* went by him.

I moved on to Alexis, whom I also couldn't imagine resorting to murderous violence. She wouldn't see it in quite the

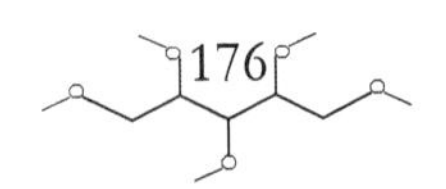

same way as Miranda, but would surely find killing someone to be the least rational solution, knowing that she could find a better way. I wrote her name, followed by *not good enough.*

Lastly I put *Jack*, but only because he was here on campus. *Come on, it's* Jack, my inner voice shouted. He could do no wrong, hurt no one, make no mistakes. *Again, the opposite of me,* I thought, unconsciously writing *big mistake* next to his name as I replayed what I'd done to him. I hurried to move on before I got totally bogged down by guilt.

Having closed out the old friends category, I moved on to the new ones.

First came Xavier, who was simply too nice, too warm and welcoming, to be a killer. Then again, that same magnetism drew people to him, and he could've easily lured Larson and Nate into a trap. Not wanting to make the mistake of misplaced trust like I'd done with Janet, I left the space next to his name open.

Next was Rae, another person I knew absolutely could not have committed the crimes. *But why?* I forced myself to ask. *Because she's a girl?* That was a cop-out, with her being as strong and agile as any of the other jocks. And like Ford had said, both she and Xavier had arrived at a very curious time. I left her line blank, too.

That leaves only eight-nine more kids to go, I thought wryly, *of which I know pretty much zero.* I could lump them into groups and apply the same reasoning I'd done with my friends – assume that none of the stars would be willing to break a nail, that the jocks were just too "jocular," and that the heavies would be under-motivated – but we all knew what assuming made out of *u* and

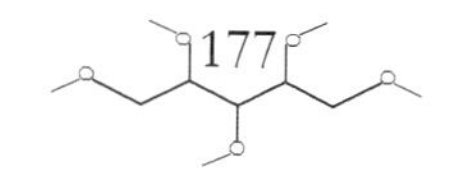

me.

I could probably get a full student roster, then attempt to talk to and get a read on each person, but Ford had already done that. Plus I'd have to get the list from Ford, which would require talking to him – something I was not yet prepared to do.

I decided to leave the kid section for now and move onto the staff. Again, I found myself with a short list of officers I knew, followed by a much larger group of unknowns.

I knew I could immediately dismiss Ford, Clark, and Trudy as suspects, since their sole focus was *catching* the killer. Plus the "camp" was almost as much Ford and Trudy's baby as Clark's, and they had nothing to gain by terrorizing its occupants.

I didn't know enough about any of the other staff members to make judgments one way or another, but I had to believe that if Major Lombardo was a real candidate for the murderer role, Jack would've picked up some sort of suspicious vibe from him. Likewise, Garrett and Alexis would've noticed if something was seriously off with Coach Sikes or Captain Dolan, wouldn't they? Then again, Alexis didn't have any concerns about Major Godwin, who'd gotten my hackles up from the very first time she'd cat-walked to the front of the great room to speak to us.

After those few, there were so many other campus employees, from Job at the med center to the myriad of behind-the-scenes people who worked security, catering, and maintenance, that I couldn't even begin to name them all. The staff list was quickly running its course, too.

Not that the next grouping yielded any more promising

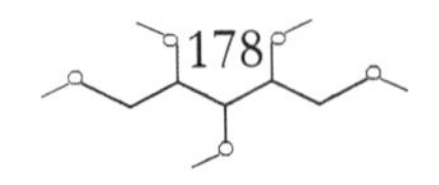

leads; now that I'd worked my way out to the fenceline, I had to confront the possibility that the killer might be an outsider. I'd heard about the hate-mail flooding in from people protesting everything from the tax dollars wasted on us to our right to walk freely in society, "freaks" that we were. And those were the ones satisfied to blow off steam writing letters. *What about the real haters who wanted to take action?*

Then came all the people who had a beef with the Army, or even the whole government. Throw in everyone on the planet who had a problem with the United States, and we had a potential suspect pool of thousands.

I dropped my pen in defeat.

If only C9x had given me some kind of super-genius ability, I thought, *I might be of some help to this investigation.* But at my current skill level, I could bang my head against this wall all night and be no better off in the morning.

Not entirely, I realized, unfolding my arms and legs from the writer's pose I'd been hunched in. Putting down some of my thoughts had taken some of the weight off my mind. I stretched out across my bed, trying to focus on the highlights of the day. I'd made up with my friends, reconnected with my mom, and even cleared a little space in my head. *Not a total loss,* I had to admit, allowing myself a small smile before finally letting sleep take me away.

EIGHTEEN

Saturday morning, I went to meet the others at the large clearing where we used to gather for stealth group. Of course, that was long before we called ourselves stealths, before we even knew we could disappear. The long-unused space provided the only flat, open area large enough to accommodate all the kids, staff, and food for a barbecue.

There used to be a giant event tent overhead, like the kind they used for outdoor weddings, only ours had been camouflage instead of white, which we later found out was to conceal us from unwanted eyes in the sky. Since that threat hadn't gone away, I surmised that Miranda must've thrown a serious fit to get them to take down the canopy, even for one day.

When I reached the designated spot, the caterers were already setting up both the food stations and the check-in area, where the tables featured our handiwork from yesterday. Ten in the morning was too early for them to put out any food, but they had plenty of other prep work to get done.

Miranda had requested our help with the final decorations – the ones she hadn't wanted to put up too far ahead and risk getting messed up before the main event. She was busy dictating streamer position to Bliss, Garrett, and Xavier when I walked up.

"This would be so much easier if these were plastic instead of paper," Bliss mumbled under her breath as a length of blue tissue snagged on a pine bough and tore.

Her complaint had been barely audible, but it didn't get past Miranda. "Easier for you maybe," she scolded, "but not the environment."

I waited for Garrett to shake her boss pedestal – although if he took too long, I may do it for him – but Xavier spoke up before Garrett had a chance to. *And he agreed with Miranda.*

"Easy usually means bad," he chimed in. At first I couldn't decide if he was sucking up or *flirting*, but when I looked at his face, I realized that, unlike my special gift of regurgitating idiocy, it was in his nature to be supportive. *It must be an extension of his ability,* I mused, which of course led me down another of my over-thought and under-resolved philosophical paths. *Were we all* who *we were because of* what *we were? Had C9x predetermined our personalities along with our abilities? Or had the drug worked off of our already-set genetic material – given us abilities based on who we were already set to become?*

I could see the logic in both possibilities – that the stealths, for instance, seemed to all be the blend-into-the-crowd-and-vanish type long before we knew we had the ability to actually make it happen, making disappearing a logical next step for us. At the same time, that same shirking behavior might really have been our subconscious minds trying to tell us what we could do all along.

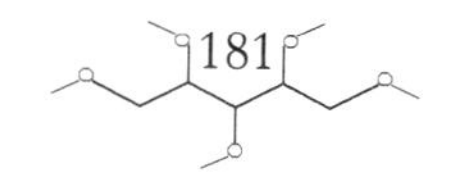

I looked at Xavier and thought about his situation. *Would he be so engaging if people hadn't always been inexplicably drawn to him? If they hadn't kept him surrounded until he'd become charismatic out of need or habit?*

And if I'd reacted to the drug differently, would I have morphed into whatever Xavier is instead of a stealth? Would I be able to talk to people like he could?

The what-ifs were endless, so I backed away from the slippery slope while I still could. Yesterday with my friends had been such a nice brain-break from my worries, and I wanted today to be a continuation of that. I wanted to be able to free my mind like the others and just enjoy the beautiful day.

"Where's everybody else?" I asked the decorating trio.

Bliss was happy to fill me in, beginning with Jack, who was, of course, working. Today would be a big one on campus, and Lombardo needed all hands on deck. Miranda was twistedly stoked by this code-red status, as if he'd just dubbed her barbecue the Oscars of the campground.

"Rae and Alexis are both retaking the polygraph," Bliss continued, and I froze in place. "There was some sort of malfunction with one of the machines," she rushed to explain, "so half of Graham's roster has a do-over." Yet another reason for me to be thankful I'd been on Lombardo's list and not Ford's.

I couldn't help but find it curious that it'd been Ford's machine to break down – the same one he'd shown me in his office before..., well, *before. Had the problem really been with the equipment, or could it have been Ford himself that'd messed up? Had yesterday's encounter unsettled him as much as me?* I wondered, feeling strangely thrilled at the prospect.

"Which leaves us short-handed," Miranda interjected. "Let's get these streamers up."

"Ugh, bee," Xavier complained, swatting and ducking away from the small attacker that had appeared to buzz around his head.

Bliss's reaction wasn't quite as benign. "Worst fear! Worst fear!" she screamed in terror, scrambling up Garrett's back as if scaling a mountain.

Her panic must have also triggered some sort of uncontrollable defense mechanism in her, because she suddenly began *flashing*. It had to be the most bizarre thing I'd ever seen – her blinding brilliance blinking on and off like a lightning bug.

Only after we were finally able to tear our eyes from her did we determine that the bee had flown away. Once Miranda declared the coast was clear, Bliss carefully climbed down and returned to her normal non-firefly state.

I was about to ask her if she'd been aware of the flashing when Garrett jumped in.

"*That's* your worst fear?" he asked, trying to keep the laughter out of his voice. "What about crocodiles? Clowns? Crazed killers?"

"Clowns?" I scoffed, both to rebuke him and to gloss over the third item on his list.

"Clowns," he confirmed with wide-eyed solemnity.

"They stab you with those little stingers," Bliss huffed, trying to justify her reaction.

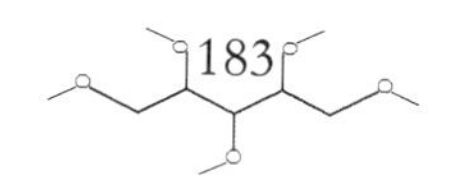

"Speaking of stabbing…," Garrett began, looking around wickedly. *So much for keeping the conversation fun and light,* I thought. Apparently even Mother Nature was bent on bringing up the subject of murder. Or getting Garrett to do it for her.

"Let's not and say we did," Bliss interrupted quickly. When all eyes turned to her, she added, "I'm already scared enough about being out tonight after dark."

Miranda rolled her eyes, but at least she had the decency not to make fun of her.

"I'm not," Garrett tossed out lightly. "I have inside knowledge."

"Really?" Xavier questioned, raising one skeptical eyebrow. "Please enlighten us."

"You got it," Garrett replied, going on to explain, "My gramps watches *Law and Order.* Killers always have a pattern. Seems we've got ourselves a Tuesday-Wednesday guy, so we're safe 'til next week."

"Unless the pattern is kill two days, take two days off, repeat," I contradicted him out of reflex. "That would make the next attack tonight." *Why'd I say that out loud?* The damage I'd done was clear in Bliss's complexion, which went instantly from perky pink to ghastly gray.

"If we're talking patterns," Miranda interjected, "don't forget we had seventeen years of normal before we came here. So we had some crazy," she said as flippantly as if we'd had a little snow in June, "and now we're back in the long calm part of the cycle – like locusts." Some color returned to Bliss's face, showing that the buggish fairy tale, spun by the most unlikely candidate to do so, had cleaned up some of my mess.

"Right," Garrett agreed, grabbing the story thread and winding it into a new kind of knot. "Life was dandy, then we came here, to a new place, and *Bam!* Janet tries to kill us."

Xavier tried to shut down this line that was sure to re-upset Bliss, but Garrett was unstoppable.

"So we recover from the Psychster, and life goes on. *Hakuna matata.*" Even though he was quoting Disney movies, I had a feeling this was going nowhere good.

He continued, "Then we pick up new jobs and *Cablooey!* We're back under siege. Seems to me," he summed up, "the common thread is *new* stuff."

"So you think if we just stop trying new things, we'll be alright?" Xavier tried to grasp Garrett's theory.

"All I'm sayin'," Garrett responded, turning both hands palms up, "is that I'm gonna start today by not trying the soy burgers."

"Genius," Miranda snorted.

"I feel good about it," he answered with a self-satisfied nod.

"Maybe this isn't the best time to make jokes," I suggested gently, keeping my eye on the still-wobbly Bliss.

"Au contraire," he disagreed. "It's always funny time." To demonstrate, he scooped up Bliss like a fireman saving a girl from a burning building. But instead of running away with her, he turned to the nearest oak, dashed ten feet up the side of its massive trunk, then flipped off, depositing them both safely back in the spot from which they'd started.

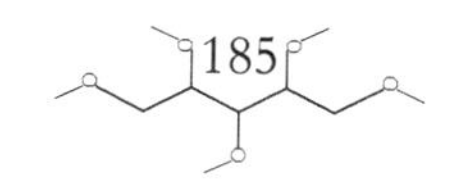

The ostentatious feat left Bliss in a fit of giggles. Garrett winked at me over her head as he placed her back on her feet. His look said, *Mission 'Distract Bliss' accomplished.*

"So who'd you get for music?" I hurried to ask Miranda before Garrett could run us off the rails again.

"It's under control," Miranda answered evasively, not making eye contact.

"Some local flavor?" Garrett pursued. "Bon Jovi? My Chemical Romance?"

"They're from Jersey?" Bliss asked.

"Everyone's from Jersey," Xavier chimed in. "Forget NYC; this is where the magic happens."

"So who is it?" I asked again, my curiosity now more than peaked.

"No one!" Miranda shouted, stunning us all into silence. I couldn't see why she'd pass up such a prime opportunity for bragging by acting all secretive.

"What do you mean, no one?" I finally asked when no one else would.

"I mean, no one is coming," she replied slowly and deliberately.

"So Bruce said no?" Garrett joked.

"Everyone's too busy," Miranda admitted with a dejected sigh. "They're all on tour, in the studio, whatever."

"Maybe you should've asked nicely," Garrett suggested, earning him a full-wattage glare. "Just sayin'."

"You could still find someone," Bliss said hopefully. "Stacey Kent's local; why don't you try her?"

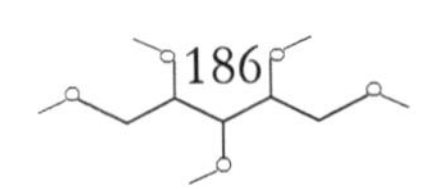

"For tonight?" Miranda snapped. "Don't be ridiculous."

"See, that's the attitude that got you in this mess in the first place," Garrett pointed out, making me seriously worry for his safety.

"I've got the music," Xavier jumped in. "I've already made the playlists and hooked up the wireless." He pointed out the short posts mounted with small speakers ringing the area that I hadn't noticed before.

"Hey!" Garrett complained to Miranda. "Why didn't you ask me to deejay?"

"Because you said you'd do the fireworks now that Nate's out, remember?" she reminded him.

"That was before the spin gig opened up!" he argued.

"Like I said, the playlists are set," Xavier assured him. "I just have to switch them at the right time."

"Okay," Garrett proposed a compromise, "how 'bout I still do the fireworks with J-Bird, but when we're done I get to bust in and be the after-hours mix-master."

"Deal," Xavier agreed, if for no other reason than to avoid battle.

With the music issue settled and the decorations secured, it was time to head back to the dorm to shower and change. But despite how festive things looked and how well everything was coming together, something nagged at me. I just had a bad feeling about today, tonight, the barbecue – all of it.

Maybe when we're alone, I thought, *I can talk it through with Bliss.* I turned to her and asked, "Walk back with me?"

"I can't," she answered apologetically.

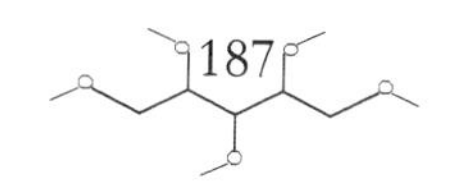

"Okay. See you later then?" I asked.

"I don't think so," she turned me down. "I've got to help Miranda."

"How'd you get roped into that?" I teased.

"I wanted to help," she said defensively, and I braced myself for the flickering to start up again. Having seen it once, I sort of expected a repeat performance. I got nothing.

"Sorry," I backed down. "I didn't know it was such a touchy subject."

"It's just that you've been busy," she added, her tone implying that the problem was I'd been too busy for *her.* I thought that, after yesterday, we'd moved past this, so I didn't like being reminded how easily and deeply her feelings got hurt. But she was right.

"I'm sorry for that, too," I apologized again. "And I'm not doing it anymore. Let's meet up after, okay?"

"It *is* Miranda," she pointed out. "*After* may not be until tomorrow morning."

"So we'll do breakfast," I promised. "Belgian waffles and ice cream."

"How about we skip the waffles and add hot fudge?" she negotiated.

"You got it," I agreed and hugged her – a good, solid hug that I hoped told her I would be a better friend from now on. *Fixing takes a little longer than breaking,* I reminded myself, and left to get ready.

NINETEEN

Late afternoon found my stomach growling with both hunger and trepidation. Talking to Bliss had reminded me that real friendship meant putting it all out there – the good and the bad in one big pile – and going through it together. There may not be a together for me and Jack after this, but I knew I had to tell him about Ford. Tonight.

It didn't really matter if the kiss had meant anything or not; it'd happened, and Jack deserved to know. Not that I had an answer for him if he asked why I'd done it. *Bad judgment? Hormones?* That didn't really matter, either. Just like I'd said to my mom last night – *no excuses.* I needed to put on my big-girl pants and fess up.

My festive attempt at said pants was a pair of navy blue shorts embroidered with tiny white stars. I added a spaghetti-strap white tank on top, then let my hair be the red of the patriotic trifecta. Not bad for being somewhat fashion-challenged. Although, between the excitement of the big event and the bomb I was about to drop, I was pretty sure nobody was going to care what I was wearing.

When I got to the picnic area, I saw that I was no competition for Bliss, whose red, white, and blue tinsel tiara would've commanded plenty of attention even without the white lights she'd woven into it. If we'd gotten ready together, I'd have told her to abandon the headdress and turn on her own inner spark, not that she'd have gone for it. The tiara itself was pretty over-the-top for her, so I figured it must be either a photo-op piece supplied by her mom, or an event uniform of sorts provided by Miranda. Either way, she looked like Miss America serving at a soup kitchen, which was really not that far from actuality.

The white lights of course reminded me of Jack and the constellation he'd created for me in his ceiling. I scanned the crowd for his familiar form, but he was nowhere to be found. *He couldn't possibly still be working, could he?* My answer came in the equally attractive form of Xavier, who met me with a basket for two. I saw the big X over Jack's name right away, not sure if it was meant to X-out Jack or to X-in Xavier.

"He asked me to stand in for him," Xavier told me. "He's not gonna make it."

I felt bad that the disappointment on my face might hurt his feelings, but I was also glad I'd kept hidden my relief at the temporary reprieve. On the one side, I wanted to put off confessing as long as possible, knowing that Jack might not forgive me, or even speak to me ever again. On the other hand, the worrying was eating me from the inside out and I was tired of avoiding things. I wanted everything out in the open so that I could at least go on, no matter how bad the fallout.

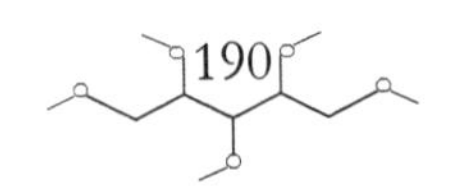

"There's a note," Xavier added hopefully. He handed it over, and I read:

Have to go straight from treehouse to set up fireworks – sorry!
Meet me at launch site at 9 and we'll watch them together. ♥ *J*

Seemed my stay of execution would be short-lived.

I followed Xavier to the spot marked on the map tied to our basket. Miranda had laid out the area like a wedding planner, gifting me a private – and now wholly unwarranted – site at the far corner of the field, near the treeline. Of course, I knew better than to try and move now and face her wrath.

Only a scattering of spots were occupied, with most people in the food line. Our closest neighbors were two jocks, both with dates. My quick visual survey found that most of the guy stealths seemed to be paired up as well, probably due in part to the serious shortage of boys on campus.

I turned to my newly-assigned "date," realizing that he had to be the most coveted prize of all. I could only imagine all the eyes that must be spitting poison at me for unfairly taking him off the market, and I told him so.

"No worries," he assured me. "You're actually saving me."

"Seriously?" I asked, unable to see how.

"Let's just say, I get a lot of attention," he explained. "Sometimes more than I'd like."

"Come on, I bet you love it," I teased.

"The girls are alright," he admitted, "but their boyfriends

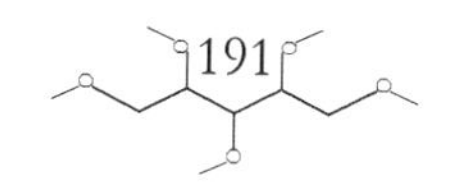

aren't my biggest fans."

"Oh," I said with dawning comprehension.

"They especially don't like when I tell them if they'd just listen and pay more attention, their girlfriends might like them, too," he added.

"I bet not," I agreed.

"Plus, I never know who likes me for me, you know?" He let that sink in as he smoothed the blanket over our patch of grass.

"Well, I like you," I finally said.

"I like you, too," he answered with a smile, then we both called out at the same time, "But not in that way!"

He gestured with his hand and a tilt of his head toward the food line. "Shall we?"

"We shall," I accepted, following his lead.

Initially, I'd been grateful for the long walk we'd have to make back and forth, thinking we'd need it to eat up some time and take away from the awkward feeling that this was kind of like a date. But I shouldn't have worried; Xavier was easy to talk to and I was happy to find we had a lot in common.

After I'd asked him where he was from – New York – the conversation flowed from there. We talked about how long he'd been there, where he'd lived before, places we both knew and liked in the city. By the time we reached the front, I'd managed to push all my current woes to the back of my mind.

As we stepped up to the end of the food line, I spotted Colonel Clark. I was glad to see he'd made it out for the event, but equally happy that he was surrounded by his mom and some

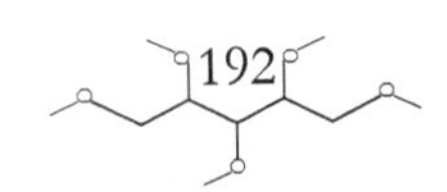

other staff members. This time Xavier was the one saving me; if I'd been alone, I would've felt obligated to go sit with the colonel, making me the only kid at the grown-up table. *Not my first choice.* He waved to me over the crowd and I waved back, but kept moving.

Garrett passed us on his way out and I couldn't resist commenting on the three heaping plates balanced precariously on top of his basket. "That's it?" I teased.

"Oh, I already ate," he answered. "This is my launch snack." He threw a "see ya" over his shoulder as he loped off.

When we got to the food table, everything looked so good that I wanted to try it all. I had to remind myself to take small scoops before I ran out of valuable plate inchage. Xavier did not have the same problem; he seemed to be looking for something specific, though I couldn't imagine what could possibly be missing. When we were almost at the end of the line, he complained, "No pizza?"

"It probably wouldn't have been what you were looking for anyway," I consoled him.

"Why?" he asked. "They're world-class chefs, right?"

"As in, poached from the White House," I clarified.

"So not schooled in street food," he picked up.

"Ballpark, maybe, but not pizza," I confirmed. "Definitely not New York-slice good."

"Not *sitting-on-the-curb-and-not-even-caring-that-tourists-keep-kicking-you-on-their-way-by* good?" he said with a grin, solidifying that I liked him for him and not his pull.

I ended up with an almost Garrett-worthy plate that

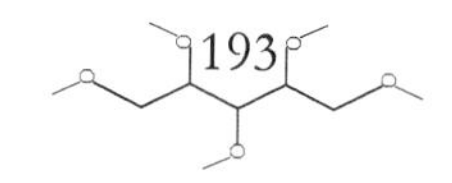

barely held the chicken, hot dog, soy burger, and every salad from leafy to Jell-O. I hoped I could make it all the way back to the blanket without dropping the motley mountain.

When we made it back with our plates, I found myself now grateful for the peripheral spot. I was having fun with just Xavier and wanted to keep it that way.

He poured the lemonade, trading me a cupful for a napkin-roll of silverware that I'd dug out of the basket. Before I could dig in, I was startled by the blinding flash of a camera.

There's press here? I wondered, though it seemed highly unlikely. Miranda may have touted this as the event of the year, but it was hardly what I'd call newsworthy.

Then, at the same time she and Xavier called out "Hi" to each other, I realized that I recognized the photographer from campus. Xavier quickly introduced me to Lindy, who, as was evident by her hesitant greeting, had to be one of the heavies.

Until now, I'd assumed the heavies were all the same – musicians and artists. It'd never occurred to me that their affinities might reach out to other creative outlets as well. And now, realizing I'd been so wrong about their group, I couldn't help but wonder what world of talent there might be among the other stealths. Just because I didn't have any special skills, didn't mean the others didn't either. As Lindy moved on to photograph the next pair, I made another mental note to stop making generalizations.

"Are you musical?" I asked Xavier curiously.

"Well, I play the piano like everybody else," he answered.

"Not everybody plays the piano," I pointed out.

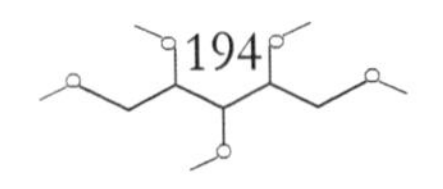

"Really?" he said with surprise. "I thought everyone's parents forced at least a year of lessons on them."

"Not mine," I disagreed. "My mom never really forced me to do anything. Except move," I amended.

"Ha – so you are like the rest of us!" he cheered.

"Why would you think I wasn't?" I asked, confused.

"You know, because you're not an Army brat...," he trailed off, giving me the feeling that there was something more behind his words. *Had Alexis told him about my second ability?* I didn't want to ask; if he was willing to drop it, I wasn't going to be the one to resurrect it.

"So you're not musical then?" I resumed my earlier line of questioning.

"I like to sing," he said unassumingly.

My immediate reaction was, *Of course.* Singing made perfect sense for him, since just listening to him talk was almost like being serenaded.

"Like what?" I asked. "Sing me something."

He purred the opening lines of *Falling Slowly*, a song I recognized right away, since it was one of my favorites. Losing myself in his hypnotic tone, all I could think was, *Good thing he's keeping his voice low, or girls would be fainting left and right.*

I wanted to make a clever allusion to the character in mythology that sang and mesmerized sailors, but the only thing I could think of was a mermaid. I knew that wasn't right, and I definitely wasn't about to tell Xavier that's what I thought of him. Guess I had another reason besides the muses to study up on the ancient Greeks now.

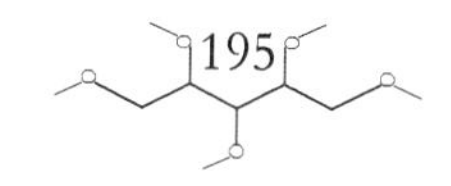

Hearing his natural talent also reminded me how extraordinary many of the kids here were – how many gifts they boasted beyond their C9x abilities. Which in turn made me feel wholly inadequate. Like, if Miranda decided to put on a camp pageant, not only would I botch the Q and A part, but I'd have nothing for the talent portion either. Throw in the swimsuit competition that I'd have to boycott just on principle, and I wouldn't even be able to enter.

I must've inadvertently shared my gripes out loud, because Xavier mused, "Now I get that saying, *The mind works in mysterious ways*." His eyes met mine briefly, before he raised them to my forehead. "It must be like a carnival in there," he said, as if he were examining a fascinating specimen.

"Oh, yeah," I laughed, not sure if I should be offended. "There," I paused to drape a long strand of hair across my face, "is a total freak show inside this tent."

"That's not what I meant," he said, smiling and shaking his head until I realized that he was actually interested in me, though not in a romantic way.

"I meant that your Ferris wheel of a brain's always turning," he clarified, "and I never know what'll get off the next car."

"Half the time, neither do I," I joked back easily.

These past weeks, I'd been so happy – and felt so lucky – to have made such good, fast friends on campus. Each member of my eclectic circle – Bliss, Garrett, Miranda, Jack, Alexis – was so different, yet so equally vital, that I'd loved feeling I was a like a small part of a greater whole. *Complete.*

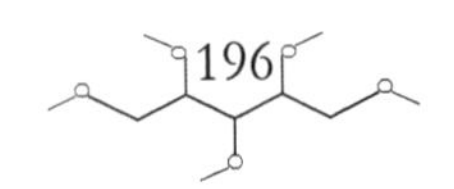

But then along came Rae, with her infectious laugh and generous heart, to claim a space I hadn't even known was vacant. And now here was Xavier, filling yet another gap that I hadn't realized existed.

We are a circle, I realized, *just one that never closes.* Looking into Xavier's beautiful face, and knowing who we would've missed out on if we'd closed our ring, made me suddenly thankful for that open-endedness.

"I've got to get going," he said, rising to his feet. "Time to switch playlists from *Barbecue Beats* to *Firework Favorites.*"

He started picking things up, but I told him, "I've got this." I'd offered not just to be nice, but also because I wanted to stall for just one more minute.

As he shook the crumbs from his shirt, I looked in the bottom of the picnic basket to make sure it was empty before I stuffed the cloth and dishes back inside. It wasn't until I saw them that I remembered about the parting gifts. I pulled out the dark blue velvet pouch that I surely would've missed in the encroaching darkness if not for the embroidered stars that sparkled with the last rays of twilight.

I eased open the drawstring and upended the bag, spilling the two sets of dog tags onto my open palm. Miranda may have changed the name on the basket, but she hadn't switched the bags, and I found myself holding up first my chain, then Jack's. Twirling them on my finger to see both sides, I found that one said *Calliope* on the front – I would've preferred Clio, but surely she'd gone for authenticity with the full names – and *Stealth* on the back.

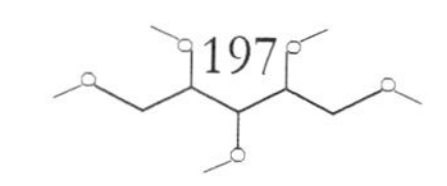

I hesitated before turning the other, marked *Jack*, not sure what I'd find on the back side. I was surprised to see the imprint *Special Forces. How perfect,* I smiled to myself. *And people say she's thoughtless*, I mused before carefully slipping them back into the bag.

"Are you okay?" Xavier asked, and I blinked up at him. I hadn't even been aware he was still there. *I definitely have to get better at masking my feelings*, I realized, not missing the irony of my being able to physically vanish, but being a window as far as emotions were concerned.

For a moment I was tempted to tell Xavier what was wrong – to tell him everything from my betrayal of Jack to my emerging heaviness – but I refrained. I knew it would be just another excuse to put off what I had to do.

After making one last offer to help, he left, and I finished cleaning up. I added my full basket to the growing pile and headed for the launch area before I found another reason to stay.

It took me a good ten minutes to reach the guys at the launch site, which was situated a safe distance from the crowd. Plenty of time for me to overthink everything until I'd rubbed my nerves so raw that I almost imagined I could taste blood.

No, I corrected myself, *the blood's from the gorge your teeth just carved in the side of your mouth.*

"Hey, look who's here to run the countdown!" Garrett called out as I approached.

Jack turned to face me, revealing a broad grin that practically glowed in the dark. He enveloped me in a warm hug and I felt my courage prepare to run, but my mouth stepped up

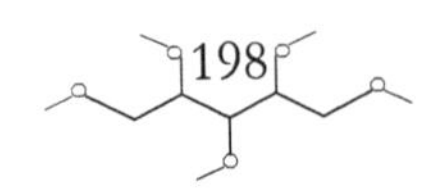

first.

"I need to talk to you," I said gently, easing out of the embrace.

"Sure," he said uncertainly, then looked to Garrett, who nodded his assent. He let me lead him a short distance away before he started apologizing.

"I'm sorry I haven't been around lately," he said softly, taking both of my hands in his.

"That's not it," I tried dissuading him, but he kept going.

"No, I know you've been going through a lot and I should've been there for you," he insisted.

"Really, that's not what I need to talk to you about," I said again, pulling back my hands.

"Have you ever read any Jules Verne?" he asked, completely throwing me off.

"Um," I stammered in my confusion, "that's the guy who wrote *Twenty Thousand Leagues Under the Sea*, right?"

He nodded, waiting for my answer.

"I'm not really a sci-fi girl," I admitted.

"Is that so, Miss Invisible?" he teased, and brushed a strand of hair out of my eyes. "I don't see how you could be any *more* sci-fi."

"Oh, right," I conceded, my face opening into the smile he could always coax out of me. And I was about to return the favor by nailing him in the gut.

"So he wrote another book called *The Kip Brothers*," he went on.

"And it was good?" I asked, still clueless.

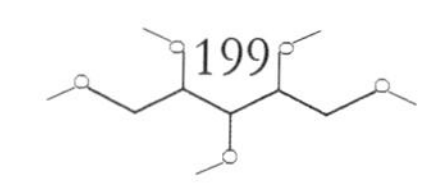

"Eh, it was okay," he answered dismissively, then continued, "but the point is that the story is about a captain who gets stabbed to death, and the Kip brothers are wrongly accused of it."

"Okay?" If he was going to keep pausing and waiting for me to catch up, we could be here all night.

"But then an old friend of the victim asks the photographer to blow up a picture he took of the body so he can have something to remember him by, and the photo reveals the real killers."

"How?" I asked, growing interested.

"Because their images imprinted on his irises, kind of like how pictures burn onto your desktop if you don't have a moving screen-saver," he explained. "The moment of death froze the last thing he saw onto the surface of his eyes – the murderers."

"That's crazy," I replied, not sure what else to say.

"Well, the last chapter kind of explains the science behind the idea," he added before finally getting to his point. "Anyway, I think it works both ways; that seeing death is burned onto the seer's eyes, too, and that it changes you forever."

"I don't think that's my problem," I disagreed, and as I shook my head, I could feel my defenses starting to go up – could feel myself start to push away from him.

"I can see your wall," he said softly. "I know that you're becoming a heavy, and it's okay."

I took a step back, unable to speak.

"It's okay that it's happening, and it's okay that you didn't tell me yet," he continued, moving forward to close the gap I'd put between us. I didn't see what was coming until it was too late.

"Clio, I love you."

You love me? my mind shrieked. How could he possibly love *me*? Jack, the gifted seer who didn't even know it yet – yet another screw-up on my part since I'd been too busy kissing another guy to help him put it together. He had to be blind to see anything lovable in the horrible person standing in front of him.

Despite the mix of shock and horror washing over me, and for quite possibly the first time in my entire life, my words came out simple and direct.

"I kissed Ford."

TWENTY

"I mean, Lieutenant Graham," I stammered, then bit down on my lip to stop myself from making things worse. Of course Jack knew who I was talking about; confusion wasn't the reason for his silence.

He remained completely motionless – his eyes unblinking, his hands still in front of him, palms up and empty since I'd removed mine from his hold.

I wanted to take it all back – to undo the last few minutes, return my hands to his, and go watch the fireworks together. But I knew in my heart that five minutes wouldn't be enough. Two days probably couldn't even take me far back enough to fix everything, since kissing Ford hadn't been my first mistake. I could see now that the kiss was merely the culmination of all the issues that must've been gathering inside me for a while.

With no words to say, no moves to make, I also stayed still, keeping my hands clasped in front of me in an almost defensive stance. Not that I had any reason to believe he'd move closer to me, particularly now that his eyes seemed to have filmed over in a protective shield of his own. No, it was like my body just needed to put something between us – even just my hands – to keep me from hurting him any further.

He opened his mouth as if to say something, then closed it again. I waited nervously for him to put his thoughts together, not daring to prompt him with any of my own. He repeated the sequence twice more, still unable to speak, before finally releasing a defeated sigh. His usually strong shoulders sagged forward, his unheld hands retreated into his pockets, but he said nothing.

The painful moment dragged on until I couldn't take it anymore – the hurt in his eyes, the crippling silence, the feeling I was going to vomit any second. I opened my mouth to excuse myself, but, much like him, I had no words. So I did the only thing I could think of – I left.

I started walking, not back toward the picnic revelers and the fun and music and laughter, but toward the surrounding forest. I needed a dark, lonely place to curl up and rip myself a new one.

I didn't look back – I couldn't – but I had a sick feeling that I'd also ruined everything in front of me, too.

As soon as I was out of Jack's sight, I broke into a run. Every part of me begged to go further, faster, as if by doing so I could get away from my own disastrous self. Even my breath seemed to taunt me, coming out in accusing *wha-wha-whats*, as if to say, *What have you done?*

My out-of-shapeness finally forced me to slow down and catch my breath. And at almost the exact moment I bent forward to rest my hands on my knees, the silent night was shattered by an explosion overhead.

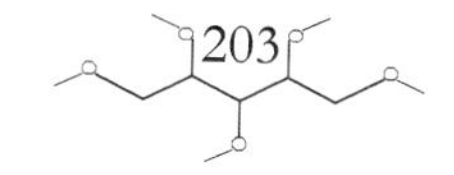

My head fell back reflexively to take in the spectacle above. A giant spray of gold illuminated the night sky, then somehow managed to hang there an extra beat, as if it were a solid thing. As gravity caught up with fireworks and the sparks faded away, my mind belatedly registered the image I'd just seen. Two distinct trails had arched up and out from the center, creating a rounded letter *M. It couldn't be, could it? An M for Miranda?*

Another blast split the night, and I watched as one rocket, heading straight up, was soon chased by a second one of the same bright green. Both trails turned right, then the higher one arced down, the lower curved up, and they came together at the middle of the original line. The entire image then burst outward into a deliberate crescent that briefly held its shape before disappearing. This time the outlines were unmistakable – *B for Bliss, C for Clio.*

I stood mesmerized by the display that was unlike any I'd ever seen. Miranda had taken the fourth to a whole new level, and I held my breath as I waited for the next character to appear. This time two violet lines shot up from distant points on the ground to meet at the top center, while a third appeared from nowhere to cross the middle. After a full-second pause, the center of the *A* exploded out to the four corners, creating a perfect *X. Alexis, Xavier.*

I didn't know if Miranda'd consulted professional pyro-techs to make this happen, or if I should credit Garrett's gift for both rockets and math. However they'd done it, the result was beyond belief.

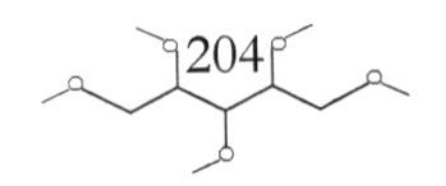

Each metamorphosis more spectacular than the last, I watched as next a brilliant crimson *R* burst out into a *G. Rae, Garrett.* Yet what I found even more amazing than the sky art was that Miranda had chosen to share her moment of glory with all of us.

Suddenly a beautiful blue flash materialized mid-sky, swooping down and then curving up and around into a *J*, completed by a second rocket shooting a finishing line across the top. I stared at the image, holding its shape as the others had before disintegrating. *Jack*, alone. It seemed like the cosmos was sending a message directly to me. *Where was he now? Was he watching the show? Waiting for me to return?*

I knew I had to go back to him. To offer an apology, even if I couldn't give an explanation. I'd promised myself that I wouldn't do this anymore – run, hide, coward-out. At least I knew that, as such an inept runner, I couldn't have gone far, and even if my return pace might be slower than my departure, the trip shouldn't take too long.

I headed back the way I'd come, thankful I'd bolted in a fairly straight line since I had no bread-crumb trail to guide me. Not that it would've helped; the blackness of night had fully descended, making sight little more than a memory. Though I was now too focused on getting back to Jack to keep watching the fireworks, I was hugely grateful for the sporadic illumination they provided to help me find my way.

I knew I'd found the spot where Jack had been standing as soon as I reached it – his sweet, soapy smell still hung in the warm air. Then my foot caught in a large divot that almost sent me sprawling, meaning that I'd stumbled into the exact place *I'd* stood before, grinding the toe of my shoe into the dirt while I'd pensively waited for his response to my confession.

But there was no sign of Jack. He must've gone on to catch up with Garrett for the launch, which gave me pause. That meant he'd probably told Garrett what I'd said and done by now. The thought of having to face both of them made me doubly sick.

No excuses, I reminded myself. I would face them both, and my entire circle of friends if I had to. I'd screwed up; now I had to deal with the consequences.

Now that I really needed the intermittent flashes, I realized the sky had been dormant for too long – it must be a break in the show. Before I could begin picking my way down the trail to Garrett's spot, my ears caught a low, muffled noise. Unable to see even my own body, I stood stock-still and closed my eyes – an instinctual move that I hoped would help me focus on the sound. *It's breathing*, I figured out, moving cautiously toward the source to investigate. *Strangled* human *breathing*.

My eyes were finally starting to adjust from the bright fireworks to the black night, but I still almost stepped on the person before I saw him. *Jack*.

He was curled up on his side, I figured out as I dropped to my knees and tried to feel out the situation. I put one hand on his shoulder and the other at his waist to turn him toward me. As he rolled onto his back, my lower hand slid across his stomach and into the warm, stickiness of his blood.

"Jack!" I cried, screamed, and called for help all in one.

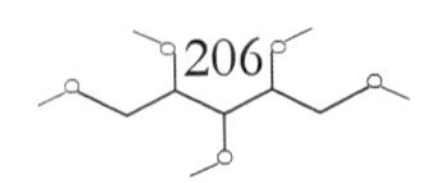

There was just so much blood – too much; his torso seemed to be covered in it. And now it was all over my hands, too. I frantically wiped them on my thighs, but it just spread the horrific mess across my skin.

Not being able to see further intensified my fear. I used my hands to carefully feel my way up his chest, at the same time whispering his name. "Jack? Can you hear me? Jack?" My only answer was his continued rasping, which at least gave me something to hold onto.

My hands found his chin, his jaw, his face – his beautiful face that I wanted more than anything to be able to see at this moment. I couldn't keep my fingers from sliding gently across his eyes, and was overwhelming relieved to find them closed and not frozen in a stare of death.

What'd happened to him? He must not have met up with Garrett after all, staying instead right where I'd left him, alone and vulnerable. Now he lay bleeding, fighting for his life, and it was all my fault.

He needed help, but I couldn't leave him, and I was having an increasingly hard time beating down the hysteria that was threatening to overpower me.

Before I could give another shout, I realized that his breathing had changed. Each inhale was more deliberate, each exhale with a sound behind it. Unbelievably, he was trying to *say* something. I leaned down, putting my ear as close to his lips as I could without blocking his air flow.

All I heard was a low hiss. When I didn't respond, he tried again, and then a third time, but with no better results. Even

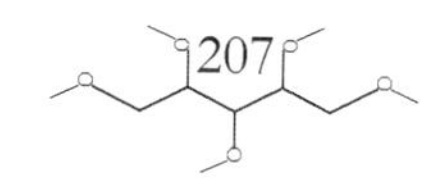

in the dark, I sensed his eyes fluttering open and then shut again, so when he fell silent, I started to panic that he'd used the very last of his strength. As my heart begged him to stay with me, my mind tried to work out what he'd been trying to say.

"Sss," I ran the sound over my tongue. *Sick?* I guessed. *Is that what he meant to say?* That didn't make sense.

Stay? I tried again, knowing that couldn't be it either. He had to know that, even after everything, I would never even consider leaving him like this.

Sorry? Was he trying to tell me he was sorry? That would be completely insane, but at the same time completely Jack. And would also make me the worst person in the entire world.

Suddenly Garrett burst onto the scene. Miraculously, my cry had been loud enough after all – loud enough to reach him, at least, and hopefully that would be enough. His eyes seemed to be in better focus than mine, as he ran straight to us without a misstep.

"He's been stabbed!" I screamed. "Go get help!"

Garrett didn't pause to question the order; he pivoted on the spot and took off at a full sprint.

I stayed with Jack, stroking his hair, not sure what else to do. He was so still, showing no signs of life besides the soft, shallow breaths. I wanted to offer words of comfort, but all I could say was, "I'm sorry," over and over again. I didn't dare break the chant, sure that his silence would be more than I could take.

Thankfully, only moments passed before Garrett returned with Bliss and Rae at his sides. He'd caught them on his way to

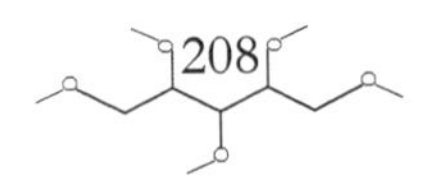

the clearing; along with Miranda, they'd been on their way to him to find out why the second wave of fireworks hadn't gone off. After hearing the horrific news about Jack, Miranda'd gone back for Trudy and anyone else who could help.

"Which way did he go?" Garrett shouted, and it took me a second to figure out what he meant.

"I don't know!" I cried, shaking my head to shift the clear thoughts to the front. I told him where I'd been when the fireworks had started, knowing that at least the attacker couldn't have gone that way, or I'd have seen him.

After brief deliberation, Rae and Garrett took off toward the treeline, leaving Bliss behind to help care for Jack. She crouched beside me, her face frozen in shock, but her body moving on auto-pilot. She had a picnic blanket in her hands and we tried to use it to stop the bleeding, though we still couldn't see exactly where the wounds were. I felt dizzy from the déjà vu – we'd been in almost this same situation not that long ago. But substituting a knife wound for a bullet hole and Jack for Colonel Clark made this so much worse.

When I looked up again to see if help was getting close, a glint in the nearby grass caught my eye. I left my post for one minute and crawled the few feet to find myself staring at a silver blade just like the one Colonel Clark had described.

At the same moment, Jack sputtered back to life. I hurried back to help Bliss calm him down. "It's okay," I murmured, "help will be here soon."

But he was determined to get his word out and, unbelievably, this time I heard it. "Stealth."

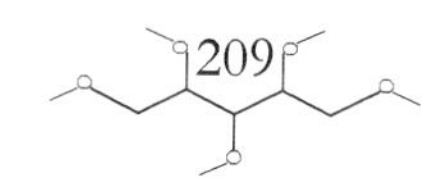

A stealth? The killer? One of us? A kid? My mind began to spin wildly, then came to a screeching halt with the realization that, if the killer was invisible, Garrett and Rae wouldn't be able to see him.

But I will, it dawned on me just as suddenly. Stealths could see other stealths when they were in vanish-mode just like they were still solid; that's why it took us so long to figure out our ability in the first place. I had to catch up with the others – they needed me. Now.

Jack had lapsed back into silence, his breathing barely pushing against the palm I'd placed on his chest. He needed me, too, but I had to leave him. Even though I felt like it would split my heart in two, I had to go after the murderous stealth.

"Bliss, I have to go," I said, struggling to my feet.

"No!" she shrieked. "You can't leave me!"

"I have to." It took everything in me to keep from shouting at her. "Help will be here any second," I tried to assure her.

Bliss continued shaking her head as if this were a bad dream that she needed to wake up from. I grabbed her by both shoulders and forced her to look at me.

"Bliss," I said evenly, "the killer is a stealth. Garrett and Rae won't be able to see him; they need me."

I couldn't waste any more time trying to convince her. I knew I had no chance of catching up to them, but Rae and Garrett also ran the risk of overtaking him and not even knowing it. My only hope was to get in front of all of them, then cut back.

It's almost shocking how much better my brain works in a crisis, I

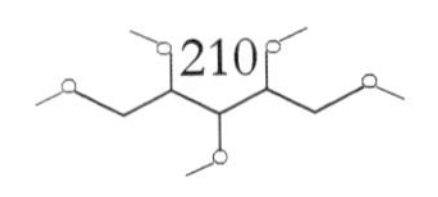

thought wryly. *Probably because I have to act, leaving no time to think, re-think, and over-think some more.*

I took off across the center of campus toward the main gate, which I figured had to be the killer's destination as well. Since my gut told me he'd taken the long way to avoid common areas, I hoped I still had a fighting chance to get there first.

TWENTY ONE

I bolted across the middle of campus, hoping I was right about this. Even at a dead-run, I couldn't help but notice how strangely abandoned the courtyard felt as I blew through it. There were always people here, no matter how early in the morning, or how late at night I'd passed by. Well, maybe I'd never been here *early*, but I was sure someone had.

I'd hoped to find at least one person there that Miranda hadn't been able to convince – or force – to attend her event; someone to claim for my team so I didn't have to go in alone, but it seemed luck had decided to sit this one out.

I'd never been to the main gate at night, which further fueled my anxiety. The more I thought about it, I was pretty sure I hadn't come back to this part of campus since the day we arrived, daylight or otherwise. Either way, my eyes were totally unprepared for the stadium-bright lights that greeted me, washing the grass in a stark white, almost as if there was a dusting of snow on the ground.

My mind flashed back to a Friday night last fall when I'd driven down the winding road to Angola with a boy from school on a dare. When we'd crested the final hill of the twenty-mile entry, we'd been practically blinded by the spotlights illuminating the prison. Dave had thrown the car in reverse and gotten us out of there before we'd had to be escorted out. We'd definitely gotten a story to tell out of it, but I hadn't been in a hurry to go out with him again.

Knock it off, one side of my brain reprimanded the other. The last thing I needed right now was to be reminded of yet another dumb situation I'd stumbled into, especially with the danger I was about to face. And Angola had been Dave's dare to take – I'd just gone along so he wouldn't think I was a wuss. This was different – this choice was *mine*. I hadn't blundered into this mess after someone else, but run in full-force by my own volition. I wasn't sure which way was more frightening. I shook my head to focus my eyes and mind on the current situation.

Aside from my own breathing, the area was eerily quiet, and the gate itself was closed. The solid metal fixture stood before me tall, imposing…and completely out of place in the middle of the woods. It may block road-bound vehicles and warn off potential trespassers, but thanks to Jack I knew that the fence extending from both sides into the trees didn't encircle the entire property. And anyone determined to get in could figure that out easily enough, too.

There was supposed to be an officer standing guard twenty-four-seven – usually more than one since the attacks began – but I didn't see a single soul. *Where were they?* I couldn't believe Lombardo would've moved every soldier to the clearing for tonight, especially if it meant leaving the gate unattended.

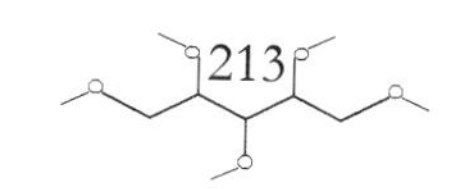

I heard a shuffle, turned, and saw them, all at what felt like the same moment.

A uniformed guard stood facing me, but in such an unnatural pose that I knew immediately something was wrong. If not for the rustling, I may not have even seen him at all – between his camouflage fatigues and his position just beyond the light, he was little more than a ghost.

"Hey!" I called out, waving at the same time to be sure he saw me, even though I'd be virtually impossible to miss in the fluorescent bath. My hand had only made half an arc when I caught the shadow of a figure behind him. The officer's broad frame almost completely concealed the second person, who instinct told me was not staying behind his back for protection.

As if in response to my thought, he stumbled forward and to one side. He took the shove with a protesting stiffness, not the limpness of defeat – a wooden soldier, not a ragdoll.

The jerky movement also revealed first the gun pointed at his side, then the face of the person who held it there. I involuntarily gasped.

The girl was dressed like me, like the rest of us. Not patriotically for the fourth, but in shorts and a t-shirt. My first thought was, *How could a complete lunatic – a multiple murderer – look so much like me? So* normal? She could've easily walked into any crowd of kids without earning a second glance.

Her long face was almost swallowed up by her thick tangle of curls – hair that, at any other time, on any other girl, would've made me totally envious. The tendrils snaked out in all directions, almost as if the wind had whipped the strands into a

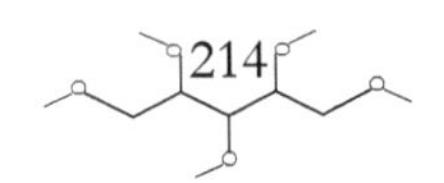

torrent around her, though the night remained perfectly still. I couldn't make out the color of her eyes; the light at her back veiled her face in shadow and forced her pupils to dilate until they practically overtook her irises. If I didn't know better, I'd have sworn I caught a glint of red.

For some ridiculous reason, I thought of the words Bliss would use to describe her if she were here: *She'd be so pretty if she'd just smile.*

As if she'd heard my thoughts, the villain's lips drew back in a grin so wicked I wished I could go back and un-think the suggestion.

Her coloring was warm, but her voice was ice cold when she greeted me with a purring, "Hello."

I couldn't manage any kind of response as my mind struggled to wrap itself around the scene. The girl was significantly shorter, smaller than the guard, but she held complete control thanks to her loaded equalizer. *How'd she pull that off?*

Then I remembered what Jack had fought so hard to tell me – that she was a stealth. She must have grabbed his gun from his holster while she was invisible; he'd probably never even seen it coming. And right now, she must think I was struck dumb by fear at the seemingly disembodied voice that had spoken to me. That she didn't know I could see her might be just the edge I needed to shake her control.

She chose that moment to give the guard another hard shove, and I could tell by the way his leg buckled that he was hurt. *Had they struggled? Had she shot him? And why didn't he say*

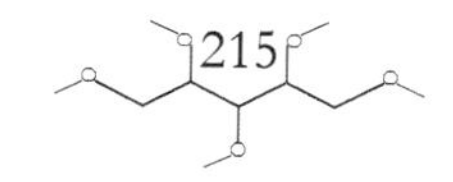

something? He hadn't given a shout to warn me off, no explanation now that I was here. I could only hope he was working on a plan and not going into shock. I couldn't imagine how bizarre it must've been for him to take a bullet from an invisible gunman.

Make that gunwoman. I kept coming back to what had to be the most startling part of all – that the killer was a girl. *Never saw that coming.*

As gun-girl and I both contemplated our next move, Rae and Garrett ran into view.

"Clio!" Garrett called out in relief.

"How'd you get here?" Rae launched straight into question-mode. "Did you see him?"

As one, they both spied the hunched guard, and I watched as first anger, then fear, and finally confusion passed over their faces.

"Is that…?" Garrett started a question, but trailed off.

"What's wrong with him?" Rae jumped in.

Having put together that they weren't facing the killer, Garrett asked, "Did he get away?"

It took several moments of their jumbled questions to remind me that nobody could see the murderous girl but me. She stood so clearly before me that I'd almost forgotten again that she was in stealth-mode. And she was good; I'd seen what'd happened to Bliss in a panic – total breakdown of her ability. But this girl had complete control of her shield, even when surrounded.

"She's right there," I explained, pointing straight at her, but they didn't catch on until I explained, "She's a stealth."

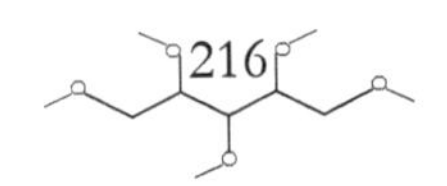

As Rae and Garrett's expressions registered an identical mixture of comprehension and fear, the killer's face fell in utter disbelief. She must've realized that she'd just lost her secret weapon.

"What, you thought I was looking at him?" I asked her, nodding at the hostage. Though I was shaking inside, I tried my best to channel Miranda's self-assurance.

She didn't answer right away, and I knew she was trying to decide whether or not to believe me. I wondered what her next move would be. I decided not to give her the chance to come up with one.

The only one who could, I began to approach her like a cornered animal. Not that I had any idea what I was going to do once I reached her, but I felt I had to keep up the brash front. "I'm not bluffing," I assured her in my best talk-down-from-the-ledge voice. "It's over. You can't escape." I kept my tone soft and even, though my words were far from soothing. It's not like I could tell her everything was going to be okay.

"It's not over," she hissed back, and Rae and Garrett's heads both snapped in her direction at the sound, like bats using echolocation. They slowly began moving in her direction, blind as bats as well.

"All those scientists wasting time making bombs," Garrett muttered as he inched forward. "Why haven't they been working on stealth-vision glasses?"

"Who are you?" I asked our target, trying to guide the others to her with my voice. Instinct told me to keep up a steady dialogue, but I didn't actually expect her to answer. I figured

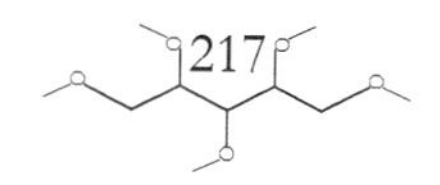

she'd deflect the question, say it was none of my business. I was wrong. It seemed she *wanted* us to know who she was by the way she boldly asserted, "I'm Ivy."

"Ivy?" Garrett repeated with a harsh laugh, not letting the small inconvenience of not being able to see her get in the way of his trash talk. "Come on – you're setting up the creeper jokes way too easy. Make me work for it a little."

"Nice to meet you, Ivy," I jumped in for both our sakes, leaving off the *not* that my brain wanted to tag on at the end. "Why don't we make it face-to-face?" I suggested in the most casual tone I could muster.

"Sure, why not?" she answered too readily. I stopped my forward progress, trying to see the trap she must be leading me into. I suddenly realized that I might not want her to show herself to everyone. I knew how this went down in the movies; killers only took off their masks when they weren't going to let you live to tell anyone. As of right now, I was the only one she knew could see her, and she wasn't even a hundred percent convinced of that.

I'd never witnessed a transition, so I could only guess it would happen one of two ways: fast, like the yanking back of a curtain, or slow, like some sort of reverse-fade. And nothing happened that I could see; she stood before me as clearly as she'd been this whole time. But whatever she did, it definitely shocked Rae, who let out a gasp and took a stumbling step backward.

Garrett, on the other hand, acknowledged the emergence of Ivy's solid form with an appreciative wolf-whistle. "If this was a movie," he said approvingly, "I'd give mad props to casting."

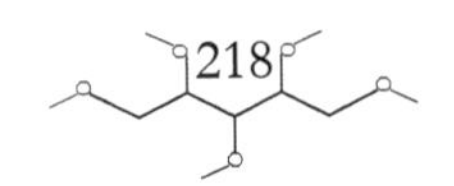

"You think you're so funny, don't you?" Ivy snapped at him in response.

"Sure do," he admitted, "and if you'd been around all summer, you'd be a fan, too."

"Oh, I've been around," she sneered.

"Believe me, I'd remember seeing you on campus," Garrett disagreed. "You're not just one of the girls." I couldn't tell if he was baiting her or flirting, but, either way, he had her attention.

"You've got that part right," she agreed, but her voice was filled with disgust, not congratulations.

"What does that mean?" Rae asked, making no pretense of niceness.

I decided to take advantage of the distracting banter to go for my phone. I may have lost my chance to call for help, but I suddenly realized there was something I could still do. Alexis had put a one-touch record button on my home screen so that whenever lyrical inspiration struck, I could save my ideas. Now I was hoping to use it to save our butts.

I put my hands on my hips, pretending to be interested in Ivy's answer, then subtly slid my pointer finger until it bumped the edge of the hard plastic in my right pocket. I'd shoved the phone in face-out and top-first like always, so I only needed to move a millimeter across the screen to reach the icon. I pressed lightly and prayed I'd successfully turned on the recorder, never moving my eyes from the trio's taunting exchange.

"It means that I might've been part of the big *experiment*," Ivy answered Rae, "but I'm nothing like the rest of you."

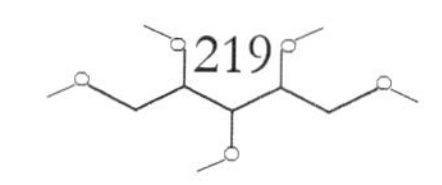

"Why don't you tell us what you are like, then?" I tagged back in.

"Yeah," Rae agreed. "And where you've been," she followed up.

"Here," Ivy said simply.

"In Jersey?" Garrett tried to clarify her answer.

"No, right here, you moron," she snapped.

On campus? The idea struck us all silent for a moment as we realized how spot-on Garrett's creeper remark really was. *Here? All summer? As in, lurking around for weeks without anyone knowing?* The tiny hairs on my arms bristled at the thought.

I wanted to believe that if she'd been around me, I'd have noticed – sensed her somehow. But even invisible, she'd have been as clear as day to my eyes, and no different from any of the other kids I hadn't paid much attention to on campus. She could've been sitting at the next table at lunch, passed me on the stairs…the thought was even more disturbing than being watched by the security cameras. At least those lenses only captured images; apparently, Ivy could've reached out and touched me – or stabbed me – any time she'd felt like it.

"Why didn't you just come normally, like everyone else?" Rae was the first one to find her voice.

Again, I didn't expect a real answer, but again, Ivy surprised me.

"I didn't want the Army to find out what I could do," she said. "That was when I thought I was the only one who could disappear."

"You *knew* you were a stealth?" Garrett asked, some of

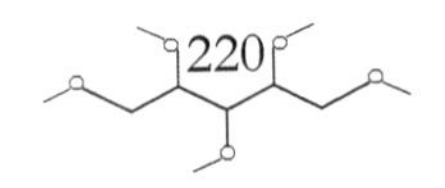

his cool dropping along with his jaw.

"A what?" she asked with irritation.

"A stealth," I explained. "That's what we call ourselves."

"Cute," she replied, though the word sounded anything but as it fell from her lips.

"So you said you weren't coming, but then you did after all?" Rae asked again, and, like every time I heard it, the idea struck me as completely alien. I knew the Army had said it was our decision to make, and Ford had reiterated that just this week, but I still never felt like there'd been a choice.

"That's right. I told them no," Ivy said, as casually as if she'd just turned down a date. "I knew that once they figured out what I could do, they'd lock me up and stick me with needles. Or worse, they'd find some kind of antidote that would cure me and I'd end up a nothing."

"So where do your parents think you are?" I asked, still trying to fit the pieces together.

"What parents?" Ivy made the word sound like an obscenity. "I live in a group home."

"Yeah, I could tell this wasn't your first criminal rodeo," Garrett said, nodding. "What'd you get busted for?"

"My loser-abuser drunk of a dad killed my mom when I was ten," she answered without missing a beat. "And then he killed himself. Is that funny enough for you, joker?"

I'd thought my feelings had been in turmoil before, but Ivy'd whipped them into a category five. I couldn't even wrap my head around her story – probably the worst I'd heard in my entire life – yet she didn't even seem fazed by it.

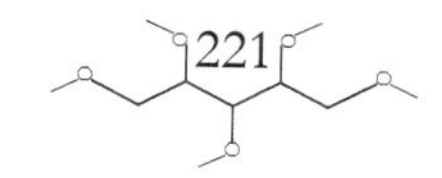

Apparently neither was Garrett. "So you've been secretly living here? How?" he pried for details.

So we were just going to move on to the next subject? *Really?* This girl was seriously messed up; she'd just told us most, if not all, of the *why*, and we were going to drop it? It's not like I expected her to burst into tears, toss aside the gun, and fall into our arms for a group hug, but I also couldn't stop thinking about what she'd said. I did my best to put my thoughts on hold to hear her explanation of the *how*.

Or maybe *wow* was more accurate. I listened as she explained to Garrett how she'd been sleeping in a string hammock that she tied between a new set of trees each night. Even more surprising was hearing that she'd found out about the invisible fence at the beginning, and had been careful to never go far enough into the woods to cross it.

"What about when it rains?" I channeled my inner Bliss to come up with a random-detail question.

"I sleep behind one of those big dryers in the laundry room," Ivy answered. "I don't know everything about how the disappearing works, so I don't know if I stay invisible when I'm asleep."

Huh, I thought. No wonder she'd gone undetected for so long; she'd thought through so many things that'd never even crossed my mind.

"What do you eat?" Garrett asked next, going along with our unspoken plan to keep her talking, get answers, and hopefully buy enough time for the cavalry to ride in and save the day.

"Same stuff as you," she sighed, beginning to lose

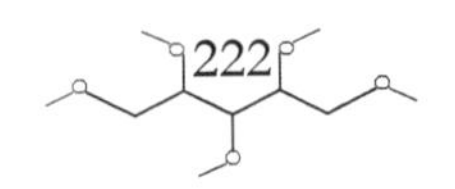

patience with this interrogation. Luckily, our three sets of curious eyes were enough to convince her to go on. "The dining hall's always open so you can graze like stupid cows all day. I just wait until nobody's there. Mostly I eat right out of the pans," she added, "so that if somebody comes in, they won't see a meatball float by or anything."

As much as the idea of her picking through our food grossed me out, I knew it would've caused Miranda to explode. I debated whether or not I should tell her, then quickly realized I might not have a say in that. *If Ivy has her way, none of us may be telling anyone anything ever again.* I had to force myself not to go down that road, instead returning my attention to her explanation of how she'd been getting clean clothes.

Not that it was some amazing revelation. It made perfect sense that she just took new outfits from one of the dryers at night and threw her dirty stuff on somebody's waiting pile. Like she said, the things found their way back to the right people eventually. But thinking of her pawing through my underwear, then wearing it, was foul. I gave her a once-over and was relieved to find that I didn't recognize anything she had on right now as mine.

Garrett, of course, had his own take on the subject. "Why don't you just go naked?"

"That's disgusting," Ivy spat back.

"Seriously?" Rae snorted. "Nudity's wrong, but murder's okay?"

Of all the insults, this was the one to finally hit home. Ivy seemed to grow not only in volatility, but also in actual *size* when

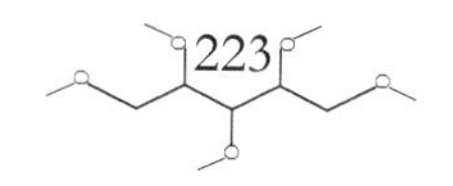

she roared, "They deserved it!"

Up until that moment, even after the tragi-horror of her backstory, I'd been unable to see how this girl – this damaged, but intelligent young person – could've stabbed someone, let alone three men. But now, witnessing the flash of rage in her eyes, the snarl pulling back her lips – the transformation of her entire being from girl to monster – forced me to see it. And it rocked me to my core.

Again, it was Garrett who broke the silence; he'd always had a hard time with that concept.

"If you're going to kill us, why don't you just get it over with?" Poking the tiger seemed to be his signature move.

The quieting of Ivy's voice only intensified the threat behind her words. "I only want to get rid of *her*."

TWENTY TWO

"Me?" I choked, dropping any attempt at bravado. *What had I done now?*

"They were going to close campus after Captain Quirk snapped," Ivy informed us. "Everyone was supposed to go home – no more questions, no more research, all back to normal."

"But *you* had to ruin everything by keeping this place open," she went on, "so I had to find a way to shut it down on my own." The mention of Janet made me see that, even though they had different agendas, the two crazies had one thing in common. *Aside from being complete lunatics.* They both just couldn't seem to stop talking about themselves.

We all listened in fascination as Ivy regaled her tale, beginning with her recognition that Larson was the key. She'd looked him up online and found that he was a serious researcher with big degrees, looking for a big discovery. She knew once he figured out what caused our chromosome mutation, his next step would be to recreate C9x. Then he'd patent it, sell it – soon everyone would have super-abilities. And for Ivy, that would mean losing the one thing that made her special.

"Why'd you have to *kill* him?" I asked. "Couldn't you have tried *talking* to him?"

"I did try to talk to him, to *convince* him, but he wouldn't listen," she said, but the excuse rang false.

Rae must've thought so, too, because she asked, "So why'd you bring a knife to a convince-ment?"

"I think knives are pretty convincing, don't you?" Ivy sneered, her sick candor evoking even more fear in me after I thought I'd already maxed out.

"But even after I took Larson out, you idiots still wouldn't leave," she scolded us, as if lecturing naughty children. "So I took a shot with Nate."

"*With* him?" Rae interrupted. "Don't you mean you took a shot *at* him?"

"No," Ivy corrected. "I thought he was going to take my side."

So she must've found out about Nate's temporary alliance with Janet. That realization brought with it a startling afterthought; *she might've even been there the night Janet and Nate jumped us – watching, listening, probably willing us all to die.*

"But he turned me down," she went on. "He was going to turn me in for brownie points with that colonel. Can you believe that?"

Um, one criminal stabbing another in the back? No, that never happens. I wanted to tell her that even I could've seen that coming, but I found the strength to keep my mouth clamped shut.

"Nate's no prize," Garrett sympathized. "I've been saying that this whole time."

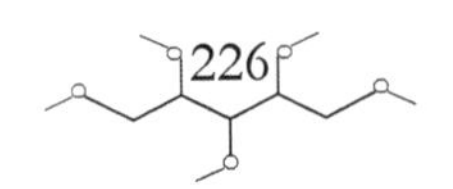

"Well, neither is she," Ivy spat back, cocking her head at me. "Do you even know what your little friend here's been up to?"

My heart fell to the pit of my stomach, but Ivy's face brightened in the flickering flame of her dropped bomb. Her eyes locked on mine and she flashed me her nastiest smile as she asked, "Who's Ford?"

When none of us uttered a sound, she tried again. "If nobody knows who Ford is," she drew out slowly, evilly, "then why is it such a big deal that you kissed him?"

Garrett's head whirled to look at me and, in that split second, I saw his hatred for Ivy turn into hatred for me. "That's why you led him away? To tell him you cheated on him?" he raged. "Then you just left him there to get stabbed?"

I couldn't find any words to defend myself. Maybe because there weren't any. *What'd happened to Jack was all my fault.*

"I didn't want to hurt him," Ivy said with wide-eyed innocence, turning her full attention to Garrett once she saw that she'd succeeded in dividing us. "I heard them fighting and saw someone take off. I thought it was *her*, but I couldn't tell in the dark. When I got closer and saw that it was Jack, I was going to leave him alone," she promised, expertly weaving together the lies.

"But he saw me," she said, getting to the part she still couldn't figure out. "How did he do that?" she asked, looking back to me.

"He's special," I answered simply.

"Shut up," Garrett snarled at me, but Ivy ignored him.

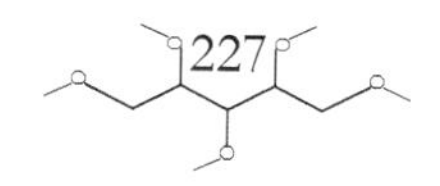

"*Special,*" she spat with disgust. "I'm sick of hearing how special you all think you are, when you're not. Not like me."

"Well, maybe your cell-mate will appreciate you," Rae offered.

"Like I'm not going to jail," Ivy disagreed. "I'm going to get rid of her," she said, giving me an indicative nod while still keeping her gun hand in position at the mute guard's side. "And then I'm going to walk out that gate and disappear."

"You know we can't let you do that," Rae spoke up again, this time with even more conviction.

"How do you think you're going to stop me," Ivy countered, "when you won't even be able to see me? And once I'm gone, no one will ever find me, even if you tell them what to look for."

"Is that a challenge?" Garrett stepped up beside Rae. I was relieved to see that, while he may not be on my side, at least he hadn't gone to Ivy's.

"Sounds like you've got it all figured out," I jumped in before he irritated her enough to get himself added to the elimination list.

"I do," she confirmed smugly.

"But what if you get caught?" I asked.

"I won't," she said, dismissing the possibility.

"But what if you do?" I persisted.

"Okay, just to humor you – I have a pretty solid defense."

"Insanity," Garrett filled in knowingly.

"Do I *look* insane?" Ivy hissed.

"Do you really want me to answer that?" he threw back.

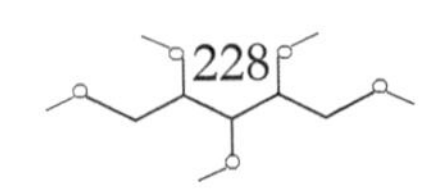

"You're the crazy ones," she countered, "to want to stay here."

"Have you seen the gym?" Rae piped up, only half-joking. "Food's pretty decent, too."

"Stop it!" Ivy shouted, for the first time moving the gun from the still-silent guard's ribcage to point it at us.

"I bet you don't even know how to use that," Rae taunted.

Without flinching, Ivy shot the ground inches in front of Rae's feet. "I grew up with guns," she told us. "That's the one thing Daddy Dearest did for me. I could shoot better in third grade than you can now." I didn't know about Rae and Garrett, but that was true for me. I'd never even held a gun before – this might actually be only the second time I'd even seen one in real life – and I was terrified.

"Then how come you missed?" Garrett jeered. "Gun must be too heavy for your poor little hand."

"How 'bout I bring it up a little?" Ivy's arm came up and sent a second bullet whizzing past his ear. "Spare me your *women are the weaker sex* crap."

"Hey, I never said you were the weaker sex," he disagreed, holding both hands up in his defense. "*Crazier* sex, that's what I said."

"Did you really just say that out loud?" Rae turned to him in disbelief.

"Uh, did you see her fire that gun at me?" Garrett responded. I couldn't tell if this was their normal back-and-forth or some kind of good cop-bad cop routine they'd worked out on

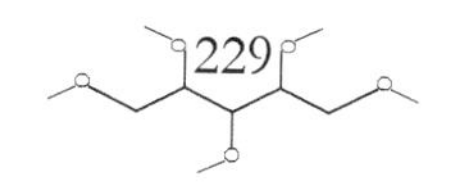

the way here. I just hoped Ivy was having as hard a time following as I was.

With each volley, Rae and Garrett subtly inched toward Ivy. But as sly as they surely thought they were being, Ivy saw immediately what they were up to.

"Don't come any closer," she warned.

Garrett and Rae proceeded as if they hadn't heard, but I knew Ivy was serious even if they didn't. She hadn't hesitated to stab three people. I may not watch all the crime shows Garrett's grandfather did, but I could put together that the brutality of plunging a knife into another human being took serious mental disturbance. And someone who'd so easily broken from reality would have no qualms about pulling a trigger.

"Stop," Ivy ordered one last time, then I heard the unmistakable click of the gun hammer being cocked back. The small but deadly sound triggered a rage in me unlike anything I'd ever felt. It was as if a newly-awakened monster burst hulk-like from my body as I launched myself directly at Ivy. And the gun.

Rae and Garrett's mouths rounded in identical *No!*s – neither of which I could hear over the explosion of the bullet leaving the barrel. From there, everything seemed to move in slow motion. As in, completely unreal, eighties-movie *slo-mo*. We all watched in amazement as the bullet shot across the short distance between Ivy and me, then abruptly stopped mid-air. My hand rose in wonder toward the metal capsule poised only inches from my chest, suspended as if embedded in a Plexiglas wall.

What? Was? That? my brain stuttered.

As if in a daze, I swept my hand in a downward arc and

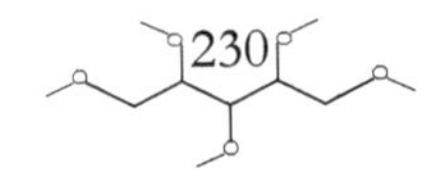

knocked the bullet away. Without my wall to slow its velocity, it drilled deep into the ground at my feet.

While all of us, including Ivy, stood frozen in shock by what we'd just witnessed, the guard finally seized his opportunity to act. In one expert movement, he twisted Ivy's arm behind her back, pinned her hand between her shoulder blades, plucked the gun from her fingers, and turned it on her. Clearly the silence and crippling injury had been for show; he must've played it up so that she'd forget he was a threat.

"It's about time," Garrett grumbled, but the relief that washed over his face betrayed the pretense.

"I was waiting for the right moment," the guard informed him. "What were *you* thinking?" he yelled, whirling on me. "I was just about to make my move when you lost it."

I couldn't get in a word of apology as he continued shouting at me. "If you hadn't done – whatever that was – with your hand…or your mind…you'd be dead right now. Do you get that?"

The words hit me the way the bullet had failed to and I crumpled to the ground with the impact. As tears sprang up to blur my vision, a row of headlights appeared, chasing away the rest of the shadows.

Ford leapt out of the point-vehicle, hitting the ground at a full-sprint, gun drawn. Lombardo and half the security team followed suit, likewise armed and ready. The guard had to yell over the dying engines to tell them the situation had been diffused.

I didn't need to see clearly to know that Ford was headed

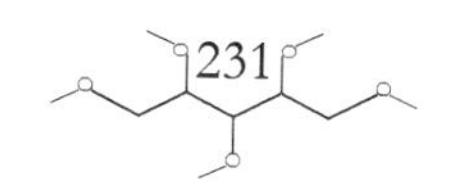

straight for me; I felt him coming before he knelt down in front of me and said my name. "Clio! Clio, are you alright?" His strong hands clutched my shoulders and I looked up into his panicked face.

"I'm okay," I answered, trying to force a smile, trying to look brave despite the rush of tears spilling down my face. His intense blue eyes searched mine for a solid minute before moving over the rest of me. Anyone watching would've seen nothing more than a commander inspecting a victim, but I did. I saw the raw emotion and fear in his eyes, and it filled me up and knocked me out all at once.

Every part of my body yearned to press myself against him and be swallowed up by his strength, enveloped in his protection. But I fought the urge to go to him, wrapping my arms around myself instead.

Assured that I was physically unharmed, he released my shoulders and rose to his feet. He opened his mouth to say something, but I shook my head to stop him. The jumble of questions and conflicting answers I saw in his eyes reflected the chaos in my heart. *No, this wasn't the time for anything to be said between us.*

As I watched him go to Rae and Garrett, I knew that I'd been right to stop him. I also knew that I may not get another chance – that I may never hear what he'd been about to tell me – but I could live with that. I'd put enough people in harm's way for one day.

I watched soundlessly as first the now-handcuffed Ivy was taken away in a jeep, followed by a blanket-wrapped Rae in

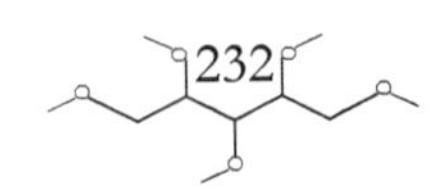

another. I could feel the heat of Garrett's burning gaze as he passed, but I didn't look up to meet it. I didn't need him to tell me everything was my fault for being so selfish. Ivy was right; *I* was the one who'd fought to keep the campus open because *I* wanted to stay. So I should've been the one hurt, not Jack. And worst of all, all I selfishly wanted at this moment was for him to hold and comfort *me*.

Only once the others were gone did I lift my eyes to take in the aftermath. I looked from the doctor bent over the injured guard, tending to the wound, to the yellow crime tape going up around the scene. And there was no way I could ignore the stolen glances at me – the last kid to leave the scene, the one who was responsible for all of it. The only thought I had left was, *Look at all the damage I've caused.*

TWENTY THREE

I sat alone on the bench in the middle of the empty courtyard, unable to avoid the irony of all that time I'd wasted hiding in my room, avoiding everybody, when now that I wanted nothing more than to be around other people, nobody wanted to be around me.

My life seemed to have gone the way of a bad TV movie, and I couldn't find the remote. The know-better me had to watch the scene in Ford's office over and over, yelling, *Stop! Don't do it!* But mistake-making me couldn't hear. *Could I have stopped me anyway?* I wondered. Now I'd never know.

To kill time until the debriefing, I used my phone to look up the band Alexis had told me about the last time we'd hung out. *Far Behind* seemed to be their most popular tune, so that's one I chose to download, thinking that was the one I'd have the best chance of having heard before, even if it was from the nineties.

I liked the piano intro, followed by the drums that had to be what Alexis loved. And she was right – two seconds in, I knew I wanted to hear more stuff like this. I paged down to launch a new station of similar stuff, titling it *Heavy*.

But once the vocals started, the opening lines knocked the breath right out of me. *Now maybe I didn't mean to treat you bad, but I did it anyway*....That couldn't be any more timely, appropriate, and aimed right at me. My first instinct was to throw the phone, but I made myself hang on to it. The song kept playing and, like a bad accident, I couldn't close my ears to it. As hard it was for me to listen to, I knew that I had to put it in my lyric journal. It wouldn't be a happy entry, or one I'd revisit often, but it'd sure be an honest one.

I sighed, finally turning off the phone and shelving that project for another time. Unfortunately, time was something I had too much of these days, as proven by my harshly blank calendar. My routine these days consisted mainly of going for solo walks, pathetically hoping for Garrett to intrude, and taking al fresco meals with no Bliss to share and no Miranda to criticize. And no Jack at all.

At first, I'd gone to the hospital every day, hovering outside his door when the nurses wouldn't allow visitors, settling for watching him through the window. Seeing him in the bed tore at my heart, particularly the way his arms lay on top of the blanket – stretched down along his sides, palms up, hands open – so painfully much like the last time I'd seen him before the attack. And even more than then, I'd just wanted to put my hands in his and hold on.

Then the third day changed everything. I'd shown up to take my regular post, only to find Jack in his room *un*alone. My heart leapt when I first saw Bliss at his bedside, knowing that had

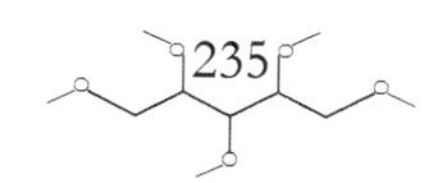

to mean he'd taken a turn for the better. But the thrill was short-lived. Before I could go in the room, Miranda's face had appeared on the other side of the glass, pausing long enough to scowl at me, then snapping the blinds closed to shut me out.

I'd waited a long time – an embarrassingly long time – for the girls to come out and give me the good news. Instead, I'd found myself being quietly escorted to the elevator by a stone-faced nurse. On the ride down, I tried to figure out what I could've done wrong today to be forced to leave, but I came up empty.

I found my answer seated at the reception desk with an evil Cheshire grin. I knew the second he met my eyes that Job had called upstairs to order my removal, no doubt at Miranda's request. I should've known he'd be happy to side with the candy-striper and the Hun once they'd told him their side of the story.

So, with no other options, they hadn't needed to make today's assembly mandatory to get me here. I'd hoped that by hanging around right in front of the door to the main building that I'd get a chance to catch Bliss's eye, or maybe Miranda's. Anything to make one tiny step toward rebuilding our now nonexistent friendship. But they'd either gone in really early, or were holding back to avoid me. That Bliss would be willing to risk drawing attention to herself by showing up late said it all.

I hurried into the great room before the session started to make sure I could slide into a seat without drawing too many stares of my own. I should've known that all the chairs along the back and down the edges would be full, forcing me to walk the long center aisle to the front row.

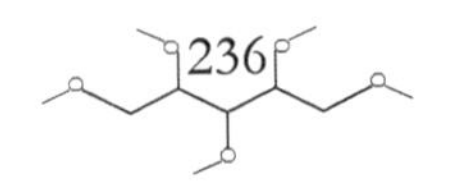

Though I had to walk right by them, I tried not to stare at Miranda, Garrett, and Bliss, as they were seated in order from the outside in. I couldn't help but feel like they were in defensive formation, from toughest to most vulnerable, against the enemy – me.

As I passed their row, I kept my eyes trained on my hands clasped in front of me. Even so, I saw, out of the corner of my eye, Garrett's hand covering Bliss's, which was resting on his thigh. *What's that about?* I wondered. *Something going on there?* Maybe their hatred of me had brought them together.

I took a seat alone in the front, where nobody else ever wanted to sit. I tried to make myself feel better about it, thinking that at least here I was so obviously available that one of the group might finally decide to come talk to me. Nobody moved.

At the very front of the room, facing the audience, sat Rae and Xavier. I wanted to send them a signal, but both of their eyes stayed focused on Ford's back as they waited for him to begin.

I hadn't seen them since the night of the barbecue, after which they'd been moved to another area. The official reason for the temporary arrangement was that, as late-arrivals to campus, they needed extra help processing this trauma. Apparently this meant the rest of us were old pros at handling our post-traumatic stress.

I found it amazing that Major Godwin or her boss or her boss's boss – whoever made the final call on these "statements" – continued to confuse seventeen with stupid. Especially since it was the kids they had to thank for taking down another psycho.

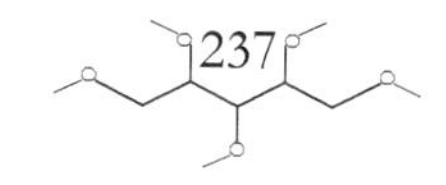

But it didn't really matter what the higher powers thought; everyone on campus knew the real reason for keeping Rae and Xavier out of circulation was to find out if they'd known Ivy before coming here. More specifically, if they'd ever talked to her or, worst case, helped her with her plan. Since being relaxed and easy-going hadn't served the Army all that well so far, I had a feeling that things around here might be taking a turn toward un-kinder and un-gentler.

On the other side of Rae's escort sat Alexis, followed by Captain Dolan, and then Major Godwin, who would surely be speaking after Ford. I'd learned to recognize the debriefing pattern; he always went first, going over the action and filling everyone in on the details, and then she'd swoop in to gloss it over and wrap it up.

Finally, Ford adjusted his collar microphone and began to speak. I had a hard time looking at him and I sensed that he felt the same way, since he looked into every face but mine. Pretty hard to do with me sitting front-row, center.

I knew he didn't really need the notes stacked on the podium in front of him; he'd know the information cold after surely having had to report it dozens of times over the past week. And I didn't really need to listen, either. I already knew everything he was going to say, having been on the front line for most of it.

We all knew that, at seventeen, Ivy could be tried as an adult, and between my recording and Jack's positive ID, she'd most likely be convicted by a jury. But she wouldn't be facing a civilian court; the Army was keeping this mess in-house, and

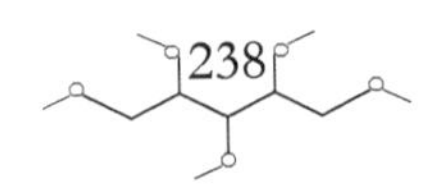

there were already rumors that due to her "special circumstances," she might not even serve time. Kind of like Nate's deal.

It'd been bad enough when Nate had gotten no real punishment for threatening to shoot us, but I'd tried to see the Army's side of that decision. He'd been manipulated by an officer, and, in the end, at least he hadn't hurt any of us. Ivy, on the other hand, had stabbed three people and shot a fourth. If they didn't lock her up – and for a long time – the government had a serious misunderstanding of justice. Victim of Heigl's experiment or not, I couldn't see any justification for killing another human being. Just the thought of it churned waves of nausea in my stomach.

As Ford wrapped up, I noted that he'd carefully avoided discussing Ivy's current whereabouts. *Had she been moved off-campus, or was she still here somewhere?* Maybe they'd put her in the same undisclosed place where Nate had done his "time." Not that it mattered; it wasn't like I was planning to bring her a candy bar on visiting day or anything. Although maybe I should consider it; she might be more likely to speak to me than most of my friends at this point.

As Major Godwin launched into her prepared statement, I still didn't find much worth listening to. Alexis had already filled me in on most of Ivy's backstory; she'd told me how Ivy'd been able to lure Larson to a private meeting – how his desire to solve the mystery of C9x had made it pretty easy for her, actually. All she'd had to do was text him that she was a student with special insight into the experiment. She'd used a disposable cell and been careful not to divulge any shady details, like the fact that she was living on campus unregistered and invisible, which had helped her keep her identity secret.

Anonymity had also given her a major card to play when she'd next approached Nate. Lucky for her, he'd been treated well enough in his faux confinement to retain most of his arrogance. Otherwise, she may not have had the edge she'd needed to take him out when he'd turned her down.

And Ivy'd told me herself what'd happened with Jack; he'd been in the wrong place at the wrong time, and she probably would've left him alone if he hadn't made the mistake of *seeing* her when she was supposed to be invisible.

But Major Godwin did manage to recapture my attention when she started talking about the last two kids who'd never shown up at campus. Of the original hundred, ninety-five had reported on day one; then Rae and Xavier made their joint late entry, followed by Ivy creeping in on her own terms. *But what about the others?* When Godwin said the Army was actively working to locate them, which sure sounded like they didn't know where they were, I had to stifle a cry. *Seriously? Like you've misplaced them?*

But my frustration was tempered by exhaustion. I was just beat. I'd been through too much over these couple of months, lost so much hope in so many people at so many levels. Not that I had much right to criticize anyone else, with all the mistakes I'd made this summer. Since I hadn't been able to deal all that stellarly with my ability and the changes that'd come with it, how could I expect perfection from the Army? I could practically hear Trudy's voice in my ear, saying, *Clio, it sounds to me like you're growing up.* Those were the exact kind of phrases she'd been shoveling onto me lately, which is why I wasn't spending all my newfound free time with her.

I lost track of how long we'd been sitting there, but when Major Godwin wrapped things up with one of her typical don't-worry-everything's-under-control statements, the other kids couldn't get out of the room fast enough. But I stayed in my seat. I wondered if I was the only one who thought these press conferences seemed to go on forever, dispersing so much "information" that by the end you might not notice that you hadn't gotten any answers. Not only had I learned nothing new today, but I almost felt like I had more questions than ever. *What about campus life? Us? School?* I looked around, but there was nobody left to ask.

I watched my friends go out the door without a backward glance. *Maybe it's the heaviness*, I tried to convince myself, though not doing that great of a job. It would be so much easier to believe that they weren't really avoiding me, but that it was my new ability pushing them away. At least that would be something I could fix.

Not that I'd given up hope. I knew they might never forgive me; might never even speak to me again. But I also knew that if you work hard to prove you're sorry, your friends can forgive your mistakes. I liked to believe that I'd be able to, if I was in their shoes right now.

Maybe I was meant to be with Jack and maybe I wasn't, but I did know that I wasn't meant to leave and never see him again. He was supposed to be in my life, along with Bliss, Garrett,

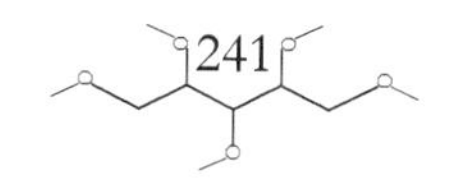

and Miranda. I couldn't have been brought here to find them, to go through all we had, and then *lose* them. The best things were worth fighting for, and all I knew was that I had to stay on the field to play. I needed to be here now more than ever.

After everyone else had gone, leaving me the only person in the room, I let the tears I'd been holding back slide down my cheeks. I'd never wanted to be different, or exciting, and definitely not the center of attention. But I'd learned to come to terms with all of that here. Now I realized I'd become the one thing I'd wanted even less than being "special" – *alone.*

"Don't you think it's time we showed the world what you can do?"

BOOK # 3 OF THE "SOLID" SERIES

COMING SUMMER 2012

SHELLEY WORKINGER was born in Maine, educated in New Orleans, currently resides in New Jersey, and considers all of them home. "Solid" is her first series.

VISIT HER AT:
WWW.SHELLEYWORKINGER.COM

Made in the USA
Lexington, KY
03 December 2011